ECHO OF
A CURSE

The DANCING TUATARA PRESS
Books from RAMBLE HOUSE

ECHO OF A CURSE

R.R. RYAN

Introduced by

John Pelan and D.H. Olson

RAMBLE HOUSE

Echo of a Curse ©1938 by R.R. Ryan

Introduction © 2014 by John Pelan and D.H. White

Cover Design © 2014 by Gavin L. O'Keefe

Edited by John Pelan and D.H. Olson

The editor and publisher would like to express their gratitude to Mr. David Medhurst for his invaluable assistance with this project.

"Not anything to me comes strangely . . ."
James Thomson

ISBN 13: 978-1-60543-714-9

Dancing Tuatara Press #41

ECHOES OF R.R. RYAN

Eleven years have passed since the publication of the Midnight House edition of *Echo of a Curse* by R.R. Ryan. Not surprisingly, as *Echo of a Curse* is arguably Ryan's masterpiece, that edition has long been out of print. In the intervening years a funny thing happened: after all this time R.R. Ryan's true identity was revealed? or was it?

Let me back up a bit for those just coming on board. R.R. Ryan first came to the attention of modern readers via the famous list of the thirty-nine best horror novels authored by Karl Edward Wagner. Ryan was notable for appearing in all three categories, non-supernatural horror, supernatural horror, and science-fictional horror. Obviously, Mr. Wagner thought rather highly of Ryan and his recommendation was sufficient to get other "students of the game" such as Ramsey Campbell, D.H. Olson, and myself to seek out Ryan's work for ourselves.

What we found was impressive. Wagner had not overstated the visceral power of Ryan's novels; they ranged in quality from terrible to brilliant, with the mid-range material still being pretty good by any standards. Now here's where it started to get real interesting.

R.R. Ryan seemed to be a complete cipher, no information on the person behind the name seemed to be available. At first there was conjecture that the author was "Rachel Ryan", who had written one novel many years before the R.R. Ryan books appeared. Years of literary detection followed, with scholar James Doig finally producing evidence that the author was theatre manager and playwright Evelyn Bradley, who also wrote under the names Cameron Carr, Noel Despard, and John Galton. There the matter would seem to rest until contact was made with descendants of the author, one of whom claimed that "R.R. Ryan" was actually Bradley's daughter, Denice

Jeanette Bradley-Ryan, who authored several novels under the name of "Kay Seaton."

So who *was* R.R. Ryan? There's an intriguing blurb from "Kay Seaton's" publisher commenting on her father helping her with her books. What does that mean? Were all of the Ryan and Seaton novels collaborations? How about the others? Thus far I've only had the opportunity to read one Seaton novel to compare styles and from that small a sample size I can't be 100% certain. My gut feeling is that the first R.R. Ryan book was a solo effort by Bradley as was the Noel Despard novel. The strong female characters that are hallmarks of Ryan's work began appearing with *Death of a Sadist* and got progressively better as more books appeared. At this point it seems pretty clear to me that everything from *Death of a Sadist* on was likely a father/daughter collaboration. It's also interesting to note that after Bradley's suicide in 1950, no further books appeared, though it is of course quite possible that Bradley-Ryan used another pseudonym which has yet to come to light, it seems more plausible that without her long-time collaborator she simply gave up on fiction writing.

The present book is considered by me and several other Ryan aficionados to be his/her masterpiece. At this point I'll bow out and turn the introduction over to my colleague D.H. Olson . . .

The elevation of R. R. Ryan into the pantheon of collectable but forgotten authors is due solely to the efforts of one man: Karl Edward Wagner. All of the Ryan titles populating the numerous "wish lists" that often vex collectable book dealers are based on his own lists of "Neglected Masterpieces" from *Twilight Zone Magazine* in 1983. The Wagner List, as it has since come to be known, was made up of three separate lists of thirteen books each. Ryan, then completely unknown, has the distinction of being the only author to appear on all three lists. Those listings, with their short descriptive paragraphs, are worth quoting here:

Of *Echo of a Curse*, Wagner wrote: "Undeservedly forgotten, Ms. Ryan was the best of the British thriller writers—a group who wrote popular fiction for the lending libraries, roughly parallel to the pulp writers in America between the world wars. This novel of lycanthropy and vampirism rates with *Fingers of Fear* as one of the best."

If Ryan was aware of the flaws in both *The Subjugated Beast* and *Freak Museum*, it's clear that she learned from her mistakes. *Echo of a Curse* (1939), her sixth novel, is the first of Ryan's works to be so essentially flawless as to be considered a true classic. It is also the first, and only, of her novels that is inarguably supernatural. True, both *The Subjugated Beast* and *Freak Museum* include passages that border upon the paranormal, but neither clearly crosses over that line, at least not to the extent of *Echo of a Curse*. While it would take some doing, it would even be possible to argue that both earlier novels are mainstream, their more fantastic elements readily explainable by more mundane (or psychological) means. A stretch perhaps, but not an impossible one.

Not surprisingly, *Echo* is full of themes and characters familiar from earlier novels. Mary Border is in the classic tradition of Ryan heroines: not stupid like Mary Bootle in *The Right to Kill*, but rather unexceptional, and given to bad choices made worse by a highly-developed, and some might say out-dated, sense of honor and propriety. Terry Cliffe, the man she should have married, is also cut to the traditional Ryan pattern: a nice man, bound by his own strong sense of duty to the woman he loves. Like Robert Litherland, in that earlier novel, his loyalty to Mary goes beyond what would normally be considered reasonable, while his own sense of morality and propriety is above reproach. To this is added the character of Vincent "Vin" Border, and with him the perfect R.R. Ryan triangle is thus complete.

Vin, not unexpectedly, is another quintessentially Ryan character: the sadist and madman. Yet, Vin is also more than that. In fact, he is one of Ryan's most finely-drawn, well-rounded and memorable characters. His sadism is intense and disturbing, far over-shadowing earlier Ryan creations like Selwyn Maine or Boris Gregorovich. But Vin also has a softer side and, at odd moments, the reader can hardly help but feel a twinge of sympathy and even respect for his poor, tortured soul. He is also the first of Ryan's characters in whom true growth can be seen over the course of a novel, an achievement made all the more amazing by his obvious inhumanity in other respects.

To this "romantic triangle," Ryan adds hints of vampirism and lycanthropy, an ancestral "curse," and repeated references to THE INEXPLICABLE, a hideously deformed side-show freak. She also returns to the use of a two-part story line, with the second half of the action occurring many years after the events of the first.

Ramsey Campbell, in his article on Ryan in *Necrofile*, speculates that Ryan also wrote *Echo of a Curse* while under the influence of, or at least after becoming familiar with, the writings of H.P. Lovecraft. Such may not be provable, especially as Ryan makes no references to anything explicitly Lovecraftian, but a careful reading of *Echo*'s text does provide a strong circumstantial case in support of such influences. Note, for instance, the ceremony of "The Black Commune" early in Book Two, or the appearance of Mr. Govina in the next chapter:

"An odd figure awaited her. Tall. Drooping. Gaunt—in so far as one could judge; for, despite the time of year, the visitor was swathed in wrappings. Immediately Mary had a strong revulsion from her guest, who stood strangely still, strangely impersonal. Round his mouth was woven a muffler of soft, fine material. His head was bare, revealing a tough-looking black thatch, which was almost too coarse for human hair and resembled nothing so much as what is known in theatrical circles as a scratch wig. Perhaps, Mary thought, it is a wig. He may have lost his hair. With his mouth definitely concealed and his eyes masked by special dark glasses, which had side-flaps to prevent all hurtful rays reaching his eyes, the stranger's face reminded Mary of a carving rather than of a human head. One hand, she observed, was gloved, the other not. There seemed, for an instant, something baleful in his stillness. It was impossible to determine the newcomer's age."

Shades of Henry W. Akeley in "The Whisperer in Darkness" or Randolph Carter in "Through the Gates of the Silver Key"!

Another implicit reference may be found in Chambers' belief in a "foul, forbidden world," that rides "parallel with ours and which was inseparable from the unimaginable vast in whose enormity we are lost." Yet another passage, even more indicative of the authors having been contaminated by the taint of Lovecraftian Yog-Sothothery, may be found at the very end of Book One, when reference is made to Vin's unorthodox religious beliefs and his discussion of them with his daughter, Faith:

". . . But it was also true that at times he told her queer fables, propounded impossible doctrines of eternal life. And these tales of future existence were far from being founded upon orthodox principles of religious people, but were odd, outré, grotesque. Mankind in the bulk died — but there were those who need not die. The secret was vouchsafed to few; but he, Vin, possessed it. He would live forever and Faith should share his eternity."

Other, classic Ryan sub-plots are also very much in evidence: the untimely pregnancy, a World War I setting for some of the early action, decaying family finances, animal abuse. Also still in evidence is a trace of the Weird Menace influence so prevalent in *Freak Museum*. The first half of *Curse* is definitely not for the squeamish and is, in many respects, far more disturbingly perverse than anything written in the sixty-two years since. The "puppy episode" and the earlier tableau in which Terry discovers the true, violently dysfunctional nature of Mary and Vin's relationship, are scenes that retain the power to shock even after all these years. Moreover, their power is such that, once experienced, they will not be soon forgotten by any of Ryan's readers.

John here again. We plan on releasing all of Ryan's novels as well as the four thrillers that appeared under the "Kay Seaton" by-line. The current plan is to issue two books at a time, so that the companion volume to this book will be the flawed, but still exciting, *Death of a Sadist.* In this economy, few people want to spend their money on a literary curiosity. In the case of R. R. Ryan, the novels break down like this: *Echo of a Curse* and *No Escape* masterpieces; *Freak Museum* and *The Subjugated Beast* excellent; *Devil's Shelter* and *Death of a Sadist* flawed, but still well-worth reading; *The Right to Kill* okay—I'll be completely honest, this merits the designation of "literary curiosity"—it has not one but several major flaws and in the final analysis is a failure. For readers wanting to see just how far the author(s) came from such inauspicious beginnings the novel is a case study that shows just how many mistakes a writer can make and learn from them.

However, enough about R.R. Ryan's worst book. You have in your hands one of her two best. Enjoy!

John Pelan and D.H. Olson
New Mexico and Minnesota
Ides of March 2014

BOOK ONE

CHAPTER 1

TERRY LOVED MARY and once believed she nearly loved him, would have loved him, had not Vincent Border risen like a new star in her particular firmament. He suffered from the disadvantage of having known her since childhood. Familiarity blunts the edge of any thrill. He had little more sex-appeal for her than a brother.

Mary was the daughter of a doctor, Terry the son of a lawyer; they were neighbors in a large provincial town.

Terry's was one of those old-fashioned loves—that last, like gold.

Mary was not beautiful by any standard, except her own, and by that—for Terry at least—she was beautiful. Or perhaps she might be said to have inherited all the forms of female beauty because her face never looked the same three minutes together.

She was tall, undulating; had that curious grace one associates with the more lovely forest creatures, and tantalizing, quizzical eyes which put Terry in mind of deep pools flecked by shadows. There were hollows under her cheek-bones that gave her face an inimitable charm.

Gay? Yes, she was gay. Sunshine? Terry was as accustomed to seeing Mary smile as he was accustomed to see the sun shine; as accustomed to hear her gay songs as to hearing the birds sing.

The desire that accompanies even the most spiritual love awoke in him when she first wore evening dress. That was in 1912, almost the end of perhaps the happiest period this earth will ever know. Men still believed in the superiority of the hu-

man race and did not credit that man can be more savage than
the fiercest beast.

Mary was eighteen then, Terry two years older. No thought
of love had entered her care-free heart—until that night when
he, a Territorial, marched to the station *en route* for France.

That night, had he spoken, perhaps his luck would have been
in. He thought so then and has done ever since. Mary was full
up with warm emotion, which, if not love, was its kin. She
would, Terry believed, have said yes; and once her promise had
been given, she'd have been true. That was Mary.

They'd been tremendous pals, constant companions, into all
kinds of scrapes and out again—mostly by the gooseflesh of
their skins. They'd lied for each other, suffered for each other.
Often he'd been her Sydney Carton, she his Grace Darling.
And bit by bit he'd grown to long for her until the longing became almost unbearable. But he said nothing, because it was
clear to him that her only interest was life itself. However, that
night he stood on the platform with his father (himself killed
late in the war) and mother and sister (now married and living
in Brazil), his shoulder touching Mary's, when she suddenly
looked up at him in quite a new way, as if some exalting realization had lit her soul.

The others were watching a high-spirited group, laughing at
their antics; for that instant Mary and he were utterly alone.
Alone on earth. Alone in the universe. Her teasing eyes were
gentle.

"Terry!" He'd never heard that sound in her voice before.
"Let's steal away a minute."

They linked arms and moved off unobserved. She was trembling. Presently her eyes were again raised to his with that ear-
nestness so strange in Mary.

"Oh, Terry! I've only just realized what this means. We may
never see each other again."

It was then he saw the birth of love in her gaze—or believed
he did. That was the moment when he could have bound her for
life . . . But he wouldn't. White honour. Chivalry. Selflessness.
All that kind of thing. It was, he told himself, no time for a
chap to grab all he could get. It was the time of supreme giving.

A man was rotten who tied up a girl with tragedy and complications.

So all he said was:

"Don't you believe it, old thing! We'll be hitch-hiking when we're a couple of gummy old guys."

It was on that reckless note he went away, leaving Mary damped and curiously disheartened, though she failed to comprehend why she felt as she did, attributing her sudden and alien depression to the loss of one who had more than helped to fill her days and keep her gay. Never has chivalry so deserved its purpose. Had Terry burst out with his love instead of so nobly suppressing it, foul misfortune, appalling terror would have been averted.

Terry was a bundle of contradictions, for, whereas in both appearance and manner he was far from robust, his will and physical strength were uncommon. Fragile in appearance, his manner was deprecating, shy, diffident. His charming, friendly, modest eyes totally misled strangers in regard to his steel-like disposition, just as his nervous, fine-drawn bodily lines belied his true quality of muscle, sinew and constitution. His gentle ways pleased his superiors, even while filling them with doubts as to his fitness to handle men. But their qualms were speedily silenced. Though quiet and friendly with his men, he ruled them as if possessed of hypnotic powers. They obeyed him, they worshiped him. After they had followed him into battle they apotheosized him. His scorn of danger fired his men with the spirit of emulation and they performed prodigies of valour.

Perhaps because Fortune favours the fearless, or is piqued by indifference, Terry was not wounded until early 1917, by which time he was a captain, much family trouble had overtaken both Mary and him, and he had met Vincent Border.

Vincent was a few months older than Terry and had come to fill young Norrey's place, left empty by a direct hit.

Major Black himself brought him, which was typical of the major, a man without side or egotism and a most capable officer.

"This is our new Lefty One Pip, Terry. Don't let him get hit, he's too beautiful."

And this, Terry silently agreed, was true. And more: Mr. Lefty One Pip knew it. He was lovely. Tall, slim, well-shaped. Perfect features were crowned with clusters of sunny-brown curls, which even a military barber could not crop straight. His brilliant blue eyes were as gay as Mary's, but larger and more heavily lashed. A delicious round chin lent emphasis to a mouth that reminded Terry of a bud about to break into some luscious flower. Small ears, delicate hands, slender feet were all in perfect accord.

"Welcome to Paradise Lost," Terry said gravely and in rather a hushed voice.

Major Black grinned.

"You mustn't speak to Mr. Border as if he's holy, Terry. I'm told his very soul is washed in blood. Seen almost as much service as you, my boy."

Terry glanced at the new-comer, who smiled. Now, indeed, he did not look holy, but satanic. His teeth, small and rather pointed, were plainly all his own and undecayed. Yet . . . However, a second glance discovered nothing wrong with the smile and nothing sophisticated in Border's gaze, which was as ingenious as his unflawed beauty. This a soldier! It sounded fabulous.

"Well," the major said, preparing to take himself off, "you'd better dig out the Psychic and a spot of tea."

"The Psychic," Terry explained to Border, "is our orderly."

"Why Psychic?"

His voice, too, was attractive, almost purring.

"Wait till you get to know him—you'll understand. He's a bit weird, that's all."

Corporal Huges was a bit weird, in looks as well as in mentality. He looked like a man with a permanent grievance. An exiguous morsel, nature had assembled his features to scale, given him a pair of globulous eyes that were at once peevish and frightened. A somewhat fluent moustache hid a puffy, obstinate mouth. Whether it was true or not, the corporal had acquired a rather unhappy reputation for dismal prophecy that had an awkward way of proving true, and, seemingly, extraordinary powers of assessing the true natures of those with whom he mixed.

"Pore Mr. Norreys, 'e's for it," Huges had announced the night before that direct hit. " 'E'll be blown to bits termorrer."

Boots were thrown and Huges fully instructed as to the desserts of bloody pessimists; but Norreys *had* been blown to bits next day.

Dug out, Huges stared at his new superior as if with awe—though it might have been merely astonishment; on the other hand it might have been for some reason quite apart from the commonplace.

"Gor bli!" he breathed; then fell silent.

And that was how Terry met Vincent Border, who was destined to become much more than a casual contact in his life.

The newcomer talked informedly about the various danger spots with which he had been associated from the war's early days; and it soon became apparent to all concerned that we *was* a soldier in more than name. Indeed, he was as fearless, as careless of danger as Terry himself. But he was more. He was a devotee to violence, bloodshed, frightfulness. The horrors of these front-line trenches were his sacrament. Mars was his deity.

In their dug-out Terry and the others found their new comrade placid, non-assuming, and each acknowledged his curious charm.

But Terry was strangely fascinated by "Second Lieutenant Adonis," as he had been almost immediately nicknamed. It really seemed as if Border possessed a nature corresponding to his appearance, and an easy, agreeable mind, sufficiently well-informed. Life in the front-line had become more bearable, Terry concluded, for the coming of Vincent Border. But then two events happened that modified his views.

The first of these occurred one night quite soon after Border's advent and when Terry was turning round the corner of Bone's Lane into Dead Man's Causeway, off which lay his dug-out. The uncertain illumination of Very lights had momentarily failed, but, as he turned into the Causeway, it seemed to Terry that two pin-points of light gleamed catlike in the gloom.

Like a flash, someone turned and ran, lightly, soundlessly; but not before Terry had detected a strong smell of spirits. The truth was hardly in question, for he knew well that his better-known companions were not only temperate by nature but also entirely minus supplies. That lurker had been the new man. What had he been up to?

There had been something almost uncanny about that silent lurking—coupled as it was with that odd impression of shining eyes . . . Imagination, of course; or an illusion associated with the sudden ceasing of the Very lights.

Tired, and for some reason dispirited, Terry decided to get into bed without delay. They all had beds, curiously and ingeniously arranged by the admirable Huges, whose shining gift was extemporisation. Everyone was asleep except Border, who, in his night kit, sat with feet dangling over the side of his makeshift couch.

He stared at Terry in a strange, fixed fashion, his eyes alight, but expressionless. Something dead, but miraculously animated, might have been seated there. Terry realized at once that in an odd, contained, *compos mentis* way the man was drunk, dangerously, savagely drunk. Neither spoke and, half asleep in his fatigue, Terry undressed and got into bed.

He had, perhaps, been asleep an hour when that extra sense which war vouchsafes to its helots warned him of immediate danger. He awoke. Looked up. The glazed, drink-mad eyes of Border stared down at him with the fascination that blinkless eyes have for the startled.

Poised for instant descent was a wicked-looking, opened clasp-knife. A second more and that keen-edged knife would have ripped open his throat.

But, used to the alarms of war, Terry habitually awoke unflurried, prepared to grapple swiftly with any danger; and, drunk-strong or not, Border was immediately helpless in a grip cruelly powerful. The knife fell. Terry twisted the other's somewhat fragile wrists, till anguish brought some sanity to those uncoordinated eyes.

"I'll give him a little of his own medicine," Terry thought. And taking Border by the throat he half-throttled him before

changing pressure into violent shaking. Under this treatment
Border's whisky-elevated state suddenly subsided. He began to
whimper and would have embraced Terry, had the latter consented. Instead he mercilessly slapped the drunk man's cheeks.
Subsiding on to his bed, Border began to mumble and Terry
tossed him into his blankets, tucking him comfortably up. This
done, he sat awhile on the edge of his own bed, watching for
any fresh demonstration; but none came. Soon it was clear that
Border had succumbed to the claims of drunken sleep.

The next morning nothing could have exceeded the humility
and regret with which the culprit approached his senior officer.

Expecting penitence and disliking any drunkard's abject repentance, Terry eyed the approaching figure quizzically.

"Hell of a hang-over, eh?"

"I say, please forgive . . ."

And now came the full flood of humility and confession.

"I should never touch whisky."

"Hanged if you should. A few nips of special are not worth a
man's life."

"I attacked you?"

"Oh dear me, yes. All but knifed me."

"It's my second warning. I swear I'll never touch the beastly
stuff again."

"Certainly you're no end of a fool to bring it into the
trenches. It wouldn't have made any difference to you last
night had I been Number One Brass Hat. It's my duty to report
the matter."

And then Border's eloquence burst into full flood. Despite
all, Terry had a strong reaction in his favour. The sinner's penitence was as charming as his lapse had been horrible. Finally,
at a plea for help, the stronger nature capitulated entirely. Terry
never could resist an appeal for aid.

"The thing is, have you any more of the stuff?"

"No. I swear I haven't."

"Will you let me search your kit?"

"You doubt my word?"

"I doubt any whisky-addict's word."

"But I'm *not* an addict."

"So you say; but, if you've none hidden, why this obstruction?"

"Go ahead. Search me and my things."

Border's reproachful dignity had the ironical consequence of making Terry feel guilty. Nevertheless, he took the other at his word, searching not only his person, but his kit with care. It seemed pretty evident from the empty bottles that Border had no secret reserve.

"Well, I don't suppose you're likely to get a new supply while we're in the line. It's when we're relieved that you'll get your chance . . . I warn you, Border, that I'd not treat a repetition leniently. You're lucky I didn't shoot you last night. I'd have been justified. It would be well to remember we're here to kill Germans, not each other."

"Look here, I see you guess. I have a craving; but, honest to God, I'm fighting it. You know, Cliffe, a hell of a lot goes on inside chaps out here that no one guesses. We're all scared more or less; and it affects us in different ways. Some pray—secretly; some gamble; some drug; some drink. It's to stifle imagination . . . Those chaps who have none or little are lucky. When we're in camp, will you watch me? I'll fight like hell; and I believe I could win through—with a pal. Someone strong to talk with and keep my mind off blood and bombs and mess in leisure hours. It's the leisure hours that get me . . ."

And so Terry promised, half cursing himself for a fool. Wasn't everything hell enough without saddling oneself with a troublesome responsibility like Border's fear-complex?

However, he accepted the fear-complex with cordiality, glad to do so; for his conscience-charge had won his warmest regard. If he could help this lad, (no younger than himself), he'd be proud. He was a chap worth reclaiming. Trench-nerves demanded sympathy, however they expressed themselves. He could well understand this sensitive-looking, yet undoubtedly brave, young fellow suffering from suppressed terror, dread of noise, dread of sights, dread of slaying, dread of being slain; and the general circumstances, not least of which—the rats. Yes, he'd look after Border when their lot were resting. He'd try and disperse this accumulated carnage-dread.

Or at least so he determined until he discovered that the object of his sympathy had no fear of war, of blood, of human offal lying about; but, on the contrary, a gruesome appetite for all. This occurred when during a push their regiment had captured some important enemy trenches after an exhausting and ferocious fight. Corpses of both sides lay piled upon each other. The slaughter had been so severe that some confusion now resulted. Border was needed, but seemed to be missing. Terry set off to find him and, while so engaged, let his thoughts dwell upon the subject of his recent commiseration. He felt puzzled. During that mad rush across No-man's Land, he had turned to shout general encouragement and looked full into Border's face—convulsed with sheer, demoniac joy, with murderous ecstasy. His eyes were as unfocused, as alight, as upon the occasion of his drunken bout. He was drunk now. With the delight of slaughter, with the smell of blood, with the sight of indiscriminate human butchery.

"Hell," Terry thought, "I believe the fellow's a dangerous devil, an evil fellow, a conscienceless liar."

And then the idea occurred to him that perhaps the very effect he had seen during that short, sharp trip across hell was the off-spring of those causes in regard to which he had offered Border his sympathy and help.

Abruptly passing from one to another of these muddy, bloody corridors, he discovered Border, stooped over a body rent from neck to groin. For that instant they were isolated, he and his conscience-charge, who, absorbed in his grim survey, failed either to hear or to see the suddenly-arrived witness to his preoccupation. He was smiling at the flowing blood and presently glanced from left to right; but it was plain he did not see Terry, despite the fact that his gaze fell full upon him . . . He muttered. A little froth had gathered at his lips. Bending, he dipped his forefinger in the blood . . . then immersed his hand.

"Border!"

As if electrified, the possessed man shot erect, an exclamation that might have been pain issuing from his lips. He seemed literally to hurl himself out of his tranced condition, back to cognizance of his immediate surroundings and circumstances; but not before Terry had seen a flame of excited glee suffusing his eyes.

"What am I to think?" the would-be Samaritan asked himself later. "Was he temporarily off his head? Had his nerves gone?"

These seemed the most charitable conclusions. And there was one thing; even if he had not a sufficiently tough mentality to face war in its more ghastly forms, at least he had neither shirked the fighting nor fought badly. Terry knew many soldiers who literally exalted themselves into Ajaxes, Hectors, Hannibals, Davids when zero hour arrived and they must either kill or run.

The next day both Terry and Border were wounded and returned to the base where both woke to consciousness in neighbouring beds.

Simultaneously they rolled languid heads to see what manner of comrade they each had and lo:

"Hello!"

"Well!"

Even in pain, even affected by illness, Border's smile, Terry thought, was ineffably sweet.

"I was a fool to believe rotten things. He wasn't normal. Maybe I was not myself."

This kindly opinion strengthened during convalescence in England, where both men became more than commonly intimate. Closer relationship with Border revealed no sinister qualities. Whisky might be poison to his lovely nature, Terry decided, but fundamentally he was as pure as his profile.

CHAPTER II

GREAT CHANGES had taken place in the homes and lives of both Terry's people and Mary's people since the beginning of war. His father was himself now a soldier, his mother matron of a recreation home for wound-recovered soldiers, his sister nursing in Mesopotamia; Mary's father, the doctor, on active service. But she still lived in the warm-hued provincial home where she had grown up next door to Terry.

Till now the latter had scarcely considered Border's material affairs, taking him and his circumstances for granted in the haphazard way which war makes inevitable. But now he began to wonder a little about the earthly lot of this strange, attractive creature. Who was he? What was he? During convalescence they had grown more and more friendly. There were qualities in Vincent Border that Terry found irresistible and, just as at first he had found the former's advent into their section of the line a boon, so now he found life infinitely the brighter for his conscience-charge.

By this time he had definitely decided that whisky and fear truly accounted for Border's contradictions of character and had sworn again to protect him from his weakness, insofar as he could and insofar as the other wished it.

When the time came for sick leave prior to more active service, Terry realized that he was going to miss Border acutely . . . But need he? So far he himself had made no plans in regard to his leave; now he gave attention to the question—*where* to spend his leave? His home was shut.

He wrote to Mary. She replied:

"Come here. Aunt Charlotte's staying with me . . ."

Gladly. But what of Border? A feeling of responsibility was, rather ridiculously, never far from Terry's mind where his friend was concerned. Would he go home? Had he a home? Come to think of it, he knew nothing about Vincent Border.

"Going to your people, Vin?" (It had become Vin and Terry between them.)

The other shrugged.

"My father's dead and mother's got another man on her string. A Colonel, whom I don't cotton to."

"Well, what are your plans?"

"None. Can't we, you and I, go away somewhere? Let's go and hit the bright spots somewhere. Make a splash."

"Unfortunately I've not the needful. Hard up bloke, me."

Terry looked inquiringly at Border, who laughed.

"I've private means."

"Lucky dog!"

"Oh, I don't know. It takes purpose out of life. Deadens initiative." For an instant he broke off, then added: "I was at Cambridge when the row began."

The explanation seemed made without any particular purpose, but it affected Terry favourably. University backgrounds do lend men a cachet, he thought; seal their credentials. Border had the university air, tone, outlook. He was "all right."

"Why don't you come along with me?" He began to explain all about Mary, her nature, her curious claims to all the beauties, her definite claims to none. Vin, Terry observed, listened closely. Watching him, he faltered in his tale, struck by something curious in the other man's attitude. "Never seems quite inside things," he told himself. "Like someone artificially arranged in a group to which he doesn't naturally belong . . . But, gosh, he's too beautiful to be real, anyway." Yet . . . come to think of it, he'd noticed that strange, non-associated attitude before when they'd been talking of women. Not indifference. No. Far from it. Terrible intensity. "As if he were a being from Mars aware of special power to enjoy Earth's voluptuous pleasures."

And yet, he didn't look a voluptuous type, but more of the ascetic order, with his chiselled features, small, somewhat thin-lipped mouth.

Interested in both physiological and psychological subjects, Terry found it hard to place Vin. There was mystery in him; but also, beyond question, much that was charming and admirable. In most aspects Vincent Border was delightfully normal. Modesty, kindliness, some culture, sociability—he could claim all these.

So it was arranged that the precious leave should be spent in Terry's home town.

As the time for departure approached, he found himself looking forward with almost painful eagerness to seeing Mary again. Mary in her soft-hued home, cheek by jowl with his own soft-hued replica. A typical modest, middle-class English residence. It was nice to think of her in such surroundings, a link with that preciousness now blown off the earth by monster shells. He felt glad she was in no way associated with the war personally. Mary was hard to imagine in posts requiring bustling efficiency. She had, however, a beautiful voice, with which he knew she had done a lot of entertaining of troops. Good! Dear women with lovely gifts were rare, precious to wounded Tommies.

He wrote at some length in explanation of Vin, to which she replied:

"By all means bring him along; and between us we'll keep him on the pilgrim path of rectitude."

And so he took his odd friend with him to place in the unguarded charge of Mary, whose sex had heard no call, had lain, restful but potent, in slumber, ready to raise alert ears at the first distant note.

"*Is* there a war on?" he asked Vin as the train rolled on through vistas of bucolic peace, through valleys of misty beauty.

Mary met them. She had the gift of making simple and commonplace clothes—whether cheap or costly—appear the products of infinite thought, money and skill; and she had a stride that had captured Diana's untrammelled grace. Eyes radiant, lips apart, face alight and entire being athrill with eagerness, she came swinging down the platform into Vincent Border's life.

But for a while there was none but Terry in her horizon.
There he was! Her pal. As that, now, she knew his worth. If sex
did not respond to his appeal, other human attributes did.

She grasped his hands in her own, danced him round, voic-
ing a joy that surprised herself.

"I told Dad they couldn't kill *you*!" she cried.

All memory of the horrors of war left him. They mattered
nothing now, all those months of tense danger, suffering, filth,
pain. One moment could compensate man for the endurance of
years. The pleasure, gladness, happiness in her eyes were
strangely like love.

Marvellous Mary! Just now she was beauty embodied. Radiant. Dazzling. Incomparable.

They began to chatter, like, as she said presently, starved
monkeys, until a rather savage poke in his kidneys reminded
Terry he had brought Vincent Border with him. Being young,
he giggled, turned gaily to see his friend's eyes as alight, as excited as Mary's; to see him as starrily beautiful as she.

"Oh, Mary, this is Vin. I wrote you, you know."

"Oh, yes! How do . . . ."

She paused abruptly. Something dynamic, cosmic, in Vincent Border's stare sobered her mood. His loveliness staggered
her. This lovely god the ardent soldier Terry affirmed? World
of never-ceasing wonders! It did not seem possible that such
gracious glamour could be a killer, a licensed killer. Lyres and
lyrics alone seemed appropriate to his golden glow. And
whisky! Oh lord! Her limbs trembled. For an instant her brain
swam. Something seemed to rouse within her to almost vicious
life, to dig claws into the most sensitive part of her immaterial
self, to enslave her free self. Waves of feeling surged up to her
throat, suffused her eyes . . . And then she was finishing her
formal greeting . . . She must pull herself together . . .

But all he said was three words—which sealed Mary's fate:
"Oh lovely lady!"

Archly said, they were full of incomparable homage. All the
courting of years was in them. No woman could have escaped
him—then.

But Terry, watching, thought that, despite the intensity of his gaze, despite its directness, Vin did not *see* Mary; not as he and others would see her, coming upon her thus for the first time; that his mind and his eyes did not focus fully upon the objects they regarded—were too restless, evasive. There was possessiveness, appetite in his eyes, but no concentration, no tranquillity. Vin looked at things, received an impression of desirability and, obeying his primitive instincts, snatched without consideration, without civilized appreciation of consequences, as a child snatches at lovely wayside flowers, looks, smells, and idly drops, when drawn to the next gay attraction.

From Vin's gay, yet, somehow, indefinite face Terry glanced at Mary, to catch the startled recognition of something special to herself in this new personality. His own heart jumped. A little stream of molten agony poured through his veins. A sense of calamity pervaded him, together with a more particular sense of irreparable loss.

This meeting to which he had looked forward with a sort of exultant hope was the grave of hope. Vincent and Mary. He might have known. That almost uncanny charm! Mary, like himself, had encountered nothing similar.

But Mary . . . and Vincent Border? A dragging sense of disaster whispered that he would have been wiser to take her with him into the trenches, into the direct line of fire, rather than subject her to the poison of Vincent Border's beauty.

Yet the visitor's manner and behaviour were exemplary. Seeking for definite justification of his almost prophetic fears, he could find none. It was as if some psychic quality in himself had been stirred by Vin's aura.

And it was not to the newcomer that Mary gave her attention, but to the old pal. Almost she seemed inclined to snub her guest. And this was so unlike Mary that Terry sought wildly for some explanation. Did she perceive something odd lurking behind Vin's beauty? Something at variance with nature—the norm? Not something merely pagan; something more . . . more . . . He could not find the words to express his instinct.

And yet was there not another explanation for that almost marked ignoring of the newcomer in favour of the old? Do we not often turn away our gaze from the thing we most desire? It is one of the most common pretenses. And it is one of woman's most eloquent reactions. Women think, perhaps—Terry told himself—that this action is an effective mask.

"I've arranged dinner early for to-night," Mary explained as they entered. "I thought you'd like that. Come and meet Aunt Charlotte." She turned to Vin. "Aunt's rather lame, which is rotten luck because she's jolly, you know."

It seemed to Terry she was afraid to meet his friend's eyes, that for once the graceful tom-boy of his home-days was shy— at a loss.

She turned, leading the way, and Terry stole a glance at Vin. He was watching Mary move with the same intense regard that seemed inseparable from his reaction to women, subjectively or objectively. A faint uneasiness stole into Terry's mind. A sudden vision of this lovely, golden boy dipping his hand into a flowing red flood intensified the uneasiness. Mary! Clasp-knives and glassy eyes. The dead!

~ ~ ~ ~ ~

They were all very gay at dinner. Despite her lameness, Aunt Charlotte was obviously taken with the strange young man.

Champagne flowed, rather to Terry's concern. How, he wondered, was the potent wine going to affect Vin; but his anxiety was not justified, for, though Vin drank it without any noticeable restraint, it seemed only to make him gayer. Never, Terry thought, had Vin shown to greater advantage. His high spirits expressed themselves in humour and he kept the table in roars of laughter, not only by his quips and tales but also by his power of facial expression. He struck a note to which Mary found it easy to respond. She had supposed these two invalids would be glad of early bed, but neither showed the slightest disposition to leave the bright drawing-room with its autumn fire and pleasant air of belonging to a bygone age. Vincent revealed a light, tuneful baritone and sang many gay little, sometimes risqué, songs that none of the others had heard before. Mary sang. Then they sang duets. And Aunt Charlotte electrified them by brilliant renderings of famous composers. Terry alone could do nothing—save laugh and cheer. Mary and Vincent, he thought, stimulated each other. Now he reproached himself for his earlier misgivings. Now, he told himself, he was seeing his friend as he really was—just a happy, singing, laughing lad. Yet he was more than that: he was, above all else, fascinating, exciting. To a woman Vin himself must be like wine in the blood, exhilarating. Never had he seen Mary's eyes sparkle as they were sparkling to-night. Her whole being glowed, like a creature uplifted . . . Which she was. No one knew better than she that something vital had happened to her, that life had changed.

Vincent Border had startled her. He was an invader, had assaulted and stormed strongholds of her nature hitherto absolutely inviolate. Something in his personality roused an imp in her. Since first his glance had met hers, a recklessness beyond anything in her experience demanded expression. She felt almost indecently attracted—without actually liking or approving of Border. Not as she approved of Terry beyond question or hesitation. On the other hand, no other human being had ever made her feel so brilliantly happy as Vincent Border proceeded to do during the next few hours. She had looked forward keenly to Terry's advent: long walks, long talks; recollecting, revealing new thoughts. She had expected to be cosy and jolly; but this! Terry had brought Pan with him, out of the dirt and slaughter of lice-ridden trenches into a provincial drawing-room; and the supreme outlaw had changed her into a nymph.

Mary had poise, self-reliance and a cool judgment; but all these were now disturbed. She felt in a whirl. She felt the approach of new and ardent influences and for the first time tremulous. Terry had kissed her. Other men had kissed her; but she had experience no thrill, no sudden fire in her being. But when Vincent Border kissed her—the solid earth melted, she swam in a sea of ecstasy.

He had kissed her terribly, so that she burned more because of the memory of that kiss than she had burned from the kiss itself. Delicious shame lingered. And he had kissed her without preparation or preliminary. He had not waited until they became better acquainted or until she gave him encouragement, but had kissed her on that very first evening, after all of them except herself had said good night and gone to bed. But he had come down again—just as she was about to switch off the drawing-room light and go to bed herself.

"My watch has stopped," he explained.

And then they had just stood and stared at each other; she at him with an utterly helpless feeling.

He smiled. There was an extraordinary and uninterpretable expression on his face. His eyes challenged her.

Then he took a swift step forward and kissed her, while she stood unresisting and received it. Not a mere salute. Nothing tentative about it. A kiss that had sex as its impulse. And it was like that she received it. With his own puckered lips he parted hers and kissed her with deliberate, almost voracious, enjoyment.

"Lovely lady!" he whispered.

~ ~ ~ ~ ~

When he had gone, she wondered why he had gone; knowing full well that it was not because he respected her possible virginity, or because he was a chivalrous young man. In time she answered this question; but then she could not.

She went to bed herself to lie awake and think. For the first time in her life she had surrendered. Yes, and to a young man of whom she knew practically nothing beyond the little that Terry had told her in his letters. Father dead, mother—with whom he was not on good terms—about to re-marry, independent means, University man, weakness for whisky, inclined—Terry thought—to neurasthenia, but a daring soldier in spite of it.

Was she in love? She supposed so. No, she'd better be honest: was she in love? Yes. Which showed that love *could* come suddenly, without any preparation. But did being in love mean the same as loving? Hardly. She loved Terry, but was not in love with him. She loved Terry for his qualities, not for his physical being. And every feminine instinct loudly declared that of these two young men Terry was the worthy one, the one to be blindly trusted.

Marriage? Huh! He might not ask her . . . But some prescient voice declared he would. Well? Would she? She fell asleep debating the question.

~ ~ ~ ~ ~

Terry, of course, was best man; a rather worried one. He tried to be more than just best man. But it is difficult for a man deeply in love to warn his lady against one he had brought to her as his friend; and the rôle of mentor was never much in Terry's line. But, for that matter, it is doubtful if he could have helped Mary even if he had put into definite words his indefinite doubts; for she had them, too, and yet had not the strength to resist Vin. Terry did rather clumsily express his own sentiments regarding a man's right to tie a woman to possible, very possible, tragedy and the rest of it; but she swept his arguments a little contemptuously to one side.

"The kind of love that Vin and I feel, Terry, may never come again in life. Why, in the name of sense, should one deny oneself its consummation because it may be snatched away as abruptly as it has been offered? All acute joy is short and sharp. Physical love is generally brief; and at its best is irresistible. I'm going to marry a sinner, not a saint . . . I'd ever so much rather marry you than Vin, if I could feel for you what I feel for him. That would be the most perfect form of marriage, because you'd be a dear as well as a lover."

Terry's wound had hurt far less than these unheeding words. But then, he told himself, she did not realize he cared in exactly the same way as Vin; and, though she knew he loved her, she supposed it was the same kind of non-physical fondness she accorded him.

So they were married and went to Torquay for their brief honeymoon, which, for Mary, passed like a blissful dream and with never a jarring note.

Terry returned to France before Vin, who applied for and received additional leave. When, however, the groom returned from the warmth of his nuptial bed to the wet chill of front-line trenches, his friend could detect no change of any kind in his demeanour. He was the same rather faunlike, psychically elusive being, full of fun and charming ways and as vicious in attacks.

They talked of Mary and the future, but only because Terry introduced both subjects. To the latter it seemed strange that Vin should avoid any reference to his future plans and not indicate in some way the degree of his financial independence.

"Well, you see, Terry," Border explained in reply to a somewhat leading question, "it's difficult for me to make plans. I shan't go back to Cambridge, of course. I'm making no claims to any special ability. I have none. What I'd like is some prosaic job . . . Incidentally, what are *you* doing when things go flat?"

"I shall go into Dad's office."

"A lawyer. Gosh, it's useful to have a pal in the legal profession . . . I gathered during leave that your job's a nice fat cinch."

It seemed to Terry that genuine envy lurked beneath this supposedly humorous remark.

"No job's such a cinch as having an assured income," Terry replied with a laugh.

"Quite."

His voice sounded a little dry.

"Anyhow, my inclination is to settle down in the old home-town."

"Whose old home-town? Yours?"

"God forbid! No, yours. Nice ready-made connections there . . . And, though you may doubt it, I'd like to be near you. I've quite come to look upon you as my guardian angel."

Terry's heart gave a jump of joy. He had dreaded being parted absolutely and perhaps for ever from Mary. He was fond of his home, of his native town, of provincial life and of the two mellow houses that had seen both his and Mary's birth.

"Have you two made any plans? Where you're going to live and that?" Terry asked.

"Yes. Mary wrote to her old man and suggested that we should all carry on together."

"The doctor will like that."

"She says the practice has suffered a lot through the war."

"She told me that; and I heard it generally."

"It's rotten luck!"

To Terry he sounded as if the depreciation of Dr. Rodney's practice were a personal grievance of first class importance.

"Did Mary say why the practice has suffered so?"

"Locum's loco. Dripping with senility. Everyone who wants to live has loped off to Dr. Pugh."

~ ~ ~ ~ ~

It was some days after this that Terry, returning from an inspection, discovered Vin, rigid and livid, striding about the dug-out with an open telegram in his hands.

"The doctor's bumped off!" he shouted.

"Mary's dad?"

"Yes!"

He seemed more angry than distressed and, Terry thought, was about to burst into some invective, when either decency or commonsense prevailed. Nerves, no doubt. Vin replied to Terry's attempted condolences by walking abruptly out of the other's presence and vanishing for hours.

"Temperamental blighter," Terry reflected. "Maybe he's superstitious and has the wind-up."

A couple of days later, when once more Vin seemed his customary brilliant, diffident, but odd, self, Terry asked him if the disturbing news would alter his plans.

"No. I'd like to make a start in surroundings sympathetic to Mary. There's a home ready-made—a home with associations. Why seek trouble?"

This answer pleased Terry. It indicated that the young husband was concerned for Mary's happiness.

"I suppose," Vin asked presently, "Mary'll get the doctor's money?"

"There's no doubt of that. Only child."

"The house was his property?"

"Oh yes."

For a time there was a lull in the fighting. Inaction often, Terry had found, produced irritability; but this was not true of Vincent Border. He seemed concerned to win Terry's regard in every way, was very quiet and yet entertaining, doing much to keep his comrades cheerful. Moreover, he refused whisky, promptly and tersely, when Yovers produced an unexpected bottle.

"Good!" Terry thought. "The chap's in earnest."

~ ~ ~ ~ ~

They had been fighting furiously, holding on to their positions by, Vincent put it, the skin of their bayonets; and now they were resting, worn out—sad. It was an appropriate period for Terry to receive news of *his* father's death, instant, happily, and yet dreadful, since he had been blown to fragments.

They had been friends, this father and son; both quiet, un-demonstrative beings, but capable of hidden strong feelings. The news hurt Terry intensely, but few realized how much.

He wrote to his mother, but her reply was resigned. She had expected just this from the instant of her husband's departure to fight. Her attitude was stoic. One had to carry on. She should not leave her post while the war continued. When it ended, if ever, she supposed Terry would come home and carry on the business.

That was that.

Uneasy rest. Trenches. Slaughter. Something doing. Really doing. Something more than the interminable see-saw to which Terry and millions like him had grown inured. Something giving. Advance. Optimism again; like the sun after weeks of fog. Armistice. Delirium. Home.

CHAPTER III

THE DEATH OF HER FATHER had come as a serious and disillusioning shock to Mary, the more so because she had let him die without revealing her marriage. She had been even fonder of the doctor than she herself had known. He had been a good, considerate father, denying her little. They had permitted few secrets between them. And, now that he was dead, it puzzled her greatly to know why she had been so reluctant to announce a major fact like her marriage to Vincent Border. There were dim reasons discernible even in the fog of her puzzlement: first, if not foremost, Dr. Rodney was serving in Salonika, very distant and to her very inaccessible. It was no mere matter of getting leave and hopping home to attend what, after all, was a hasty wedding, which took place without fuss of any kind at the parish church. And then, she felt sure, unhappily sure, though she stoutly denied the truth of her instinct, that Dr. Rodney would neither have liked nor approved of Vin. Her womanhood had sensed something unstable in this risky husband—despite her infatuation. Terry had not truly liked him; and Terry thought in very similar fashion to her father. Sometimes she held her breath in an ecstasy of alarm when she considered the future . . . And yet, she asked herself, why? That honeymoon . . . a week of sheer glory. The bridal night itself, true rapture is somewhat alarming to a virginal experience. Were all men like that . . . so . . . so . . . So gloriously ruthless? Did all grooms make innocent brides gasp and blush, leave them in exhausted shame? Shamed and frightened and yet . . . oh, well!

And then this sudden deluge of disaster: not only her own father dead, not only her neat life dishevelled, but Terry also bereaved and left with a disrupted future; to which must be added this strange uneasiness about the consequences of what now seemed a short, sharp, period of madness. Not that she had changed in her feelings toward Vin. Far from it. Her vague alarm persisted *despite* those feelings. She was still very young and had not thus far preoccupied herself with prudence, method, foresight. She had wanted desperately to marry Vincent before he returned to the risks of war—like innumerable other women—and had done so in youth's unconsidering way.

But Dr. Rodney's death had sobered her considerably and left her with a curious sense of responsibility. She had been accustomed to lean absolutely upon her father's wisdom and support; now he was gone. She had to rely upon herself—or Vin. But the idea of relying upon Vin, for some reason, amused her; or it would have amused her had circumstances been less tragic. It occurred now to her as exceedingly strange that he should have made no suggestion about their future, no explanation as to his means and other affairs. Was that because he feared death, feared no return, would not speak of the future lest there be none? Was he a very superstitious man?

Terry's father had been Dr. Rodney's lawyer and now, in the absence of both principals, Mr. Stone, the firm's managing clerk, had charge of her affairs. It seemed her father had left all unconditionally to his daughter, but that did not say a great deal, for there had not been a great deal of substance for the doctor to leave. The greatly reduced practice was to be sold and, should that yield what Mr. Stone anticipated, Mary would have a small income, barely sufficient to enable her to live in a very modest way providing she continued to occupy the house that was her own property and for which she would not have to pay rent. But this did not trouble her much; Vin, Terry had said, was a man of independent means; they should be very comfortable—rich, if Vin were well off.

And then the armistice, with all its attendant delirium. Jangling peace. Men returning. Soon she would be Mrs. Border in real earnest, not in merely romantic perspective.

"Golly, I've wind-up!" she told herself in genuine alarm.

She could not picture herself as a prosaic house-wife with domestic duties. She still wanted to climb trees, indulge escapades.

And then suddenly she was longing breathlessly, with dry lips, for Vin's return, magnifying its glory beyond all possibility.

The letter she received from Border announcing his return to civilian life and her struck Mary more on account of its courteous phrasing than because of its ardour. Certainly it was not a lover's letter.

"It's the letter of a judicious, meticulous French husband," she told herself.

This epistle dashed her own high spirits and added to her strange uneasiness. The letter noticeably omitted any reference to arrangements, either financial or domestic. It took for granted that he should rejoin her at the house which was now her own property. Of course, it was understandable that he thought it better to leave all discussion regarding their future until they were again together . . . But one would have supposed . . . London! A spree! Celebrations! Even old Terry would not have proposed so humdrum a reunion. Surely it was an occasion of gladness and extreme gladness *should* express itself; has to, as a rule.

There'd be no possibility of any "do" at her end. Money was too tight. And that Vin knew. She had written fully after her father's death, explaining the position, but, though he'd replied, it was only to express sympathy and not to make any helpful financial suggestions. As it was, she'd cut down expenses and imposed rigid economy upon herself, sharing the domestic work with only one maid, Elizabeth, an ultra-respectable and rather ill-tempered person. One maid was not, of course, either sufficient or suitable for a house of any size.

But, of course, Vincent was very young, he'd never been compelled to consider domesticity. From Cambridge to the trenches was poor training in the duties of married life. Things would right themselves.

When he did come, he came alone, unannounced and naturally unexpected.

Mary saw him walking quietly up the gravel drive when she was arranging the curtains at her bedroom window. Attracted by her movements, he looked up, smiling impishly.

"Well!"

Mary dropped the curtains and tore downstairs. He met her with arms rather theatrically outstretched.

"Darling!"

His embrace was fervent yet respectful; the embrace of an actor playing his part realistically.

"Why ever didn't you wire?"

"I wanted to surprise you."

"Oh, you have!"

Girl-like she giggled, held him at arm's length, inspecting—what: lover? husband?

And yet it was all desperately disappointing. When she and Vin had last been together, neither had been normal, but exalted, first by their excited sexuality, second by the fact that his life was in constant danger and this marriage should have been a forbidden thing. But now, this creeping home, this idiotic flat meeting!

"Have you had anything to eat?"

He seemed not to hear and, when she repeated the question, roused himself from definite preoccupation with hardly concealed irritability.

"Oh, yes, yes! Food! Don't mention it!"

"Is anything the matter, Vin?"

He wrung his hands, rose, walked rapidly about, burst suddenly into tears and sank to his knees, head on Mary's lap.

She had never had a young man's weeping head on her lap and felt embarrassed. And, till now, she'd seen no man cry. It made her feel gauche.

"Vin, whatever is it?"

He raised his ravaged face, yet without directly meeting her gaze.

"A most awful thing's happened to me, Merks."

Used by now to shocks and bizarre happenings, she waited.

"It's about the will under which my income's paid," he explained chokily.

"Oh!"

She had expected death and disaster, but money! She had all youth's contempt for money and all youth's optimism.

"There's a case in Chancery to decide whether the will means capital is to be paid out or merely the income from the capital."

"Oh, then you'll get it sooner or later—your money?"

"Of course. It's mine, however they decide; but meanwhile I've nothing except my demob brass."

"Well, *that's* nothing to worry about. We can manage."

"But I've debts. A fellow runs up accounts without thought."

"I can lend you money, darlingest."

"Oh, no! I can get money, a loan from the Jews."

"You'll do nothing of the kind, Mr. Border. Mrs. Border's going to have something to say to that. Good lord, what's the good of marriage if you can't lend your own husband money? And it's not as if you can't pay it back later."

"No, that's true."

"I'll have to write you a cheque."

"There's no hurry."

"Well, I've got to go to the bank myself to-morrow, suppose I draw out extra?"

"Angel!"

"How much, a hundred, two?"

For an instant he closed his eyes. The corners of his mouth twitched a little.

"Two," he muttered.

"Poor boy," she thought, "he hates talking about it." Then added: "Terry said he was sensitive."

She liked him better for all this. Found it touching that he should cry because he was letting her down, and felt comfort in this lovely explanation of his drab creeping home.

They had a second honeymoon that night and she responded to his overtures with a spirit, a passion, that surprised him and disgusted her. He seemed to appeal to a vulgarity that she had not suspected existing in her abstract composition.

"It's coarse, this much-vaunted relationship. No wonder most people never want to discuss it literally."

A little more and it would be repulsive, horrible. Her heart beat wildly all night long—while he slept, looking as if material pleasures had never sullied his soul; looking like an embodiment of the aesthetic. Curiously, as curiously as suddenly, she wished it were Terry who lay beside her. Not this erotic stranger, this mystery who filled her soul with doubt, even while he filled her body with ecstasy.

The next day she gave him the money, which he received with gentle diffidence. His conduct was as correct as a pattern. They had three cosy, lovely, days, during which her fears began to melt away. Nevertheless, there was a certain sense of disappointment, a sense of loss inseparable from even these three special days. A sense of something lacking that Terry had unconsideringly and certainly unconsidered supplied. There was a racy tang to Terry that one missed from Vin's mere brilliance of physical glamour and mental charm. Definitely he was not intellectual, which that much-missed friend was. Moreover Terry had masses of information packed away in his mind and a manner of imparting it that was without a trace of didacticism. No tramp with Terry had ever been boring, whereas she and Vin spent half theirs in silent fatigue.

And it began to dawn upon her that he was unwholesomely erotic, prone to sudden and embarrassing impulses. These manifestations alarmed her. Was this a phase, or did he expect permanent gratification of a similar unlicensed nature?

Then came the fourth night.

Vin had been particularly charming all day, if a little too inclined towards sentiment. He had discussed the future.

"I suggest staying put," he told her. "At least for a time. We can always travel."

Mary indulged a thrill of glee. Travel! All the world's high-spots. So wonderful to her, so casual to him!

"This is a topping home," Vin continued. "It'll be nice living next door to Terry. You have a big circle of friends. I haven't enough money for us to live a real crackajack sort of life among the swells, and it's better to be a brass-hat in your own home-town than a trooper in Mayfair."

Mary was surprised at the commonsense of this outlook. One did not usually associate Vin with practicality.

Already, he told her, he had made friends, got to know "some of the boys." Who these were she did not know and could not imagine; but being so young took things for granted.

At luncheon on the fourth day she said:

"I've promised to sing at a concert for the wounded to-night. I have done every week. You'll come, won't you?"

"No, not to-night, Merks. I want to get away from anything to do with military service."

She felt disappointment, which showed in her face.

"It would be a splendid opportunity for you to get to know people. Many of my friends will be there."

"All the local swells, eh? Don't press me to-night, baby. Leave it till next time."

And that was that. She suspected there was an immense obstinacy under his easy manner and insouciance. It appeared that there was some club which he had joined. What its nature or importance were she could not gather and hardly as yet felt justified in criticizing his conduct. So that night they went each a separate way. She to her wounded; he to his "club."

Since her father's death and the revelation regarding her financial security Mary had dispensed with the late doctor's car and, like other unfortunate people in the big town, had to depend upon buses to take her here and there. To-night's concert was being held at Great Hill's Top—a threepenny bus ride. Concert done and Mary homeward bound, she preferred to sit on the outside of the bus, since it was a beautiful night, boon and mild. She gazed about her from right to left, left to right, getting peeps into variously furnished homes, into bar-parlours, smoking-rooms, saloons. In the smoking-room of Century's she saw her husband holding a peroxided woman in a lascivious embrace, while a circle of apparently semi-drunken men applauded. Her blood seemed for an instant to stop coursing, her heart to stop beating, her lungs to stop functioning. Then her blood flooded madly, hot as fire through her veins, her heart bounded in her breast, her lungs pumped dangerously. Infinite impulses, all contradictory, set her body twitching. She should jump off the bus, burst into that room. No. She would never see Vincent Border again. Shut the door in his face. She would vanish. She would—this, that and the other . . .

But she consummated none of her resolves, instead went stonily home, wrote a note bidding him keep away from their mutual room, put this where he could not fail to see it on his return—providing he could see anything—went to bed and locked the door. In bed she drew the clothes completely over her head so that she could neither see nor hear; but despite this the vision of that woman in his arms, his lips glued to hers and their bodies plastered each against the other, remained; and she heard again and again his oft-repeated assurances of love, admiration and utter loyalty.

She heard him come in—the front door crash.

"He's drunk!" she thought.

Not two minutes later he was smashing at her door. Eyes wide, the hollows under each cheek-bone intensified, abruptly she sat up and watched the door, mute, stone. His voice, continually objurgated her in the foulest terms picked up, she supposed, among the mire and entrails of war.

His tones rose—a crescendo . . .

His crashes on the panels must eventually do several things: split them asunder, rouse the night, terrify Elizabeth, a nervous woman. Her own anger flamed. The drunken beast! What manner of a woman did he take her for? What sort of house did he suppose he was in? Some continental brothel?

Tall, taut, she strode in two strides to the door; she flung it open.

His eyes glazed, unfocused, together with his unreal stance, gave him an air of being detached from his normal human self. He had stepped out of the exact. No demon could have been less of the earth. Not a man, an apparition. Occult.

Held, appalled, ice-cold, she stared, waiting. He advanced in the manner of some automaton and very slowly his lips flowed into a smile, like a snake emerging from sand. Unconsciously she backed . . . What did this mean, insult, assault, *death*? Blood? Murder?

Then she could not back any farther, unless dematerialization of solid matter miraculously took place.

~ ~ ~ ~ ~

With a single fast, deft clutch he tore off the pretty bridal nightdress and laughed with drunken lust . . . Her struggles brought froth to his lips. Deliberately he leaned back and struck her on the mouth, cutting it. Terry had once written, and destroyed, poems about her mouth. Justified inspiration . . .

With a lithe movement, she twisted free . . . But he caught her, his flaming eyes agleam with some sort of phantasy. Captured again, she felt her knees weaken with despair. As useful to protest to some obscene flux! . . . Pinning her flat to the wall with one hand, with the other he picked a pin from its tray and thrust it as far as the head into her white shoulder.

She screamed and battered at his face when she realized he was feeling for other pins; then, fighting madly, tore from his grasp—out of the room, he pursuing. Relentless, silent, intent; wearing his fixed, mischievous smile, which lent his beauty the cast of a bacchant. In the hall, redolent of middle-class calm, he caught up with Mary and snatched her two white wrists, pinning her arms behind, and, heedless of writhes, screams, tears, dragged her to the still unfastened door . . . He flung her out into the night. She crashed down the six shallow stone steps and lay, like a nude, white goddess, on the dew-wet gravel.

~ ~ ~ ~ ~

Elizabeth, chalk-white, watched from the shelter of the first landing his grandiloquent return, Puckish triumph in face and gait.

He emitted an idiotic, eldritch screech at sight of her and leapt up the stairs. She flung herself through the first door that offered, marked with two Victorian survivals, the 3rd and 23rd letters of the English alphabet, crashed to and bolted the door in his grinning face. He stood, swaying, with one brow cocked up and his falsely direct gaze fixed on the two rude letters. Presently he began to laugh and shout improper remarks at the imprisoned woman; but suddenly slumped, fell in a heap, back against the door and asleep.

~ ~ ~ ~ ~

It began to rain; a little keen wind crept and gambolled. Mary shuddered to consciousness, then to awareness. Pain enveloped her. One hip was gashed and bruised. The tendons of that leg were strained; the shoulder Vin had pierced hurt acutely; her cut mouth stung; each wrist felt broken; her whole being ached—yet obviously she could not stay naked on the gravel of her respectable little drive. The night still shrouded her shame; there was still time to gain shelter before scandal was assured.

Forcing herself to hands and knees, she looked and listened; but saw and heard no sign of Vin. Little by little she dragged her battered body up the stone steps, once used out of surgery hours by her father's trusting, cut-to-pattern patients. Mrs. This was ill, Mr. That had suffered injury, could the doctor come at once?

She'd have given a slice of life for Terry, who would at any instant fight like a Fenian in her defense.

~ ~ ~ ~ ~

She saw Vin, but he no longer slept back to the door, he had succumbed to the mat and lay on his side. He snored.

"Who's that?"

With a start, Mary realized that someone was beyond that door and then who that someone must be; besides, now she recognized the voice despite its low tones.

"Mrs. Border. Will you please let me out?"

"You must wait."

Mary continued on her way. Presently, her nudity covered, she returned and put her lips to the door.

"It's safe, cook. He's fast asleep."

Stealthily, the other scared woman emerged.

"He'll sleep now for hours," she said with a gesture at Vin . . . "I'm sorry, Mrs. Border, you must please take my notice."

"It will never occur again, cook."

"Oh, but it will, ma'am. I know that lit-up type of drinker. *My* husband was like that . . . White with it, as *he* is. Mine promised me on his honour, on his soul, on his hope for salvation, it would never occur again. He beat me black and blue three nights later . . ."

She had a lot more to say, but Mary fainted.

~ ~ ~ ~ ~

Elizabeth's prophecy of penitence proved justified. Next day, Mary, in bed, suffering acutely from pain and shock, heard a timid knocking at her door. Immediately she knew it was he. A wave of anger and disgust surged through her. She felt exceedingly confused, and had thus far come to no decision regarding her future dealings with Vin.

"I ought to inform the police," she told herself violently.

She felt he had robbed her of self-respect; destroyed something lovely and immaculate that does perish when sheltered women meet violence at masculine hands. It was not only the horror, pain, shock, that she resented so bitterly, there was the profound vulgarity of the affair. Reviewing it, Mary could find no difference between her experience and those of the police news type that delicate women avoid as men avoid mush.

Her face was hard and set when Vin crept in. He had dressed and looked spick and span, as unlike the drink-shot maniac of last night as a square is unlike a circle. Humility and penitence suited his saintly beauty, but unfortunately both his beauty and spiritual distress were lost upon Mary, for she kept her gaze rigidly averted.

"Mary!"

There was a tremor in his tones of a heart-touching quality.

"Mary, I don't know what to say."

Clearly she shared this inability of expression.

"Terry told you about me and whisky . . . I've no excuse to make . . . I swore to him I'd keep clear of the wretched stuff . . ."

So began a most eloquent tale. No counsel could have pleaded his case more subtly or with greater fervour, the better for being decently restrained.

This was only his third outbreak, he said. Terry had witnessed the second. He had asked Terry then to help him, now he asked Mary. Mere condemnation saved no souls. A little help's worth all the rebuke in Christendom. After all, they were married. They had to spend their lives together. And Mary must realize that it was not he, Vincent Border, who had disgraced the name of man last night, but the debased being created by the fumes of drink. He, the sane, sober he, would not hurt a hair of Mary's head; and to prove that, he would, if Mary wished, go now, never see her again.

Almost she bade him go. It is not easy, however, to set down in cold letters the emotional power of Vincent Border's dignified humility. Mary had not one of those boardlike souls off which men's pleas bounce like rubber balls. She wanted to be happy. She wanted everybody to be happy. She was young, full of belief. This was her first skirmish with disillusion.

She promised to help him and his eyes shone with an almost holy resolve, or what appeared to be such resolve.

He helped her disabilities with wonderful efficiency, so that eventually she was able to rise with some measure of physical and mental ease, when he wisely effaced himself. Mary descended with a renewed feeling of hope in her heart and with a sense of mission in her soul.

She felt sufficiently revived to face even Elizabeth, who, however, was wont to declare she had corns on *her* soul and no more belief in human promises than in divine fulfilments.

"Mr. Border offers you his apologies," Mary said without timidity; for she still believed in the discrepancies of class and an apology from "Master" seemed to her a very noble thing and more than full compensation for any wrong suffered by a servant.

Elizabeth sniffed, her final comment with the significance behind it of years of domestic disillusionment.

"Things are being left just as they were?" she asked in her dry voice.

Mary explained.

"Oh, yes! Well, all the same, ma'am, my notice stands. Moreover, I prefer to forego my wages and leave at once."

It was only with the utmost difficulty and after much persuasion that Mary prevailed on Elizabeth to stay until her young mistress could find other help.

"All very well, fine promises and that. However, I'll stay on this understanding: at the first sign of trouble I leave on the spot."

Yet an hour later even she had yielded to Vin's blandishments and irresistible charm.

CHAPTER IV

IT WAS WHILE on his way home to be demobbed that coincidence introduced Vincent Border's name to Terry's immediate
cognizance at a time when for once he was thinking neither of
his friend nor of her whom his friend had married. And it happened like this: Terry, while in the actual presence of Tom
Mordaunt, his traveling companion, also on his way to wave a
fond farewell to war until the next, and also a lawyer, dropped
his over-packed pocket-book from which there fell, face up-
wards and among many others, a photograph of Vin. Picking
up his fallen property, Terry proffered Vin's photograph to
Tom with the remark:

"How's that for a really good-looking chap?"

Tom Mordaunt took the likeness casually, then glanced at
Terry quizzically.

"So he's a noble British soldier now, holding His Majesty's
commission into the bargain?"

"Why, d'you know him?"

"And some." He grinned to himself. "And what, oh man of
the law, do *you* know about him?"

"Well-connected bloke, was at Cambridge when war started,
has independent means."

"How nice! He didn't happen to mention that he was at Borstal and in certain of His Majesty's guest houses, too?"

"You're kidding, Tom!" Terry exclaimed anxiously.

"I defended him before the justices on an abominable sex-
charge, Terry, old man. Young girl, under the age, grievous
assault. Three years, at the Old Bailey. More recently, eighteen
months, fraud. His independent means, you know."

"Good God!"

Tom glanced at his companion and his light manner underwent a change. Clearly his news had filled Terry with unspeakable horror.

"What's the trouble, old thing?"

"Eh, what?" Absorbed in his thoughts, urgent and anxious, Terry had not grasped the import of Tom Mordaunt's question; and, instead of answering, himself demanded: "Can it be possible that you've made a mistake, Tom? This boy's only my own age."

"Says he! Your little pip-squeak's exactly thirty-one years old."

"But he only looks . . ."

"Any age he wishes. It's no mistake, old bean. I'd know that phiz anywhere. There aren't two beautiful, saintlike criminals with those features. Dyed in the wool, incurable adventurer and bad hat. No woman's safe with him. No child's safe with him. The best, the kindest judgment that can be passed upon master Border—if that's his real name—is he's abnormal. But how does all this concern you, my bachelor lad?"

"I'd rather you didn't ask, Tom. It *does* concern me very nearly and seriously. Let it go at that, will you, old sport?"

The other immediately dropped the subject; but his information had blackened the fairest prospect of Terry's young life. He had looked forward with unqualified delight to returning home, to taking up his abode next door to Mary once more, to dropping in on her and Border for jolly evenings and arranging excursions with them both. But now! He felt terribly perturbed. If only he had known this earlier! If only . . . But there was no end to these *if onlys*. Damnable that Vincent should have had his chance to be demobbed first. Heaven alone knew what had happened to Mary by now . . . And he had not the slightest doubt of Tom Mordaunt's accuracy. Tom was a cautious chap; never made statements unless he could substantiate them. Nearly forty, Tom, not given to slack imaginings.

Anyhow, thank God he *was* going home. Thank God Vin and Mary were remaining in the old home . . . Though, of course, that was all along inevitable. That was what Master Vin had been after, security, comparative ease and comfort, a comfort very different from the unfriendly hardship of prison . . .

And how amazingly subtle the devil was! How he had taken him, Terry, in! Yet, no; to be fair to himself, not altogether. He's sensed a wrong 'un. More fool he to lack confidence in his judgment . . . Though, actually, it was a matter of instinct, not judgment. Would it have done any good to warn Mary? Unlikely. Naturally she'd have asked what he knew against Vin. And people were exceedingly sceptical about instinct, despite the constant proof of its infallibility.

Mary was now to all practical purposes alone in the world, she had no one to champion her, except her friends, the closest of whom was himself. It was up to him to do something regarding this alarming information. Wisest, of course, to be guided by the situation obtaining on the spot; but clearly he must face Vin with the truth. All kinds of difficult complications presented themselves for his consideration.

What should have been the happiest home-coming of his life now promised to be one that he would definitely have avoided had he cared for Mary less. Not only was he in for trouble, but would lack the fine judgment of his mother, who was still occupied by her self-sought duties. Impossible to say when he'd see his sister again, his father was gone forever, and there was an empty house to damp his spirits still further. However, Mrs. Cliffe had written to Thatcher, their old cook-housekeeper, who was returning specially to look after him and set everything once more in order. Things would brighten up when, with time, Mrs. Cliffe was able to relinquish work and herself return home.

However, when eventually he did arrive home, he found, except for the inevitable absences, things going on as smoothly as when he first left for France. Thatcher was there, helped by a cherubic kitchen-maid and, of all the marvels, Anne—who surely should have married—was back to carry on upstairs. Everything was orderly, bright and as his mother liked to see her house. In the latter's absence Mrs. Thatcher, who had nursed him as a boy, was a good substitute. Mrs. Cliffe herself loved Terry no better.

For the best part of an hour, during which he was doing full justice to Mrs. Thatcher's substantial fare, he all but forgot his anxiety about next door; but presently, his things unpacked and put in place, bathed and in the strange-feeling "civies," he smoked a cigarette while Mrs. Thatcher announced the various changes and imparted the most dramatic news of a neighbourhood not given to providing lurid episodes. The most lurid troubling Mrs. Thatcher's mind was that connected with next door. She was as familiar with the Rodney household as the Cliffe, little less fond of Mary than of Terry. Once she had ardently hoped these two would marry and was well aware of Terry's unquenchable love. It was for this reason she felt reluctant to wound feelings only too greatly harrowed during nearly five years of war. It was a shame, she told herself, that he should hear bad news on his first night back from the great shambles; but, nevertheless, it was much wiser to tell him, lest he should go happily hailing Mary over the garden wall as of yore; or in case some other informant, less concerned for his peace of mind, should impart a tale only to be told with tact and care.

And then, to her surprise, Terry himself broached the subject, saving her the trouble of finding the right words with which to begin.

"Has there been any trouble next door, Mrs. Thatcher?"

"Trouble enough, Mr. Terry; but how do you come to know anything about it?"

"I heard something on my way home that prepared me."

"Whatever did Miss Mary want to go marrying that devil for?"

"Devil!"

"That's what he is, neither more nor less. He tortures her."

"What?"

"It's literally true."

"Whisky?"

"Yes. It started four nights after he came home. There were terrible scenes; but that I knew nothing of. They've been repeated several times since. The last time he kicked her in the stomach and she was in bed for a week. After each bout he swears repentance and stays all right for a few days; then off he goes again. Elizabeth's left. Miss Mary's got a young girl in her place; but it seems to me she does most of the work herself. She's avoided me; however, I did see her last Friday and was shocked. All her lively looks and ways are gone."

As if it were some manifestation of the black arts, a rapidly approaching, shrill series of screams interrupted Mrs. Thatcher's recital. Made prompt by war, Terry sprang to his feet and set off to meet the out-cry. An instant later, leaving Mrs. Thatcher still petrified, he had burst open the french windows, but, as he advanced his foot to step outside, a frantic figure rushed up: a wild-eyed girl not more than sixteen. The girl from Mary's! Come the back way.

"Oh, come and 'elp, please, please; he's killing the missus! Going to shoot her!"

Like a stone the gasping child fell at Terry's feet. He rushed into the night, over the old way into the Rodney garden. But as he ran he heard no sound. At once ominous yet hopeful. No shot. No wail.

The back door stood open. Pausing in the kitchen to pull off his slippers, Terry ran on. Lights flamed. The drawing-room door stood open; Terry jerked still, controlled by the tableau visible. Mary, a bruise on her forehead, stood, in an unconscious attitude of crucifixion, back against the mantelpiece, her arms extended. Facing her, back to Terry, Vin, armed with his service revolver, stood lightly poised like a cat enjoying the terror of a mouse. His body twitched in an uncanny fashion and a flow of strange mumbling issued continually from his lips.

Clearly Mary was in imminent danger. Her display of terror would not satisfy the fiend in Border for ever. At any second he might shoot. Yet he, Terry, knew well no sudden exclamation, no abrupt attack, must startle the whisky-inflamed mind at present controlling an urgent desire to kill.

Then inspiration served.

"At-tention!"

The revolver fell, Border snapped up like a ramrod into the prescribed salute, but, almost in one wave of thought, comprehending the ruse, dipped for his weapon—too late; Terry had it.

The drunk man leapt round, spasmodically pausing at sight of the steadily-presented barrel. His eyes lit up with cunning; his lips writhed into a smile.

"You won't shoot, Terry."

With curious, mincing little steps he advanced, the expression on his face made familiar to Terry time and again when they had gone over the top together. A vague shudder passed through the sober man's being. It was almost as if the other feared no mortal weapon, defied the mediums of man-inflicted death.

Terry pocketed the revolver. Border sprang, but hardly had Mary's gasp died away than he lay, out, at Terry's feet. Simultaneously with Border's fall, Mrs. Thatcher, puffing hard, entered. She ran immediately to Mary, who still stood in her crucified attitude staring at Terry, while he, in turn, stared—his eyes expressing his heart—at her.

It was as if Mrs. Thatcher had broken some sudden spell that opened secret doors, revealing hearts, souls, lost chances and, in one instance, an unsuspected treasure that needed forcible revelation were it not to lie forever hid.

~ ~ ~ ~ ~

Vincent Border, saturated by Terry's rough treatment under the kitchen tap, dishevelled, cut, bleeding and obsequiously sober, stood silently weeping—as recently he had made Mary weep.

"Well, that ends our preliminary little argument, Border," Terry said, putting on his shirt. "Just a bit of a scuffle, observe; but I'd like to know whether or not you've ever been really and truly manhandled?"

Border, certainly suffering in as great a degree as Mary had so far suffered, remained silent. Maybe he was wondering just how this grim-eyed, lean thunder-bolt interpreted the term himself. For that matter, Border was *not* without his experience of rough usage, nor was he without an ill-directed courage; but also he had learned to know when surrender paid best, when he had met his master. Contempt for risks he already knew Terry Cliffe possessed; strength tough as steel hawsers, too; yet he

had immeasurably underestimated the younger man's ruthless-
ness when certain fires in his spirit were lit. This before him
was the proverbial British bulldog, so seldom seen with bared
teeth and its secret viciousness exposed. That one prod too
many, that one over-tantalizing twist—and, this; than which
nothing more deadly exists in human kind.

The ultimate cunning in this drunken, debased, distorted
mentality had been stirred. It was not now a case of fighting for
his physical welfare, but of fighting to retain a coveted and
hardly hoped for security. His secret mind, like a nest of
squirming vipers, needed camouflage to escape obliteration. It
must cover its true nature. He must abandon the helpless victim
that accident had provided. He had given the demon within its
fling; now he must call a halt, find secret ways to satisfy his
urge for vice—because at all cost this refuge must be assured
him. Every atom of his not inconsiderable will must be assembled for the subjection of the whisky urge. His drink must be
gin. That fired him, excited him, satisfied him, but did not release the urges that human pain alone could pacify.

The face that presently he raised to Terry's view was the
face that the latter had, out there in France, associated with me-
dieval saints and human nobility. He eyed it now grimly; but he
waited.

"You know, Terry," Border said softly, "I think you're destined to be my good angel."

"Fancy that! Mother's lost boy stuff, eh, Border?"

The latter's eyes became wary. Indeed and indeed he had
encountered the steel of Terry Cliffe's seemingly diffident nature.

"It's all that damnable whisky."

He stole a glance. The other's mocking eyes alarmed him so
that the lies died away on his lips.

"Borstal, Vincent Border. Old Bailey, Vincent Border. Three
years rape with battery, eh? Eighteen months fraud, eh?" Terry
adjusted his tie. "Thirty-one years is long enough to overcome
any foul urge, don't you think?"

The drunkard's mouth hung open. His gaze flickered, stupe-
fied . . . Somehow, almost by magic, it seemed, Terry Cliffe

had discovered everything; and Border knew well when words served no purpose.

He crept to a chair and sat, elbows on knees, chin in hands.

"Independent means, eh, Border? Not a destitute adventurer, oh no! What lies did you stuff Mary up with about all that?"

Border did not move. His eyes had grown sullen, his mouth bitter. There was a hint of some eternal quality in his pose. A close student of human beings would have known his mind was no longer grappling with this present urgent problem, but lost in the shadowy world of retrospect.

"Well, something's got to be done about things," Terry said suddenly in businesslike tones.

The other hunched still closer to himself. His gaze was hard, savage, steady.

"Nothing's going to be done about it. We were married in church, Mary and I. She insisted on that. For better or worse—that was her choice . . . I see you've had a look at my dossier . . . But that tells very little about the secret history of a man. It announces effects, not causes. To apply human justice in the life we've patterned out for ourselves on this planet it is essential to study causes. I was born awry. You weren't. Mary wasn't. Lucky you both were. I wasn't—that's all it is."

"You say nothing's going to be done about it, but the initiative doesn't lie with you, Border. That belongs to Mary. The law can and shall separate you. I should imagine it won't be long before it can divorce you—if the evidence is not already in existence."

"Mary won't do either."

"You think not."

"I know not. She's pre-14, not post. Old-fashioned. She couldn't face up to the scandal."

Terry stared at him steadily. With what seemed supernatural insight this outcast had summed Mary up with extraordinary exactness. No, she'd not face up to the scandal—unless almost forced by those who valued her welfare. *He* would force her.

"There is one person who has enormous influence over Mary. Myself. I shall exert that influence, and . . ."

"You're wasting breath, Terry." Border raised his face for the first time since sitting and looked—sightlessly, it seemed to Terry—at his angry companion. "Mary's going to have a child."

Terry inhaled deeply, standing rigid.

"That's torn it, eh, Captain?"

The brute was right. He *had* been wasting his breath, if this was no lie. He knew Mary. She'd suffer drawn-out torment till death intervened rather than degrade her coming child by public exposure.

"What a *pity* they didn't shoot *you*!" he snarled.

Border nodded.

"Yes, it would have solved the problem . . . But they didn't and life interests me."

"It wouldn't interest you long if I have you back in the trenches for five minutes," Terry said grimly. "And, if you intend to make Mary suffer, now I'm back, I don't think it'll interest you long even here."

The blank eyes flickered nervously.

"I'll leave her alone. I see I've got to. I'll definitely call off the whisky. I'll be no more than Mary's lodger, if that'll please her. I'll get work and pay my shot; but I'll not quit. Not without an exposé. The better or worse has got to stand."

Terry lit a cigarette, thinking furiously. Clearly he'd have to see Mary and discuss the situation . . . But he'd not reveal all. No need to fill her with a greater sense of degradation than she must already be enduring.

Suddenly he saw Border watching him with his curious, occult, prescient eyes—as if the creature were reading his thoughts.

"I'm in Mary's life now, Terry. Better to endure me. I'll make a definite compact—a secret one with you, if you like. You'll be wise to accept this offer; for if not . . ." He rose abruptly and stood exceedingly straight and still . . . "I have powers you little dream of, powers I've never called upon, never dared to call upon, but which I should use if you force me."

Was the creature actually mad? Yet there seemed nothing but icy sanity in Border's eyes now; they were steady, clear, penetrating.

"Listen, Terry. Sit down. I'll tell you things about myself that *are* true. Things that account for me."

Despite himself and his wish to retain the ascendency, Terry sat; and Vin sat, too, directly opposite, staring half-mournfully, half-authoritatively into the younger man's eyes with his own—unblinking eyes. Eyes. Vin's eyes. Terry was again aware of their oddness, of a kind of animal quality . . .

"A man, Terry, can only be what his father and mother make him, just as they can only be what their parents made them; with this, that or the other qualities. We are not offered the choice of what qualities we'll have . . . I'm what my father made *me*. My mother was a nondescript . . . But father was a strange being. Far shorter than I am. I get my looks from mother. Father had a head like Charley Peace . . . A big head, swelling out enormously at the crown, over-lapping at the forehead. His brain was too big . . . too big . . . and as active as a bed of snakes. He believed in and studied mystery, forbidden mystery: the hidden, dreadful secrets . . . He definitely believed in vampires, had a religion founded upon the undead. He swore by all the gods of his black world he'd still live after he was dead . . . Who knows whether he does not?"

Border ceased abruptly and sat twitching with closed eyes. Terry glanced at him uncomfortably.

"If you feel that way, Border, why don't you open his grave and make sure," he asked satirically.

"I would if I knew where he was buried. That's his secret . . . Well, that's the sort of father I had. Do you expect me to be normal?"

There was a momentary silence, then Terry said:

"You know, Border, there's been a vague suggestion in what you've said, in the way you've said it, that you've some far-down decent feelings, some human powers of emotion."

The other shot up.

"Don't appeal! Don't waste your breath! We'll make a definite commercial bargain . . ."

"Who? You, Mary?"

"You and I. You as the intermediary. You can tell Mary as much or as little as you like. It's with you I'll make the bargain; for it's you alone who can enforce it."

"Well? What *is* this bargain?"

"This is my home. To all appearances Mary and I will be the ordinary man and wife. I'll appear the respectable father of this coming child. I'll get a job. But apart from appearances we'll be strangers, living our own private lives."

"The child may die."

Border turned savagely.

"The child *won't* die. By all the dead it shall live." He paused, stared desperately at the drab kitchen wall. "Oh yes, it will live."

He burst into unrestrained laughter.

"Yes, my dear old thing, it'll live."

"You know, Border, if you're going on like this, Mary's simplest way out will be to have you certified."

Border became suddenly very still. All excitement died out of his eyes. He smiled and his smile had all its old winning sweetness.

"Oh, I'm sane, Terry, old man. It's the bargain or nothing."

CHAPTER V

IN A FAIRLY ROOMY HOUSE, Mary had always been allowed her own bedroom, leading off a charming, sunny sitting-room that overlooked the quite extensive and delightful garden.

It was here Terry found her being soothed into some semblance of tranquility by Thatcher, whose powers of comfort in times of stress he well knew.

Easier far, even with one's heart quaking like the drums of a seismometer, to go over the top in the face of anti-barrage, than to tackle Mary—with her face looking as it had when she stood in her crucified pose against the drawing-room mantelpiece. Not in all the topsy-turvyism of nightmare had anything ever appeared so incongruous as her appearance then. Mary! Arch. Gay. Radiant. Mary, wearing the aspect of a woman of sorrow!

The first glance told him she had gone, the Mary of old. This was quite another Mary. But even this Mary was lost to him, Border's words "Mary's going to have a child" had sealed the doom of sudden hope. But for that he might have persuaded her to a divorce and to a match, less of passion, more of peace, with him upon whom she had always been accustomed to lean. But the child ruled that out, bound her completely to Border. She'd never divorce him now.

The latticed windows were uncurtained; the old garden stretched away like a realm of romance, now mysteriously dark, now mysteriously silver; for the moon poured down.

Sitting in one of the latticed windows, in the curiously mingled lights provided from within by a table-lamp, from without by the moon, Mary herself seemed a study in light and shade. Her eyes were pools of shadow. The hollows beneath her cheek-bones looked like deep smudges, yet here and there her face proffered nuances of silver and gold. Thatcher was bustling; but when had he known Thatcher *not* bustling? However, as Terry entered, she turned an inquiring gaze upon him.

"Vincent's all in," he said quietly. "I've just put him to bed in the spare room."

"But . . ."

"Don't worry, Mrs. T. He's sleeping. You can take my word for it he's all right; we shall not be disturbed. There's another patient downstairs who needs your attention; and I want to talk with Mrs. Border."

"Another patient?"

"That girl. She's come over and looks rotten."

"Shock."

"Exactly, and in need of your motherly ministrations."

When he was alone with her, Terry, for the first time in his life, felt awkward, self-conscious in Mary's presence. Suffering lends a halo. Motherhood lends a halo. The Mary to whom he was used had never worn a halo—though she'd often worn his shorts, in days when shorts were naughty. But Mary had been naughty—as naughty as nice.

When directly opposite her, he could plainly see the bruise on her forehead. There was an animal look in her eyes. Contact with pain—man-inflicted. She had lost caste with herself; he could see that. And yet she had gained in beauty. She might have been painted by a master in a dream. Few women are lovely. Mary was lovely; but the source of this new quality did not appear. She had an elusive look; as if, at any moment, she might vanish. Yes, that was it, an evanescent look.

She did not smile at him and made no attempt to. Terry was glad. He could not have borne that—Mary trying to smile. Once an attempt upon her part to be serious had been cause for mirth.

"I needn't say anything about being sorry?" he asked quietly.

At this instant she knew that he loved her, had always loved her. And she knew that, in being blind to his love, she had suffered irreparable loss. She recently had knowledge of values thrust upon her. Explanations between these two had never been necessary; understanding had been mutual, telepathic.

Therefore they had no skirmishing to do; he had no need of tactful approaches, but only to go straight to the point.

"Will you consider a divorce, Mary?"

A tortured expression twisted her features; but she shook her head.

"I can't."

"Because of—the child?"

"He told you?"

"Yes."

"I've made my bed and must lie on it."

"He won't interfere with you again, Mary."

She smiled a little bitterly.

"You're thinking of the whisky; but he'll forego it now; you can rely on that, definitely. With your present approval it is arranged that you and he will 'keep up appearances' but otherwise will lead absolutely separate lives. There is a rather ugly aspect of the whole affair, yet one that offers some explanation. He told you a tale about the will from which he derives his income being suddenly involved in Chancery proceedings?"

"Yes."

"That was a misstatement. He has no money. It is a very long and unpleasant story. If you will accept my advice, you'll not hear it."

"I'm not surprised. But—what will he do?"

"Get a job. You can count on it. I can guarantee one. He'll pay so much, say two pounds, to household expenses. Otherwise your life and his, except in appearances, will not touch."

There was a long pause, then Mary asked:

"Do you think he's normal, Terry?"

"No."

Another long pause, broken by a wail.

"Oh, Terry, think of it, a child by him!"

"I *shouldn't* think of it—not that way. Remember it's your child, too. Goodness is inherited as readily as evil."

"Shall you be staying home now, Terry?"

"Yes."

She made no comment, other than a prolonged indrawn breath of exquisite relief; but that was eloquent enough.

"I shall be next door. I shall be at the office to help with your investments. You must get your Aunt back. And you must wish for a little girl . . ."

"Oh, yes! I *want* it to be a girl!"

"She'll take absolutely after you. And then you'll be happy."

It sounded simple, he thought—but was it?

Mrs. Thatcher bustled in.

"I've made you some broth and put a little wine in it," she told Mary. "I'll bring it to you in bed."

"I'm just off, Mrs. T.," Terry said. "What about your staying here? I shall be all right. Anne will be duenna enough, eh?"

"I was going to propose it, Mr. Terry. I can sleep in the other bed," she told Mary.

"I'd like to sleep with the missus."

Both Terry and Mrs. Thatcher swung round, while Mary looked up startled.

It was Ruth, flushed, lovely, like a truant petal that had yielded to a summer breeze. Her eyes were as blue as a summer sky; but just now they looked aghast with fear. Mary had obtained her from the severe and sheltered atmosphere of an orphanage and she still had the untouchable air of an *innocente*, of one more tenuously open to odd impressions than another better accustomed to life, better equipped to resist influences. She looked as if fairies whispered in her ears—and devils tried to. Now, she seemed afraid of more than she could see, more than she could hear, more than she could ordinarily know. She was AFRAID.

"What are you doing here?" Mrs. Thatcher, accustomed to handling domestic situations, who had mothered Mary quite as much as Terry, asked imperatively.

"I followed you, ma'am," the girl whispered in a way and in a voice that hardly suited even Mary's old-fashioned home.

"As if she'd stepped out of a cloister into a tomb," Terry thought.

"Mrs. Border is ill," he told the girl kindly. "Mrs. Thatcher's staying to look after her. *You* look as if you need someone to look after you, yourself. Now be a good girl and go to bed."

Ruth, awed by the kindly authority in his voice and at even being addressed at all by a cultured "gent," muttered something and respectfully withdrew. Yet, though she obeyed so quietly, Terry felt she went with fear about her like a shroud. A curious, uneasy feeling settled in his own mind.

"Nothing's *ever* going to be the same again," his spirit told him. He was thinking of the past: days of fun, uncorrupt adventure.

But there was something in Mary's eyes, when he said good night, that re-inflamed his faith that life is worth while so long as the immaterial *you* is worth while. He was not one of those who think that spiritual wishes must be confirmed by physical acts. In losing Mary he had found her and was sufficiently a survival to love once and forever. Mary was his now in all save physical contact, a satisfaction, he told himself, that was withered before the spiritual has matured.

~ ~ ~ ~ ~

Strangely one of the most profound sources from which Mary derived comfort during the ensuing days was the company of her life-forgotten little orphan, as unmalicious as spring's first snowdrop and as unaccustomed to earthly contacts. A chatterbox, too.

There was in herself, Mary found, a deep maternity, the fostering of which lent her not only tranquillity, but considerable occupation. She took Ruth under her wing, wondering that anyone could, these days, be so ingenuous and candid—until, with a shock, she realized that even in this almost transparent soul there were reticences. Perhaps her condition deepened her maternal inclination; or perhaps Ruth was an "escape" from personal consideration; for that she found to be alternately bliss and torment. Torment more often, perhaps. At times she felt fundamentally foul because inside her might be a little beast who would grow to a big beast like Vincent.

Between these two there existed a barrier almost tangible, a vague, protoplasmic sheet, transparent and, except in the imagination, unfingerable. He was there, in the house, yet he was not there. He came down to breakfast, spoke, smiled, was courtesy itself; but it was, somehow, like sitting down to breakfast with a film-figure, not a flesh and blood being. There might have been no bruise on Mary's forehead, no horror in her eyes.

Border talked with the defined courtesy with which he would have talked to a guest at a banquet, on board ship, in an hotel, and was triumphantly impersonal. His eyes reflected nothing. His smile was fixed. He was seldom in the house.

And yet, that man over there eating crisp bacon was the father of the foreshadowed life within her. In those long, slender arms she had lain. Those smiling lips had adored hers in moments of intimacy . . . She watched Ruth offer him coffee in a strange, mechanical fashion, as if compelled to do so by every iota of her will, but keeping as far from him as was compatible with duty and as if her whole body, together with the spirit in it, was rigid with abhorrence.

Was Ruth merely affected by what she had seen and heard, or had she a greater sensitiveness of instinct than his wife?

She let the girl sit with her, talked about the past, wondered about the future. Ruth could sew and darn with proficiency, an occupation inducing idle talk. Soon Ruth was committing those blunders, taking those liberties that only the naïve commit and take; but these rather appealed to Mary's softened heart. She liked the girl, was touched by her loneliness and recognized a sort of innate refinement that was not to be expected from her beginnings.

But this indulgence had its penalties, chief among which was the fact that Ruth simply could not keep away from what should have been a forbidden subject—Vin. The dreadful scene still fresh in the girl's inexperienced mind seemed to have started a complex in her susceptible nature. She told Mary again and again of her stark terror, of her certainty that, whereas she had one instant seen Mary sentient, the next she would see her dead.

And then, quite unexpectedly and very astonishingly, she had revealed that she had seen Terry thrash Border.

"It was terrible, ma'am. He took off his coat, Mr. Terry did, then his shirt and vest . . . He's ever so strong when you *see* him, and he struck frightful blows. They seemed to come from the middle of his spine, as if he had a tremendous spring there. And after he'd hit the master again and again, he beat him with the master's own belt. He howled just like I've heard a dog howl, the master did."

Caught by the girl's tale, Mary so far had listened, but now she looked up angrily. Yet the anger died as suddenly as it had generated. This telling was medicinal. It was relieving the girl's mind. Was much better out than in.

"How did you come to see all this, Ruth?"

"The kitchen curtains weren't quite drawn, ma'am. I've always kept the window open till last thing as you told me . . . so I heard . . ."

"Heard?" The question ripped out unconsidered.

"The master and Mr. Terry." She leaned mysteriously towards Mary and whispered hurriedly, in tones of hoarse horror. "Been in prison . . . and in Borstal. One of our girls had a brother in Borstal; but I never knew anyone who's been in prison until I heard Mr. Terry tell the master he knew . . . Well, he said it just like this: Borstal, Vincent Border. Three years rape with battery, eh? Eighteen months fraud, eh? . . . I don't know what he meant by rape with battery. Fraud I know means stealing in a way. But what's rape with battery?"

As she asked, she looked up at Mary, whose face was chalk white, and her eyes full of horror.

"Oh, ma'am, maybe I've said what I shouldn't . . . I never thought . . . I . . ."

She began to cry. Speechlessly, Mary put out her hand till it lay on the girl's head, where she let it rest. Borstal. Rape. Fraud. Prison . . . The father of her child. Hate began to merge with horror. She lay back praying almost savagely that the child should never breathe . . . She need not have known. Terry was hiding this hideous truth . . . But better to know! Oh much! . . . All through this child's prattle, prattle of an over-burdened mind . . . Over-burdened by the same loathsome nature.

They were both silent for a considerable time. Mary, regretting her candour with a domestic, wished that Aunt Charlotte would hurry up and come; but the latter had been inevitably detained by a fire, which, though not serious, had caused considerable inconvenience.

Ruth sat huddled up, staring at the fire, chin cupped in her hands.

"There's a fair coming to Steadman's Level."

The girl's voice startled Mary, shattering her confused reverie.

"A fair?" she asked absently.

The child's huge sigh attracted closer attention.

"Yes, ma'am . . . I've never seen a fair."

"You'd like to?"

Solemn eyes, already lit with dawning ecstasy, searched Mary's face.

"Oh *yes*, ma'am!"

"Then you shall!"

~ ~ ~ ~ ~

It almost seemed to Mary as if life was to settle down into a kind of humdrum peace. And yet she knew no peace, felt no peace. Vin got a job, through Terry's agency, as secretary to the Sports Institute; it was one well within an average person's mental and physical abilities; Vin appeared to be content.

Whenever he and Mary came face to face, his studied courtesy obtained; but behind her husband's inscrutability she detected, or imagined she did, a curious mockery.

Often she told herself she owed a debt to Terry that she could never pay; but for him, Vin, she felt sure, would have continued to barbarize her; now he had no chance. For the time being, since Aunt Charlotte was not available, Mrs. Thatcher continued to overlook both establishments and was conspicuously in evidence when Border returned for meals or to sleep—which was now about all Mary's home ever saw of him. Moreover, now every night saw the bustling guardian solidly established in what should have been Border's own bed, cunningly positioned so as to cut Mary's bed from direct approach. They kept the door locked, too. Yet, despite all these precautions, Mary never slept without fear in her heart, or with a feeling of security. She was obsessed by fear of fire; but she said nothing of this to anyone, notwithstanding that her anxiety was great. Vin, she told herself with psychic certainty, nursed an all but insane hatred for her, which would express itself sometime in some dreadful fashion. It would be like him, when unbalanced by drink, to fire the place, mocking all consequences, if not entirely oblivious of them. That she was right Border proved three days before Aunt Charlotte was due to arrive. It was Mary's birthday—though how Vin had discovered this Mary could not conjecture, since she had told none except Ruth. The fair had arrived and was to provide a birthday treat for both mistress and maid.

To this Mary had looked forward, partly because she herself was not far from the age when fairs are more important than affairs and partly because the promised threat meant so much to Ruth of whom she was fast becoming truly fond. And added to these reasons was the all-important hope of a brief oblivion from unhappy thoughts.

But Border saw to it that this pleasant prospect was destroyed shortly before its fulfilment. He sent Mary a birthday present.

There were several presents beside her place when she and Vincent met at breakfast, presents from Aunts, uncles—all more or less remote in her life; there was one from Aunt Charlotte; others from friends; and important ones from Terry, his mother, Mrs. Thatcher and even Ruth; important, not in monetary value but because they were sincere symbols of affection.

However, there was nothing from Vin. She'd expected nothing; would have been surprised had he even known this was her birthday.

And yet the parcels confessed this, so it was not surprising that he should wish her, with ambassadorial solemnity, many happy returns of the day, but truly so when he added:

"*My* present is not among those others; it's coming by private messenger."

Confused, strangely mortified—for she resented that he should assume magnanimous poses—she looked down at her plate while murmuring chilly thanks. He was staring at her. She knew that, even though her own gaze was dropped. And presently, because his stare persisted, she looked up . . . to be quite startled by the malignancy of his regard and by something that she could find no words to fit. Mythological mischief might have been peeping through the leafy shelter of a tree at a chanced-upon victim for whom it had laid a trap; or an afreet have donned collar and tie and a business suit in order to play a non-human trick upon an unsuspecting mortal. The dangerous "naughtiness" of his face was, indeed, indescribable. It was certainly not childlike, yet Mary had never seen it in any adult face.

She said an odd thing to herself:

"He's got the moon in his veins instead of blood." And then added: "What an extraordinary thought!"

Vin applied himself to the egg he was eating and made no further reference to his present.

Actually it was as Mary added the last few touches to what preparations were needed for her expedition with Ruth that the latter brought up a little basket—just left by a local boy unknown to Ruth—obviously containing a puppy, a fact Ruth delightedly announced.

"It's a pup, ma'am!"

It was plain she hoped to be allowed to see the opening of the basket, but some prescient instinct in Mary prompted her to dismiss the girl.

"Go next door, Ruth, and ask Mrs. Thatcher if she can let you have change for this pound note."

The girl's face fell, but her training held good; she went.

Despite her apparently illogical premonition, Mary felt excited as she opened the basket.

"He knew—I told him—how passionately fond of animals I am," she thought. "Is this genuine kindness?"

The lid fell back—the little occupant peeped up with pleading eyes. Lovely pleading eyes. Tears rushed to Mary's.

"It can't be true! *Vin* has given me this lovely little thing!"

She lifted it completely out, realizing in sick revulsion it had been foully mutilated. No wonder what should have been a cheeky puppy gaze was mournful query.

Why? That was its question. What have I done? All this world, all this life—and for me, nothing. Why? What have I done?

Gently she put back the injured scrap and re-secured the lid, then ran down to the phone to ring up Terry.

" . . . That you, Terry . . .? Oh, will you ask Mr. Cliffe to come to the phone . . .? Say, Mrs. Border . . . Oh, Terry. Vincent's given me a puppy . . . no wait . . . A boy brought it and went at once . . . It was in a little basket . . . Give me a minute . . . my heart's beating so . . . It's mutilated; dreadfully . . . No, not a scrap of hope. It must go to the lethal chamber at once . . . You will . . . Ruth and I are just starting for the fair . . . She brought up the basket; but I've sent her on an errand. I shall tell her it was dead. She's all excitement at the thought of a puppy . . ."

"You go to the fair and leave it to me," Terry told her. "Poor kid! Poor, poor little pal!"

"And poor, poor puppy, Terry! Such a lovely little thing!"

"Don't let your maid dwell on it, dear. Good thing you're going to the fair . . . It's marvellous, I've heard. I'll go myself before it finishes. I have been to see *THE INEXPLICABLE . . .*"

"What's that?"

"One of the freaks . . . But terrible, Mary. Not fit for public exhibition. I'd not take that kid. I'd not see it yourself because . . . You know! Might have a very bad effect, just now . . ."

"Very well, Terry . . . Yes, you're very wise."

~ ~ ~ ~ ~

How was it Vincent had known to-day was her birthday? She herself had not told him. Certainly Terry had not. Ruth never spoke to him . . . Perhaps the girl had told outsiders; when she was buying her present, for instance. Ruth was often sent on errands to the village. Did she by any chance talk? Sudden alarm rent Mary's heart. What if she had imparted details of the hideous history that had been made in the Border house since Vincent's return? Mary glanced down at the radiant, beautifully flushed, Greuzelike countenance now so happily preoccupied. Ruth would not intentionally harm her, or create mischief. But she must make sure . . .

"Ruth!"

"Yes, ma'am?"

"When you've been sent on errands, you've never spoken about . . . about what's happened at home, between the master and me?"

"Oh, no!"

"You've not said a word to anyone?"

"No, ma'am."

"You realize, of course, you would hurt me terribly if you *did* say anything to a single soul?"

"I wouldn't for the world, ma'am."

"I'm wondering . . ."

"Yes, ma'am?"

"How the master knew to-day was my birthday?"

The girl made no comment. Mary glanced down and Ruth stared at the contents of a shop window—full of puppies.

"Look, ma'am, puppies!"

"Yes, Ruth."

"I wish I could have seen *yours*, ma'am."

"You wouldn't, Ruth."

"Wouldn't . . .?"

"No, dear." There was a sob in Mary's voice and the girl glanced up, grew suddenly crimson and hung her head. She made no further reference to puppies.

Despite the shadow lying between them, they began to enjoy themselves from the instant that they entered the fair ground. It was a very big fair, with novelties and roundabouts galore, most of which Mary and Ruth sampled. Had Mary needed infecting she would have caught the contagion from her wildly excited companion but she needed none. Home, Border, sorrows, everything was forgotten in the delirious joy of whirling, falling, mounting, dipping. They whirled like crazy tops, they fell like shooting stars, they shot up like screaming rockets, they dipped like spasmodic seesaws. They bought and ate roasted peanuts; they bought and devoured sweets. And it was not until Mary came face to face in almost dramatic fashion with a curt but bold announcement that memory reminded her she was a married woman, approaching motherhood, and victim of fate's cruel whims. They both, as others did, paused abruptly and stared up at the harsh black letters. THE INEXPLICABLE. This side-show stood out from among its fellows by reason of its austerity. A plain, iron-grey frontage lent an air of dignity and emphasized the sign. For those who understood the inference of this sign, the absence of gaudy letterpress and devices doubled their curiosity and accorded the two words sinister import, which was greatly increased when a man came through the turnstile and addressed them. His very manner of appearance held attention: so quiet, so unostentatious, so lacking in all flamboyance. He was tall and dark and grave. An air of power accompanied him. When he spoke his voice was deep, quiet, authoritative; and a slight foreign accent gave it impressiveness.

He was, the man explained, a medical man. He held such and such degrees.

"In THE INEXPLICABLE I offer you true mystery. Is it a wolf? Is it an ape? Is it a demon? Has it supernatural endowment? Is it something possessed? There are those who assert it to be a human being controlled by an evil spirit who torments it at times beyond endurance, so that it screams in some kind of spiritual agony. At times it barks; at times it speaks in diverse tongues. Sometimes it merely growls. I defy the medical men of this town to form any sane opinion as to the true nature of this exhibit, as I have defied the medical men of all the other cities and towns throughout the world. I have traveled with this creature the whole world over, I have been accompanied by eminent scientists; neither I nor they are at this moment one iota wiser than when first I took charge of this living and terrible mystery. Before I invite you to witness the strange behaviour to which at any instant the thing may commit itself, I must

warn you that the sight is both morbid and horrific. Those who
suffer with weak hearts or nerves, women approaching motherhood and young people are requested to go away. At the same
time I must explain that by order of the authorities the exhibit is
caged so that no danger shall be run by any member of the public of being torn to bits. Those who have now concluded their
inspection are about to be dismissed. The signal will be given
when those who wish to view THE INEXPLICABLE may enter."

As abruptly as he had come, the man vanished; and almost
immediately a large number of people began to pour out
through the turnstile. It was obvious that twice as many waited
for admission.

"Oh, ma'am, can *we* go in?"

"No, no!"

Mary spoke sharply and turned away. Surely, she thought, if
the exhibit were of the nature that showman's words suggested,
it should not be traveling round with a country fair. Clearly
enough it paid, but . . . She would ask Terry his opinion. The
man's words had been enough! He had created an atmosphere
of sinister danger and unnaturalness . . . There was that in her
own home. Besides, standing there, outside that grey, alien façade, an unpleasant sensation of peril had possessed her. If this
child was to be *her* child, she must guard it as hierarchs their
sacred secrets.

A sudden overwhelming abhorrence of Border swept
through her . . . Hate . . . If the child *should* resemble him—
she'd leave him and the child with him. Otherwise life would
be unendurable and the only alternative self-destruction.

She realized now the completeness of the hate and horror
with which she regarded Vin, horror dominating hate, horror
similar to that she had experienced outside the iron-grey side-
show. She could trace a psychological course for this curious
association of one impression with another. Anything inimical,
anything sinister, anything declared unnatural and forbidding,
immediately took her mind back to Vin, thus allying him with
the example at hand. Wounds, for instance; the mutilated
puppy; violence; Vin's handling of her body; the unnatural:

that oddness of aura, glance, physical aloofness that differenti-ated him from the commonplace.

And at the same time she realized that Vin haunted her. He was never out of her thoughts waking and sleeping. His per-sonality seemed to pervade her house. He had got into the bricks. He was its dust.

A-nature. Dangerous. Blasphemous. He had defiled her by the human act of marriage.

Ruth, she knew, kept glancing up in puzzlement that her till now care-forsaking mistress should be so suddenly gloomy and removed from sympathetic contact . . . Ruth, of course, had not seen that puppy. By now Terry had. What did *he* think of it? What would he do? Nothing she hoped. There was only one cure for the Vincent Borderization of her life, complete sever-ance of relations; and in so far as she was concerned, was that possible? One cannot shut off memory like a radio—more's the pity. And the child . . . Oh, no! Better to do nothing.

CHAPTER VI

AUNT CHARLOTTE arrived next morning. It was good, Mary felt, to see her substantial form and somewhat bovine face, though she did not look too well.

"Well, Mary?"

"Well, Aunty darling! So glad you've been able to come at last and *so* sorry about the fire."

"My luggage is outside. I suppose I'm having the same room?"

"No, Aunty. This is Ruth, who has come in place of Elizabeth."

Aunt Charlotte laughed.

"Take her place, eh? A little difference between them."

Like that between leather and swansdown, Mary thought; but she said:

"Ruth knows where to put your luggage. Come into the morning-room until it's up and have your glass of sherry and a biscuit."

Aunt Charlotte smiled. Mary never forgot her weakness. And following Mary she saw that it was there on a little tray, the sherry; the biscuits in a little silver dish. Evidently Mary had something to tell her; and what that was seemed quite clear to the older woman's experienced eye.

But she certainly did not expect the story to which she now listened.

"What a disaster!" Aunt Charlotte commented when, with some reservations, Mary had told her tale. "It's a dreadful, dreadful pity you're having a child by such a man. I confess I'm not surprised to hear he's turned out badly. I never did like him. There's something uncanny about his eyes or mouth or expression; about him altogether, as if, though he's present, he's not there . . . As if he's not quite one of us in spirit."

These words astounded Mary. Aunt was no thinker, but guided her life by her feelings, yet had expressed in a thinker's terms exactly what she, Mary, experienced on each occasion she entered Vincent Border's presence.

"So, Aunty, I've had you put into my room. You won't mind that?"

"It's not a case of minding. If Mrs. Thatcher's giving up her double duties—and it's about time she did, I should say—someone must sleep with you in her place."

Neither woman had noticed Ruth's stealing in like an indeterminate shadow to stand and listen with wide eyes and parted lips; and both started when she suddenly spoke.

"Please, Ma'am, *please*, if Mrs. Thatcher's not coming any more, won't you let me sleep in your room? I sleep very quiet and I'd look after you like anything."

Clasped hands and intensity of pose witnessed to the girl's sincere desire. In sheer astonishment the visitor remarked:

"Well, I never did!"

"I haven't explained that Ruth's my little friend as well as our maid," Mary said.

But Aunt Charlotte's lips pursed. She did not approve of any but the usual formal relationship between mistress and servant.

"*I* shall certainly sleep with you, so that settles the matter."

"Do you really want to, Aunt? I hadn't thought about Ruth."

"If only you would, ma'am," Ruth interpolated.

There was the deepest feeling in her voice; and of this Aunt Charlotte disapproved.

"It's plain," she told herself, "that the child has formed one of those unhealthy adolescent infatuations for Mary. The sooner that's nipped in the bud the better."

So she nipped it forthwith, dismissing the matter. But Ruth's eyes haunted Mary long after the incident ended. She agreed with her Aunt that the misdirected passions of the immature should not be encouraged; nevertheless, there had been a despair, an anguish in Ruth's eyes that, no matter how foolishly exaggerated it might be, was unquestionably distressing to its possessor.

But Ruth was forgotten during the bustle that usually accompanies an arrival.

"Vin lunches out," Mary told her Aunt. "I'm having cutlets done in egg and breadcrumbs as you like. After I'll show you my other presents, shall I?"

"Yes, my dear. You know I shall like seeing them. Did Vin give you a present?"

For an instant Mary hesitated; she had never lied to Aunt Charlotte, but, on this occasion, surely a lie had more virtue than the truth—so she lied. "Terry gave me a dozen silk stockings. Altogether I've had twenty-eight pairs. I don't know *how* you knew I wanted lingerie, Auntie."

"My dear, girls *always* want lingerie."

"Where *did* you get such lovely cobwebby things? They're the most delicate I've ever seen!"

"They're ridiculous as garments, if that's anything; but I know what you girls are. Go along with you!"

"Well, I'll show you the rest of my presents."

However, she had reckoned without Vin, for each treasured stocking was laddered, the cobwebby garments were all cut in small portions. So with everything else. There remained not one present that in some way or other had not been ruined.

Mary stared at the destruction, so opposed to sanity, so opposed to ordinary human behaviour. Anger had no place in her heart; it was occupied by fear alone. She was as sure as that she knelt upon her knees in her own house, gazing at the remains of what had been delightful birthday presents, that Vin would successfully pass any test to which the world's greatest alienists might subject him. All this was not insanity; it was something else, something explained by that odd obliquity of his nature.

And now a tornado of anger swelled up and burst in her head, so that it took her a considerable effort of will not to voice the imprecations accompanying it.

White with holding back this ever-recurring tide, she re-entered the dining-room not only minus the gifts she had rather unnecessarily set out to bring down, but also minus an excuse for her empty hands; and so her confusion was doubled when Aunt Charlotte exclaimed:

"You haven't brought the presents!"

Not for a king's ransom would she reveal the revolting truth. To do so might involve her in various deplorable complications. Aunt's imagination was limited, but her powers of argument were immense.

"I . . . I'm sorry, Aunt; we'll leave them just now; would you mind? I've been sick."

Her appearance so bore out her declaration that the older woman burst into a deluge of advice, together with not a little reminiscence.

The visitor did not see her nephew-in-law until breakfast next morning. As she entered in some excitement with the morning newspaper folded back to a certain page and column, he looked up at her, his eyes ablaze with secret laughter. She glanced at Mary to discover whether there was any cause for this startling and inexplicable mirth, but her niece seemed oblivious of Vin's hilarious condition, and looked up with serious, abstracted eyes.

"Good morning, Aunt."

"Good morning, my dear. Good morning, Vincent."

"*Good* morning, Auntie. You look startled."

"I am. Have either of you seen the newspapers?"

"I haven't, Aunt Charlotte. Why?"

"A freak's escaped from the fair. Listen."

Even while her Aunt raised the folded paper to read out the news that had alarmed her, Mary grasped the truth. No need to read it out. She knew. Not only did she *know*, but had known that this would happen, that it was predestined. Her eyes askew with fear, she sat gnawing the knuckles of her clenched right hand, while Vincent watched her, the lambent laughter in his eyes wildly dancing.

"It's headed: 'WARNING!' in huge letters. See! And it says:

"Alarm has been caused by the escape from our annual fair of a mystery freak whose freedom may have sinister consequences. No doubt large numbers of local residents have already seen THE INEXPLICABLE in its cage. The actual potentialities for harm of this amazing creature can only be surmised, since no one knows whether it is human or animal. That it is ferocious and a would-be killer is unquestionable; but it may also be carnivorous.

"Residents are warned to report any sight or sign of this dangerous being. Ring up the police station: 4923 *without delay*. Hesitation may prove fatal.

"Dr. Julius Erne, who exhibits THE INEXPLICABLE, is unable to elucidate the mystery of how his exhibit obtained freedom. Because of its animal propensities the creature was kept caged by order and the bars of its prison would have defied Hercules himself. The cage door was invariably padlocked and Dr. Erne kept the key on his person. To his knowledge the key has never left his keeping and there is no sign of the lock having been forced.

"It can only be surmised that someone either provided the creature with a key, or deliberately released it and locked the cage once more . . . Unless . . .

"Unless the assumptions of Tiger Hunn, a negro attached to the fair, can be accepted. According to Hunn, THE INEXPLICABLE is neither man nor beast, but something far more terrible . . ."

"All the rest's a description of the thing. It's dreadful, isn't it?"

A curious noise from Border attracted both women. His eyes were full of faunlike raillery.

"Please, Aunt Charlotte, don't say 'thing' in that tone!"

"Why ever not? It *is* a thing."

"We are all 'things,' but this 'thing' is a relative of mine."

"Of yours! Don't be so absurd, Vincent. What *do* you mean?"

"I mean that I believe the 'thing' to be my father."

His twinkling eyes darted their gaze from one woman's face to the other: to meet contempt from Mary and astonishment from her Aunt. "If I am right, 'it' is sure to come here to see and perhaps devour his son; so should it arrive in my absence, please receive him hospitably. If he's hungry, offer him Ruth as a snack."

With every evidence of glee, he went.

"Well, of all the, well, I never did! Does he call that being funny? And why does he walk in that silly fashion? Prancing, I should call it . . . ."

Aunt Charlotte continued her harangue without observing that Mary was wrapped up in her own troublesome thoughts . . . THE INEXPLICABLE! Inexplicable indeed! Inexplicable her feelings of foreboding and shrinking when outside that iron-grey façade. Clearly some dumb part of her conscious had known that what lurked behind it was linked to her own fate . . . It was just how, had she troubled to consider them at the time, she might have foreseen events would begin: Aunt Charlotte's reading aloud this sensational item of news, Aunt Charlotte who thrived on scares and epidemics. So the thing was out—*the thing was coming.*

"I'd not see it yourself," Terry had said, "because . . . You know! Might have a very bad effect just now . . . ."

Oh, Terry, there's no escape . . . Don't you know? I am the magnet . . . I; and what I bear within me . . .

A surge of such black fear swept over her that she had a sharp and sickening struggle not to begin impotently screaming without the power to cease.

And then in sudden reaction, inescapable and welcome, she was laughing at herself for these absurd, outlandish thoughts. Daylight nightmare, due, perhaps, to her state of health. A good thing Aunt Charlotte could not read her mind. The good lady would have a fit . . . She must be strong-minded. She owed it to the second personality forming . . . Did every mother at this period have such a pronounced sensation of responsibility?

Unfortunately Aunt was so given to harping upon a subject and without being either unkind or rude or both one could not check her. On and on she pursued the matter, dealing with it from every angle. And, to do her justice, she was not only apprehensive on Mary's account, but also deeply afraid herself.

"At any moment you might turn round and find it behind you," she whispered nervously.

But Terry, looking in, "breezing in" as he himself put it, to a great extent dissipated the unhealthy anxiety of both women.

"It's been fully realized that the thing's got to be found and secured. The police are being very active and, if it's any comfort to you, both approaches to this road are under observation. As you're nervous, keep your windows closed and both front and back doors locked."

He stayed some time cheering them up and the thought occurred to Mary what an immensely desirable thing it would be could she by some magic change Vin into Terry. Why had it never occurred to her that he had all the attributes of an ideal husband and father? He'd only been Terry, her pal; never, in her eyes, a potential lover. Yet why not? Especially since, as she now realized, he did love and always had loved her.

That night in Horder's Cut—an exceedingly narrow alleyway uniting Pool Road and Century Parade—a woman was ripped to pieces. No clue presented itself to the murderer's identity; nevertheless, little doubt obtained in the public mind. Erne's freak.

It was all in the paper, which at breakfast Aunt and Mary, coming down together, found Vin reading to the detriment of his food. Without being able to observe visible reasons for her surmise, Mary believed him to be in a state of desperate excitement.

He did not go to work at his usual hour, but began to prowl round the house in a curious, restless fashion. Mary was insufferably aware of him and felt his restless energy inwardly. He roused in her a feeling of hysteria. Screams! Glorious relief . . . Or was it *not* Vin who disturbed her, but a feeling of imminent calamity? She, too, felt a desire to prowl. From room to room. Away from something? Or because of a desire to know that they retained their normal characteristics—and were empty?

Vin went suddenly. He went laughing. A low, hardly audible mirth.

She sank against the staircase wall, holding her heart.

Twenty minutes later, Terry phoned.

"Seen the papers, Mary?"

"Yes . . . Terry—I'm frightened."

"Attaboy! Listen, the police have matters well in hand. All special constables are being mobilized and a most intensive search will be made. Moreover, dozens of volunteers are pouring in with offers of help in combing the district. I'm one of them."

He waited for her reply, but waited so long that at length he asked:

"You still there, Mary?"

"Yes . . . Oh, Terry, I wish you'd be *my* special constable."

It was his turn to pause before replying.

"You want me with you, dear?"

"Yes. Especially at night . . . If I knew you were on guard . . . I dread the night. Last night I couldn't sleep . . . I kept imagining . . . something was in the room. I *had* to keep raising my head and looking, listening."

~ ~ ~ ~ ~

Vin came home drunk that night. Mary, still looking and listening, heard his entry. He was in his hilarious faunish state . . . She heard him creeping about, sometimes running and breaking things.

The most ridiculous contradictory gladness possessed her. It was good to know that Vin was drunk, breaking things, making comprehensible and unmistakable noise. *Anything* was better than the early hush during which the foulest danger might be creeping upon her. Here was a danger she could name and understand—even combat. Her soul was still numb with fear of a danger she could not name, could not understand, could not combat.

Far away she heard him laugh outrageously . . . and then a crash. A terrific crash. She knew its nature. Knew as certainly as if present what had occurred. Vin had pushed over the dresser together with its burden of crockery. No doubt he was dancing among the debris.

Simultaneously with the crash, Aunt Charlotte, a sluggish sleeper, woke with a scream of alarm, followed by a cry of pain as she sat up.

"What was that noise?" she asked.

Despite her troubled mind, Mary laughed.

"That noise" was sheer din; but Aunt's questions seemed to reduce clamour to the scratching of some mouse.

"Vin's come home drunk and is smashing things."

"What?"

The older woman twisted to obtain a better view of Mary, whose words she suspected were ironic but as she moved a second crash occurred, whose noise drowned her own fresh squeak of panic. She seemed, however, unaware of her own small outcry in giving her whole attention to the problem suggested by what was taking place below.

"The man's a lunatic!" she whispered.

"No, just drink-mad."

"Will he attack us?"

"The door's locked."

Aunt Charlotte glanced at the heavy, solid, massive door whose lock was supplemented with a bolt. They were safe. Giantlike strength would be needed to batter down that door single-handed.

"What about Ruth, Mary?"

Anxiety flooded the girl's mind. She had forgotten Ruth.

"I think she'll be all right, Aunt. Her door's thicker than ours and I've told her to lock it."

"Well, pray goodness he doesn't set light to the house."

This had been Mary's fear; but at the moment its significance seemed small. Flames would bring the fire-brigade; fire and numbers would ensure protection from . . . Suddenly she began to doubt her own reason? Surely she must be unbalanced to welcome the thought of such alternatives!

The noise below had ceased. Complete silence had supervened. Vin was creeping . . . But she was not afraid of Vin, Mary told herself. Violence held little horror for her . . . *It was a manifestation of human nature.* She glanced at her companion, whose pallor alarmed her. Aunt Charlotte's face was drawn with pain. She looked exceedingly ill.

"Auntie, is anything the matter? I mean, with you? Are you ill?"

"Never mind me, Mary. I've got a pain, but I often have it . . . What's he up to?" she asked with a wail.

"Shall I go and see?"

"No, no! For heaven's sake don't open that door!"

And, as if in justification of the alarm contained in her words, they heard him softly laughing immediately outside their door. Aunt Charlotte rose and, assuming an unconsciously majestic pose, laid her hands upon the water-jug as if it were a bomb.

Strange, slithering sounds succeeded—like hands laid flat upon the wood and moving.

Then this ceased. Silence once more reigned—only to be broken by a scream of indescribable laughter; not near, however. Perhaps from Vin's own room.

A thud beside her jerked Mary's mind to things immediate. Aunt Charlotte had fallen, as if dead, almost at the girl's feet. Symbolic. Her world tumbling about her feet. Devastation that had begun with her union to the wrong man—while the right one looked on.

The fallen woman groaned and opened her eyes just as Mary stooped to feel her heart. She smiled faintly with the courage that all good women, even the stupid ones, have at their command.

"Don't worry, my dear. Have you some sal volatile?"

"It's this pain," she gasped when presently, by her own efforts and with Mary's help, she had achieved the bed.

"What pain?"

Aunt Charlotte indicated its region.

"I've had it for weeks now."

"You should have seen a doctor."

"I expect so."

"I'll phone for Dr. Grove in the morning."

"Very well." She rolled her head restlessly. "Isn't it very close."

"Yes. A storm coming."

"What's that man doing?"

"I imagine his frenzy's over and he's gone to bed."

They listened; but all remained quiet . . . The brooding menace of silence—again.

"Mary, Mary, why ever *did* you marry him? When will you modern girls learn how much wiser, how much safer, it is to marry the man whose good qualities you know than the romantic stranger whose evil qualities you don't?"

~ ~ ~ ~ ~

Next day there was no news of the freak, so the paper said, and that despite a complete combing not only of the town itself but also of its suburbs. It appeared to have vanished with the ease of mist.

At breakfast Vin received Mary's entrance with his gayest smile and was his usual debonair and pagan self. He made no reference to the ruin Ruth had reported: pounds' worth of crockery smashed to smithereens.

"Auntie not coming?" he asked in his politest tones.

"She's ill."

"Ill! I'm *so* sorry. I like Aunty."

Mary glanced at him. He looked immaculate and cool, yet she herself felt hot, stifled. The thick, sultry air impeded breathing rather than aided it. Her hatred of the irresponsible mimic man opposite her swelled. Had she sense, she'd take steps to protect herself and her home. They were her plates, her dishes, his drunken ecstasies had destroyed. But how could she protect herself without publicity, from which she would shrink at any cost. And of what use to call upon Terry to deal with Vin's extravagances? What could he do except thrash the culprit and, since that expedient had failed as a preventative, it must not be allowed to degenerate into a medium of revenge: that would be a fresh abomination—on her side.

"Were you frightened last night?" she asked Ruth a little curtly.

The girl glanced askance at her mistress and mumbled.

"You keep you door locked, as I told you?"

"Yes, ma'am."

"I can try and arrange for you to get another situation if you like, Ruth."

The other burst into hysterical tears, for which she would accord no explanation; and, while Mary was still trying to pacify her, the front door bell rand loudly.

"That's the doctor for Aunt Charlotte . . . No, don't you go, Ruth. He'd think *I* illtreat you. I'll go."

Half an hour later Dr. Grove said to Mary:

"Your Aunt is very ill and I'm almost certain an operation's necessary. She must be very minutely examined and I would suggest her removal either to hospital or a nursing home."

"Have you told her?"

"She seemed to expect some such opinion and mentioned a nursing home herself."

"Very well, Doctor."

"Shall I make the arrangements?"

"If you'll be so good."

"Very well, I'll arrange for her to be moved tomorrow morning, about eleven."

"Thank you."

Another prop gone. Another refuge closed. She had depended upon Aunt Charlotte, who, if old-fashioned and a little dull, was, above all else, kind and a most proficient nurse. Was there any danger of being deprived of Aunt Charlotte's aid when the child was born? That would be a really bitter blow. There was something solid and protective about her Aunt's ample body and solid sense. Even Mrs. Thatcher would not be so welcome as Aunt Charlotte at *that* time.

Suddenly she realized with extraordinary clarity what was taking place within her—the production of another human being—and to her amazement a wild pang of love rushed into her heart and tore at her womb. Her child! What an immeasurable compensation if only it were *her* child; not his, not another sort of satanic imp. She could, then, well afford to ignore Vin and his incomprehensible annoyances. She would love as deeply, as steadily as great rivers flowed to their destiny.

Aunt Charlotte! Poor thing! How the young wrapped themselves up in their own concerns! But who knew what agony

and suffering might await Dr. Grove's new patient in his nursing home?

She must go up and talk to Aunt, explain about the doctor's
wishes and . . . But just then the phone rang. It *was* the doctor
to say that a suitable room at the home would not be vacant until the next day but one; would Mary explain to her Aunt? No,
it was not urgent that the patient be examined within so many
hours, or even a week; but the sooner the better.

As she mounted the stairs to the invalid's room, Mary
caught sight of the lowering sky through a landing window.
Great balls of indigo clouds with nuances of tarnished brass
and dull oxide, with occasional bursts of angry silver. The
whole sky had a metallic look and a weight seemed to be pressing down upon her head, a weight of compressed, almost solid,
air. A forbidding sky. Dangerous. Angry. Full of hate. Full of
spite. A tablet of wrathful prophecy—and to Mary of more than
harsh storm and deadly lightning. An hour to suit deeds contemplated by something more awful than nature—cruel though
that can be.

"Aunt must not get up," she told herself. "But I don't think
she wants to . . . Let us pray heaven Vin behaves himself until
the poor soul's gone."

~ ~ ~ ~ ~

"If only the storm would come and disperse," she cried to the
matt agony of her head. "I shan't sleep . . . I shall just twist
about in terror . . . Such a night creates terror out of its own op-
pressiveness. My head feels full of colourless lead . . . It's just
as if the whole of life's turned evil . . ."

Aunt Charlotte was asleep. Mary could hear her stertorous
breathing. Probably Dr. Groves had put some opiate in that
medicine . . . Almost she wished that Vin were in one of his
drunken ecstasies . . . Any noise would be welcome. But *no*
noise broke a stillness that to her too conscious mind seemed
uncanny . . .

And then there was a noise: muffled tramp, tramp, tramp . . . It died away. Came again. Tramp, tramp, tramp . . . And again. From East to West, from West to East.

Now it was gone . . . She strained her ears hard. Yes, after all this time, again; but from the back . . . From East to West, from West to East . . .

And then once more from the front . . . Now, gone.

Suddenly she understood.

"It's Terry, keeping guard. Over me! Oh, bless him, bless him!"

The love that she had been suppressing burst through her control . . . He'd be coming round to the back. She'd watch for and signal to him . . . Aunt! Still sound . . . She drew back the blind of the smaller window that looked on to the big back garden . . . How exceedingly dark the night was, a pall, thick, impenetrable. Not a gleam . . . And then she realized her mistake. There were gleams, gleams of light. Two. Tiny, luminous glints. They came from the bushes above the stream. A cat? Then she heard Terry—coming. From East to West. Her blood chilled. Her heart halted . . . Terry coming . .

She saw his torch. He jerked it this way, that, at the bushes whence she had seen the luminous eyes; then continued his march, satisfied.

~ ~ ~ ~ ~

Mary did not go down to breakfast. Aunt Charlotte was again in pain and needed attention.

"Have they caught that thing, Mary?" she asked between sips of revolting gruel.

"I haven't seen the paper, Aunt. I'll go and get it."

"Yes. I'd like to know. The night was quiet, wasn't it?"

"Yes, Auntie. Inside and out."

She heard the rumble of men's deep voices as soon as she opened the door. Now who? Now what? Definite knowledge that something sinister was afoot grew in her mind until it was a great white certainty.

She ran swiftly down.

Ruth, trembling, crying, her eyes alight with hardly sane horror; Vin, his stance one of some creature overvital and his entire face agleam; a police-sergeant and a constable—these stood an absorbed group in the hall.

As by one impulse and as if one corporate being, they turned towards Mary as she descended.

Ruth, seeing, perhaps, a refuge, or instinctively driven to a fellow-woman's side, rushed to the new-comer, throwing frantic arms round her.

"Oh, ma'am, they've found . . ."

"That'll do!" The sergeant's deep voice boomed Ruth's hoarse whispering into silence.

Mary felt her whole body blanch, her heart, her very blood must have gone white . . . Terry. They'd found him dead, torn . . .

"This is your wife?" The sergeant asked Vin, sharply.

Mary knew at once he did not like Vin, was prejudiced against him . . . Thought him too flippant in the midst of tragedy.

"Yes, this is the missus."

Vin grinned at Mary.

A glance at the latter's face assured the officer that here was a much more estimable type than her wise-cracking ape of a husband. His feelings for Vin were rude.

"Guts all run to beauty, I should imagine," the sergeant mordantly concluded. Anyway he hated beauty in men. They should be beasts and hairy. He was, himself, and took deep pleasure in scratching his pelt at night. The sports columns called him gorilla, or a great bear; said he resembled both in the ring. But Mary was gentle, almost beautiful, and even during his first glance became beautiful. It was impossible to associate her with deeds of violence, deeds of horror.

"Were you disturbed in the night, madam?"

"No, sergeant . . . At least . . ."

"Yes."

"I lay awake and heard someone patrolling round the house . . . outside, I mean."

"Yes, that was your neighbour, Mr. Cliffe, on special duty. You heard and saw nothing else at all unusual?"

Mary faltered.

"I got up and looked out of my window at the garden."

"Because you heard the footsteps?"

"Yes?"

"Did you notice anything?"

"I saw two eyes, which I took to be cat's eyes, gleaming from the bushes above our stream."

There was silence for a while. Vin, Mary thought, seemed almost unable to restrain some secret mirth.

"I regret to tell you that the mangled body of a child was found in those bushes this morning, madam."

Mary felt Ruth clawing at her arm; terror!

"The freak, sergeant?"

"We assume so, madam."

~ ~ ~ ~ ~

"P'raps he suffers from a tapeworm, Mary."

"Who?"

"Terry."

"Why?"

"To make him so ravenous."

She stared at his eyes full of brittle laughter, laughter that seemed to gleam and die like sparks from an anvil. She was aware of the venom in her gaze.

"What a pity it was that child."

"And not me, darling?" He came a little nearer. "I'm tough, pet. Besides, didn't you know it was my father? Demons aren't cannibals . . . I shan't eat our child." He thrust his face close to hers, so that their eyes almost met. She seemed to be staring into empty spheres, which slowly filled with a glacial light.

Mary experienced an insurgence of boundless contempt.

"His whole mind, his whole being, what serves him for a soul, each is empty and lit by false humanity. He's just a mean cad! Not dangerous except to women because he's a little stronger . . . A sham! An actor! He's trying to make me believe ghastly things about himself . . . An opportunist, that's what he is. He's trying to associate himself mysteriously with this escaped freak, because he sees in it a means to terrify me."

Perhaps he sensed a change in her attitude, for he moved rapidly away. But at the front door turned.

"Quite an epicure, our wandering freak, Mary. Likes them younger each time."

~ ~ ~ ~ ~

"Nobody can account for how the child came there," Terry told her. "It came from Platt's Square, a mile away. It was supposed to be in bed. The parents are utterly mystified . . . It was a lovely child. An only one . . . And I . . . right by the spot . . . On guard till dawn. On guard when it was happening . . . Mary, it's beyond my comprehension . . . It's like, like Satanism. Every time I patrolled the back I searched those bushes. My last act before going off duty was to examine the whole garden minutely . . . There was no sign of anything wrong."

Mary shuddered. THE INEXPLICABLE! How well-named.

Her skin irritated. Prickles, she was all prickles. And every now and then a tiny thread of sweat found its way down her loosely clad body.

"I wonder if I'm going mad?" she asked suddenly, shrilly.

"Now, Mary dear, *why* do you say that?"

"Because . . . this weather . . . it only began—this unendurable oppression—after that thing escaped."

"I'd not mix up meteorological phenomena with ordinary events."

"Ordinary?"

"Well, creatures are constantly escaping from custody. True there's a sinister element attached to this escape, because no one knows what the thing's predominating characteristics are, human or bestial. Nevertheless, there's no other mystery about it."

"Except how it got out and how it's evaded capture and how you didn't come to see it last night and how it contrived to devour a child in my back garden, a child that should have been in bed and asleep a mile away."

"You're wrong in saying it devoured the child. It would be almost better if it had . . . We should know then that the creature is brute, not man; that it kills to eat, as wolves kill to eat; but it merely tore the child apart and left it so, as if one instinct defeated another, as if the brute, having obtained its prey, prepared to fulfil its instinct, when the human urge forbade."

She got up, crossed to the window and stood staring out, up at the sky, which looked to her like embossed copper—and near, even to be deliberately but surely descending . . . She would never drag through this life-squeezing day without some violent personal demonstration . . . It would be possible for her to turn upon even Terry. The violence that was gathering in that savage sky was creating violence in herself. Aunt ill. Stupidly meandering in the way of old and brainless women . . . and night gradually coming; night with its tortures: incalculable beings cloaked by the night with an invisibility that perhaps they did not require; Vin and his orgies; most of all this crushing atmosphere that seemed to grip one's heart and squeeze it. Inescapable menace.

"Will the police be bothering us?" she asked curtly. However, if Terry notice her tart tone, he ignored it.

"Oh, no! They have definitely decided that the child was killed by whatever killed that woman the other night; and naturally they assume it was this escaped creature from the fair."

~ ~ ~ ~ ~

As the day proceeded the elements' mood, as expressed by the ever-lowering sky, did indeed seem to communicate itself to Mary, transforming her from the kindly, happy-tempered woman she normally was, into a being as farouche as its own heavy exhalations. She snapped at Ruth, ignored Aunt Charlotte, lay stripped on her bed fighting for breath, fighting too with a wild revolt against the man who had trapped her with his bond that inextricably united her to him, to that preening fool, that hurtful monkey, that Adonis with Caliban's nature.

During the afternoon little gusts of wind snapped over the earth. But these were threats. Harbingers of clamour and danger. Swift, invisible horsemen speeding to announce the might of their personal war-gods.

Of course she was full of dread, apprehension; she acknowledged that. Something was coming, some disaster. It was this that so agitated her.

After tea Mary kept going, though the blinds were drawn, to look out of the window—whichever room she happened to be in; for her restless feet took her from this one to that and back to this. Great swollen masses of cloud with burning edges seemed to hang right down from the sky. At any moment one might burst and deluge the earth with its burden, whether fire or water. The compression of air increased. Her lungs hurt. Her heart felt even more constricted.

And then she no longer dared look from the windows, for night was slowly and fully developing; night—with that other menace, for which this impending storm was such admirable cover.

And yet what should she have to fear? Her gardens back and front were fully guarded. Patrols were in the roads beyond. She should be as safe as Royalty . . . But even Royalty, she told herself, is not safe from microbes and other invisible foes . . .

About nine low rumbles began, growls, imprecations, the low mutterings of destructive force . . . She went up to Aunt Charlotte and found her calm, placid, ready to talk . . .

"Aren't you afraid, Auntie?"

"Of what, dear? Thunder and lighting? No I never minded them . . ."

But then Aunt did not know about the mutilated child, nor had she seen those gleaming eyes. Aunt was old, infirm, ill; she had not in her body another life, something young, lovely or horrible . . .

And Ruth was afraid. Mary saw that when the girl came to say good night. Her cheeks were livid, her eyes black pools of terror. But what could either of them do to help each other, except pretend?

And, underneath all her own fear, she knew her soul was weeping. Life had fulfilled her wish, given her fertility, given her the gift that few women reject and the burden they desire, but not the hope and gladness that should accompany it. Only this dread of her child's nature, her coming child's nature.

She would go to bed herself. She would not . . . For, even as her decision was made, a fresh, more prolonged roll of thunder—Cerberus showing his teeth—faltered her steps . . . The little winds came lashing, savage, whispering laughter . . . She went into the drawing-room, drawn by an imperative desire to open the french windows, defy the gathering storm, the night and whatever it might hold. But she could not stay. The hysterical urge in her blood drove her out.

Passing through the hall, Mary experienced a sudden sense of insecurity . . . Rooted, she stared this way, that . . . The front door was ajar. What did that mean? Such a little thing; yet so much. So prosaic; immeasurably portentous . . .

Had Vin come back, drunk, and forgotten to secure the lock and bolts? She listened . . . All seemed still. She might go to his room; but profound reluctance gripped her, even as the thought occurred.

Now her terror swelled up fully . . . *What if Vin were not back*, had *not* forgotten to bolt the door?

She found herself circling round and round, like a clockwork figure, longing, of course, for the eyes of Argus. But she did not know, she never knew, of this reason-failing act. Inwardly she longed for belief in the efficacy of prayer, for the tangible objects by which Roman Catholics feel and express their faith. Lovely Latin words filled her mouth; but they were of no use to her, because her soul was empty. Darker thoughts succeeded. She laid her crooked fingers upon the child as if she would tear it from her womb and fling it into the abyss.

A great bellow swept across the heavens . . . Like the tongues of brazen serpents the forked lighting licked the sky.

Mechanically and without one positive thought she ran to her room and undressed. Aunt, she saw, was lightly asleep. That was good . . . And then she wondered if she had left a note in the empty bottles for the milkman. Since Aunt was going to-morrow, they'd need a pint less. A pint and a half, in fact; for Aunt had more than doubled their order this last two days . . .

Barely had her body pressed the bed than she was out again.

What if something were in the house. It must not creep upon her, not with closed doors, in the dark. Let her see it, *know* its presence, its approach. She could not lie; wander she must.

The drawing-room . . . To pace like a cat . . . And listen . . . Nothing to hear? Yes. Steps. She began to laugh. The hysterical laughter of relief . . . And a sense of triumph surged up to her head. Her house was guarded. Not by one man; by many. Boldly she walked to the windows, opened them. Closed them. Yes. The patrols were on duty. Someone called out . . .

"All okay, Mrs. Border, don't worry!"

She laughed in reply and closed the windows, drawing the heavy curtains, glad enough to shut out the boiling night, like the hot stink from a venomous animal's mouth . . . Relief? None! Her heart quaked more. But what greater security could she ask? Strong, armed men on guard. Terry, bless him, had seen to that, she might be very sure.

But there was no security. Something prescient was within her . . . The embryo? Was that it which knew? Knew she was not safe. That neither men nor guns, nor tactile protection of any conceivable sort could save her from . . . The thunder . . . the thunder . . . the thunder . . . and the lightning. Despite the thick curtains she could see it rip the sky. The night pressed upon her. Thick. Oppressive.

. . . From somewhere in the house, a cry . . . Petrified, she stood waiting . . . Another, nearer . . . Ruth! Something had Ruth . . . suddenly the wind screamed loudly, pressing like violent hands upon the window—as if it were corporate and endeavouring to force entry. Again a cry, violently approaching. If it were . . . SOMETHING . . . what was she to see . . . What was she to *do*? Her duty. Help. She should be helping now. Running to the rescue. But her feet were glued to the spot they trod. Her congealed brain offered no stimulus to her paralyzed limbs.

Now the heavens screamed aloud. The vast forces met. Their impact shook the earth, their javelins rent the night. And, as if imperial giants were shedding in relative copiousness their mighty ichor, the rain fell in one vast sheet, while the wind, not to be denied its part, whistled madly—as Ruth, bruised and virginally desperate, rushed in. The truth declared itself. Abruptly Mary knew why the child had clamoured for her protection at night; dreaded to sleep alone. This child! That beast! Little, roselike Ruth who had so endeared herself. She might have known! Vin. Drunk! Her mouth seemed dead. Words could not pass. Fitting that the storm should herald this!

The foul enormity of it roused in her a spirit as warriorlike as that shaking heaven and earth.

With a swift turn Vin locked the door. Mary needed no telling what this meant, and did not wait for assault from him, but under some frantic compulsion smashed a Dresden vase that had been in her family for years and with a jagged fragment attacked his smirking face. Taken by surprise he fell back, his face a crimson flood. It seemed the skies were harmonizing with Ruth's screams, to which the harsh wind lent a crude accompaniment.

As if roused by the raucous turmoil and a pagan love of conflict, Border swept the blood away, leapt with an untranslatable utterance towards Mary, and, to Ruth's shrill screams, ripped her nightdress from neck to hem. His blows served only to rouse his victim's fury, since, joining her cries to Ruth's screams, she fought him blow for blow. While they battled, he yelled some senseless slogan at the top of his high tenor voice. And to all this saturnalia the storm, as if challenged by such unhuman outcry, came tearing over the earth like a horde of thundering Cossacks on blood-mad horses.

With a wild push, Border staggered Mary, and she fell, giving him a chance to deal a *coup de mort*, for which purpose he raised above his head a huge brass jug. As it descended, she rolled and, before he could recover to attack again, secured her jagged fragment.

Suddenly the loathsome indignity of the scene overwhelmed her. This man whom with a jagged piece of china she wished to mortally strike, whose face she had already so gashed that it streamed with blood, was the father of her foreshadowed child;

and, perhaps in an instant of demented vision, she saw, not the face of him she hated, but the face of that child she would hate more. She laid her hands where its beginnings already thrived.

The action stayed him.

"This . . ." she whispered . . .

"Our child!" he mocked.

"Yours," Mary snarled, "not mine . . ."

Beyond the door, Aunt's voice in undistinguishable commands; on its panels the battering of her urgent fists.

"My son!" Vin howled.

"If it *is* your son . ." Mary choked. Rage seemed to knot her vocal cords. Suddenly, driven beyond control by the orgy of tumult, Aunt's madding blows, her inarticulate cries, Ruth's screams, Vin's hilarity, her own seething brain and the distraught sky, she let free all-and-every hideous impulse of her unconscious.

She laughed. Terribly.

And facing the night, as if its howling forces were the gods she worshiped, lifting her arms, as if offering the white body thus exposed to their frantic will, cried:

"If it *is* his son, may it be *cursed*. May it be born a monster—as he is a monster."

To her frenzied mind it seemed the sun, perhaps the earth, had burst. The thunder. The scream of tempest. The lashing rain. All seemed to whirl in vengeful devastation upon her, scorning human interference, barriers, checks; hurling wide the flimsy french windows thus revealing Mary to the night—and what therein might lurk; offering the window as a frame to the thing that stood within it . . . Wolf's face and body. Ape's chest. Its eyes gleamed with feline fire; but were a man's eyes.

It advanced a human hand, touching her white abdomen—and laughed.

With a crash, she fell.

CHAPTER VII

FROM WHAT was almost a swoon Ruth roused to a realization that the two french windows were crashing in the gale, that someone violently hammered at the door and that Mary lay, her long, white body stark and glistening, in the rain that poured upon it. Of Vin there was no sign.

"Open the door."

A lull rendered these words clear. The girl's mind began to co-ordinate. In a bound she opened the door, admitting Aunt Charlotte, pale, trembling, dreadfully agitated, in obvious pain, wearing the pyjama jacket of one suit, the trousers of another.

"The window, child, the window!"

While Ruth now rushed to shut out the wind and rain, the elder ran to Mary's side.

"She's ice cold. Run into the hall, girl. Get me a coat."

Ashen, Ruth recoiled. Her eyes skewing like a frightened horse.

"Quick! Do you want your mistress to die?"

With a gasp, from somewhere whence it had sunk, Ruth dragged up her courage. Yet nothing but her abounding love for Mary could have driven her into the empty hall alone. But she went, at a run, and seemed hardly gone before she was back with Mary's coat.

"Now help me."

Together they dragged off from the icy body what remnants of saturated silk still clung and wrapped her in the cloak.

"We can't carry her, ma'am."

"No. Run to the dining-room, get the brandy. Quick!"

Again the tense struggle for courage; again success.

The brandy did its work. Mary opened her eyes, struggled frantically up, stared round with the acme of horror, awe and a curious submission in her gaze.

Aunt Charlotte, momentarily strong and forgetful of her own ills, supported her on the one side, Ruth on the other.

Mary stared down at the girl's starlike eyes, in which reverence, love and gratitude were all equally evident.

"Did you see it?" she asked hoarsely.

"What, ma'am?"

For an instant Mary said nothing; then muttered:

"Never mind."

"You must come to bed, Mary!" Aunt exclaimed, a little fretfully. After all she was old and ill. "You're icy. You'll catch a chill."

"I? I'm burning." She placed a fiery hand on the old woman's.

"What happened?" Aunt Charlotte demanded.

But, before Mary could reply, a sharp rapping. Muffled cries issued from the lips of both Mary and Ruth. They each, for different reasons, stared aghast at the window.

"Let me in!"

It was Terry . . . Terry! The patrol. What had become of them during that short, sharp battle? Impossible it had not been heard by one or more of that little force. Why had no one come? Both she and Ruth might be dead . . . Any Terry, he had been one of those on guard. A strange stupor held her still. It was Ruth who admitted Terry.

"Hello, girl! What's happened to your face?" Ruth, unaware of her own bruises, turned questioningly towards Mary, who with a shrug and an abrupt gesture indicated the condition of the room: tables overturned, débris littering the floor, rugs rolled up.

"Vin?"

Mary nodded. Then asked harshly:

"Where were you?"

"How long is it since this took place?"

He in turn pointed at the floor.

"Not more than fifteen to twenty minutes ago—since it started."

"We heard screams from the direction of Victoria Road . . . Dreadful cries. We ran that way in a body; the cries receded . . . When we located the cause, it was a cat; been run over and dreadfully crushed . . . This must have happened during our brief absence."

"You need not all have gone," Aunt Charlotte said tartly.

Terry nodded. "We acted on impulse. The cries were so human and so terrible. We thought it was the freak at work . . ."

"The freak was here."

The other three turned in startled surprise towards Mary. Her eyes were glassy, as if she could still see the bewildering monster. Her long, expressive hands covered the shelter wherein lay, dumb, torpid, the child who alone might bear the penalty of this night's work.

"I cursed the child," she muttered in hoarse, grating tones . . . Then she screamed and added piercingly: "I prayed it might be a monster . . . a monster—if it was his son; because he is a monster . . . And there it stood, in the window: THE MONSTER. It touched me here! The child is cursed . . . cursed!"

At their feet she threw herself prone, frantic sobs, mounting both in volume and in key, shaking her from head to foot.

Terry, stooping, encircled her head and shoulders in his arms, hiding her face against his wet raincoat, and whispered all the appropriate arguments. Always he had the power to soothe her. He soothed her even now. The sobs checked, stopped. And, urged by sudden thought, she raised herself, gazing round.

"Where is he, Vin?"

Where was he? No one had seen him go . . . But, for that matter, where was the freak? Why had it not destroyed the three women helplessly at his mercy?

Mary rose to her feet, facing both Terry and Aunt Charlotte; her hands were clenched, her lips set, her eyes hard.

"It's my duty to charge Vin," she said in low tones.

The other two stared at her, then glanced at Ruth, who was sobbing softly.

"He attacked . . ." Terry paused; but Mary answered.

"He attacked Ruth." She crossed to the girl, knelt and laid an arm round her shoulders. "When did this start?"

"Ever since I came."

Mary whispered.

"Did he succeed, dear?"

"No, ma'am . . . I got away."

"But I told you to keep your door locked at night?"

"I did. But to-night, when I went to lock it, the key was gone . . . I was afraid and I was putting my shoes on to come to you when he crept in—like a spirit."

"Why didn't you complain before, Ruth?" Terry asked.

"I was afraid . . . He said he'd kill me."

"Swine!" Terry muttered.

Suddenly Aunt Charlotte groaned.

"Oh, Aunt! You should be in bed! This will make you worse. Will you come now?"

"Will *you*?" the old woman asked.

"Yes. It's cooler now." Until this instant Mary had not noticed that the storm had passed. It rained, but with quiet persistence, and the wind had died as abruptly as it had arisen. "But what about Ruth? She had no key. She should come in with us."

"Couldn't we take the bolt off your door and put it on here?" Terry asked.

Mary glanced at Ruth. It was not bolts the girl wanted, but human companionship, the security of numbers. This orphan was in her charge, so far she had protected her badly.

"We'll move the bolt to-morrow, Terry. Ruth can manage on my settee to-night."

She saw a wave of glorious relief surge over the little maid's face . . . Something would have to be done. Ruth must be moved from Vin's immediate presence. But just now she felt too involved in her own cataclysmic problem to think clearly and benevolently.

"Just as you think best, Mary," Terry said quietly. He realized she had been through some mind-shattering experience. Something had somersaulted in her spiritually. Behind the forced calm of her eyes he could see profound horror lurking. Her whole face, her whole attitude, was one of unbearable strain. Both Mary and Ruth bore evidences of Vin's savage treatment. He, too, saw clearly some other measures would have to be taken in regard to one who was without question an undisciplined drunkard. No use to rely upon force. It solved nothing. No use to accept even Vin's most solemn assurances: they were as reliable as snow in heat. "I will stay in the house to-night," he added. "The three of you be off to bed. You all look as fit as cripples."

None of the three expostulated. Each was too profoundly thankful for his personal guardianship. Despite his diffident manner, his genuine modesty, Terry had the power to promote confidence in his mental and physical efficiency; and Mary knew her friend, knew his prowess, had seen him fight again and again, knew that notwithstanding his slim appearance his was a frame of steel, his muscles were whipcord, his courage was superlative.

Few more words passed between their silent acceptance of his offer and their departure. But, though none was more thankful than she to lay down her aching body in repose, Mary expected no sleep and did not until nearly dawn even close her eyes. She could still see that obscene appearance; her flesh still seemed to burn from its touch. Amazing that no scar remained as a brand to mark its contact. But, if her body had escaped all witness of its visit, had her soul, her mind? Had that silent embryo within her body? She was a doctor's daughter. Useless to deceive herself . . . Till the days of labour she must ask: What do I carry within me, now?

Her violent concentration upon the child, her sudden mental focus when she cursed it, with the almost miraculous appearance of an actual monster at that dramatic moment—how could what was so similar in nature to a sensitized and still unused film escape impression?

Her dry lips opened and closed in violent prayer.

~ ~ ~ ~ ~

Only Terry was about when Vin crept in and he stared at the being he meant to castigate in amazement. Stared dumbly . . . and did not even bar the prodigal's progress to his room.

Here was a being drained of all mental and much physical vitality; a creature, to Terry's eyes, completely negative and for the time being, at least, no longer the Vin he knew, impish, pervert, psychically odd. Something satanic had gone, left behind, somewhere in the night—or perhaps was merely suspended. Yes, that was it. The man looked "still," like a dynamo that isn't working; like a man who has expended himself—fully, utterly, completely; who now merely moved by automatic impulse.

Terry felt sure that, had he addressed Vin, no reply would have been vouchsafed; for this mentally evacuated creature would not have heard; or, if he had heard with his ears, he would not have heard with his mind.

~ ~ ~ ~ ~

He sat down and thought deeply about Vin . . . There was something incomprehensible about his one-time friend. There was some ugly secret concerning him; a secret that neither science nor philosophy could demonstrate . . . A dumb something in himself—in every other normal man, too, he supposed—detected it, felt it, sensed it, crawled up from its fastness, raised its head into his conscious proper and strove after it—bellicosely; as the deep-down forest instincts of a cat are at times called into actual resurrection . . .

. . . Well, there was nothing he could do that night except stick around . . . Huh! That seemed his job for life. Terry didn't pretend to himself; Mary *was* his life. He earned his bread, made money in fact, was comparatively well-to-do; had a good mother and a jolly home; but he made no bones about the truth: nothing really mattered except Mary; nothing really made up for the loss of her. And she was married to this thing about whom his very unconscious had managed to think, against whom it had revolted.

Still, there was service left. Non-promiscuous, Terry felt pleased at the idea of a quiet service devoted to the welfare of one whom, if he could not possess, he could help.

Later he stole up to the spare room, where the bed, when the door was left open, commanded a view of Mary's door. The lightest sleeper, a sound, barely audible, would rouse him; his scout training, his territorial training, his army training—each had emphasized this gift of easy awakening.

He slept lightly indeed, even in sleep on the alert, and awoke early. Outside Mary's door he could hear Aunt's stertorous breathing. Pray God Mary had gained tranquil rest. What was to be done about Vin? Police? A charge should be made. It was their duty as citizens. First, however, there were some questions he wished to put personally and alone to Vin. He slipped across the landing. Door still locked . . . Terry listened but could hear nothing. He'd wait half an hour and then rap. He sat down on a landing-chair, from which he could see both Mary's and Vin's doors . . . Surprising that Ruth was not stirring. He glanced at his watch. Seven. Breakfast was at eight-thirty . . . And Aunt Charlotte was leaving for the home at eleven . . . Yet, why wonder that one so young as Ruth—hardly out of childhood—still slept after such a night? And breakfast was unlikely to appeal . . . Except to himself.

. . . Seven-thirty. Now he'd tap at Master Vincent's door. But half-consciously, as he tapped, he turned the knob once again . . . The door was open. The room was empty . . . But—but—but how could that be? He glanced down at the lock. Its key was there, on the inside. Could he have been mistaken in thinking it turned when his previous attempt to open the door had . . . But absurd. The door *had* been locked . . . Yet had he not been seated with Vin's door in full view since seven? And it certainly had not opened! More, had that door been opened during his half-slumber . . . Still, commonsense could only assume, first, that Vin *had* come out while he, Terry, slept; and second, that the key had not been turned at his previous attempt to open that confounded door. The mind could play human certainty odd tricks. And quite clearly this room was as empty of human occupation as a new dust-bin. The wardrobe held only clothes, the window was fast on the inside . . . Well, damned odd. But then everything connected with Vin had, of course, to be bizarre.

~ ~ ~ ~ ~

Both Mary and Ruth looked pale he thought, as Mary poured out the coffee and Ruth handed his cup. Other effects showed, especially in Mary's face: it recorded the cold control her mind was exercising. Her duties done, Ruth crossed to the door, but Terry stopped her.

"A minute, Ruth."

The girl paused obediently, but her lips worked and her eyes darkened with fear. Terry turned to Mary.

"Vin *may* return at any instant now, I think we ought to decide our actions. Our duty is, of course, to phone the police-station."

"Ruth begs us not to," Mary said quietly.

Terry glanced at the girl. Tears were rolling down each cheek. God can she *love* the fellow? Possibly. There is no end, he reflected, to the complexities of human nature.

"Do you wish to charge Vin, Mary?"' he asked.

"No."

Almost he had expected this.

And, suddenly, an idea flooded his mind.

"Mary, why don't you go on a long visit to my mother and take Ruth with you?"

Mary drew a deep breath. Plainly the idea appealed to her.

"Mother's written me more than once asking me to persuade you."

"But who'll look after the house?"

"Anne and Mrs. T. And, when you return, Ruth can come to us, taking Anne's place; Anne will come to you."

"And then you won't go to the police about master?" Ruth asked hoarsely.

"We need not then, need we, Mary?"

Vin entered, in his usual, silent, buoyant way. No dephlogistication here, no lessening of that otherness. No lessening within himself, Terry decided, of that dark, striving against something a little more than that, a little less than this . . .

Twi-creature! Terry began to suspect him of being the most uncanny mortal of his experience. He seemed in no relationship with that waste soul which had wandered in during night's antelucan hour. That spent thing! That hollow simulacrum! That mindless human clock!

And yet he had met any amount of outré beings, especially sadistic drunkards . . . But Vin was the kingpin of these. One could imagine him drinking a bowl of spiced wine and blood at some magician's banquet whereat the guests had holes in place of eyes; or, suddenly revealed by a lance of moonlight, seated, wearing on his head a conical cap and on his chin a pointed beard, astride a tomb-stone; or, cut open on a slab, discovering to his dissector an acorn for a heart.

Never had he looked more Greekly gracious, younger, happier, more full of good-fellowship; or more unaware of wrongdoing. Perhaps he supposed that his present charm compensated fully for his recent debauch. But there was surely more than mere puckishness to this chap's conduct, air, thought? Suddenly, Terry's mind began to quote: "Still stranger, should, on the opposite side of the street, another Hatter establish himself . . ." Carlyle, that. Just what he was, this chap: the other Hatter. A Hatter who recked naught of time, who leapt Man's ages, using perhaps the sexual affinities—perhaps not. Or perhaps he was just addled atavism . . . Or perhaps—oh, hell!

He smiled brilliantly at the others, then strode over to Ruth and in his most winning manner said:

"I'm afraid I made a nasty beast of myself last night. But you realize, I hope, that's not the real me by a long chalk?"

"A very long chalk," Terry thought grimly; and said aloud. "That's all very well, Border, but it's not good enough. As a matter of fact we've been debating a criminal charge against you; not because we think it would benefit your mortal nature, but because it would free us of your unpleasant company for a long period."

"Now listen," Vin began.

"*Not* more promises, please. We're still smarting from the damage of your present broken ones. Look at Mary's face. Look at Ruth's . . ."

"The present circumstances are exceptional. That terrible, unnatural storm unbalanced me . . . And, then, this business about THE INEXPLICABLE . . ."

"Yes, talking about *that*—I'm talking as a special constable and a lawyer now, Border—it appeared to Mary last night, terminating. I believe, your orgy of assault, and caused her to faint because of its monstrous appearance. *You* were present at the identical instant. I'd like a formal statement from you describing exactly what happened."

Vin stared first at Terry, then at Mary with an expression of bewilderment.

"I don't get you at all, Terry. I admit losing myself last night and I admit behaving like a brute; it's certainly true that Mary fainted, but nothing appeared to her—when *I* was present. It was *because* she fainted that I sobered up sufficiently to realize what I was about . . . I *did* remember my promise, then, and in a fit of desperation rushed off to find *you*. But no one was about. I daren't trust my own self to go back, so just lost myself in the night . . ."

"Have you only now returned?" Terry asked curtly, watching Vin's face with close attention.

"About half an hour back. I've just washed and come straight in."

("Well! What sort of a liar *was* this? Or what . . . But wait! It was possible that Vin had, in some automatic condition, returned unknown even to himself. One had to be just even to Beelzebub.")

There was a considerable pause, during which Vin sat watching Terry as an eager boy would watch a bench of magistrates. And presently, perhaps rather in the manner of a magistrate, Terry passed judgment.

"I cannot accept your word, your apologies or explanations, Border. I feel sure Mary doesn't. Personally, I should charge you, for the reason that your sort ranks with the beasts . . ."

He broke off abruptly, startled by a sound that made him stare at Vin, a sound that could only be described as a brutish snarl, but certainly matched by the savage glare of the other man's eyes. In a flash Vin's beautifully moulded lids had fallen and, whatever the expression lurking beneath, Terry could not now see it. But the ferocity of both sound and look not only had startled Terry, but roused in him a curious and equally savage opposition. He leaned forward, his chin out-thrust.

"That your sort ranks with the beasts," he repeated deliberately, "and is safer caged."

A violent tremor disturbed Vin's body from top to toe. And Terry noticed that his hands remained clenched, his whole physique taut.

"However, Mary has decided to go away for some time and take Ruth with her, during which period she will come to a decision how to protect her future . . ."

Suddenly Vin looked up, his Face once more normal, his eyes clear, but anxious.

"Go away?" he repeated . . . "But for how long and where?"

"She will visit my mother, who has been pressing her to do so for some time."

"But . . ."

"How long is a matter for Mary to decide."

Vin remained very still for a time. Then, without looking up, said in a low, strange tone:

"The child must be born here."

A certain quality of emotion behind these words surprised all the others.

"Gosh, I believe he wants the child," Terry reflected swiftly . . . "Who'd have thought it?"

"You can get me a keeper, if you like, but the child must be born here . . . We are not divorced, nor legally separated . . . She shall *have* no grounds for a divorce or for any legal complaint . . . but the child must be born here . . . I still have the right to demand that."

There was another complete silence, broken by Mary who said coldly:

"I will return in time."

"Very well, we'll let things stand at that for the present . . ." He turned to Mary. "There's one excellent aspect of this decision that you've not thought of, maybe. You'll be free of THE INEXPLICABLE."

Mary rose violently and faced round, her eyes alight with an almost demented expression.

"I shall not be free. I never shall be free: the monster is here!"

She laid her hands upon the child.

Vin crashed back his chair and, erect, stared with flaming eyes at his wife.

He began to jerk and twitch, growling in a paroxysm of menacing rage; but, even as Terry sprang between man and woman, the growl changed to a scream; Vin fell at their feet torn and tortured in a fashion that none of those who, paralyzed, watched him had ever seen.

"Good God, he's an epileptic," Terry whispered.

Mary laughed.

CHAPTER VIII

IT WAS ARRANGED that Terry should phone to his mother, suggesting if possible that Mary should come at once. An informal person, Mrs. Cliffe was prepared to play hostess at any moment of the day or night; her method being: Do just as you like, and, in any plan in which I'm able to take part, count on me. Her job, just now, was entertaining and no doubt she'd welcome an attractive girl to aid in brightening up the lot of "her boys."

Things happened swiftly. Anne and Mrs. Thatcher undertook to look after Mary's house in her absence and cook plain breakfasts for Vin, who, since recovery from his fit, had disappeared.

"Let Mary do as she likes, so long as she's back here for the child's birth," he told Terry. "If she's gone when I come home, that'll be okay."

"Are you subject to epilepsy?" Terry asked abruptly.

The other turned eyes dark with evil.

"If you're referring to that seizure just now, allow me to inform you it was the first of its kind I've ever experienced; and though I don't profess to be as clever as you, Terry, I venture to suggest it was *not* in the remotest degree connected with epilepsy. And will you oblige me . . ."

"How?"

"Just go to hell, will you?"

~ ~ ~ ~ ~

Aunt Charlotte safely in her nursing home, Mary and Ruth far on their way to Mrs. Cliffe's prosaic care, it was with a sensation of great relief that Terry returned home from the office that night.

He was met by Mrs. Thatcher.

"Oh, Mr. Terry, two gentlemen called this morning just after you'd gone with Miss Mary."

"What did they want?"

"They're calling again this evening, about six."

"Why didn't you send them along to the office?"

"They said their business was not professional. Here are their cards."

"Runder . . . K.S. Runder, that's the celebrated brain man and scientist . . . Bede Touchcord . . . Yes, I'm sure he's the occultist . . . Oh, I see light. THE INEXPLICABLE. H'm, rather interesting."

"They asked me about Mr. Border. I explained he often doesn't return home till late at night, but that he usually lunched at the Clarendon Restaurant. They said they'd take a chance of finding him there."

"Yes, I expect they would . . . Well, maybe they'll get what they want from him. Anyhow, when they come, if the come, bring them along to my den."

"Very well, Mr. Terry . . . It's a funny thing they can't find that freak."

"Devilish funny! There were swarms out last night . . . We *did* think we were on the track when those screams sounded. It's hard to believe, even now, it was only a cat. Maybe to-night they'll have better luck."

"Are *you* going out to-night, Mr. Terry?"

"No. I'm having a night off. A substitute's taking my place. I want at least eight hours sleep to-night."

Promptly at six Mrs. Thatcher showed in Professor Runder and Bede Touchcord. Runder proved a hatchet-faced man with exceedingly steady and penetrating eyes. The occultist was a massive-browed, very still being, whose reddy-brown eyes had a curious opaque appearance. Both these men struck Terry as of profound mentality and, during the ensuring conversation, it became clear that they were profoundly informed men, familiar with various fields of thought and the erudite attainments of most countries. Runder introduced the purpose of their visit after the first few complimentary amenities had been exchanged.

"We are writing a book, a curious book," Runder explained with a laugh. "It's in the form of dialogue and contains the fors and againsts upon many subjects from the points of view of what you might call an exact mind such as my own and an impressionist or open mind like my good friend's." He smiled at Touchcord. "Anything in the nature of the unusual interests us; we examine it minutely from our different standpoints, then debate the matter in dialogue . . ."

"My word, I'd like to read your book," Terry exclaimed.

"I'm afraid," Touchcord said quietly, "it will be many months yet before our book sees the light. You may be assured, however, that, since you are interested, we will send you a copy."

"Certainly," Runder endorsed.

Touchcord had a remarkable voice, Terry thought; it matched his deep, still, unreadable eyes. Powerfully bass, it suggested an immense sense of personal mental dignity. His utterance was exceedingly deliberate and suggested that each word was accompanied by clear, applied thought.

"Well, Mr. Cliffe, you no doubt appreciate why we're interested in this INEXPLICABLE business."

"I do; but I hardly think I'm the man to help you. Dr. Erne, his . . ."

"Erne has disappeared."

"Disappeared?"

"So we understand . . . Vanished. As it would seem his freak had done. As a matter of fact, it is not so much about the freak we want to see you, or perhaps I should say my friend, Touchcord, wants to see you, but about your next door neighbour."

"Border?"

"Exactly," Touchcord's deep voice broke in. "It was in his garden that the last victim was discovered, so naturally we sought him out first thing. It is *I* who am interested in Mr. Border. Have you known him long and intimately?"

"We were in the trenches together and his wife's my oldest friend; but he and I are not very intimate," Terry replied carefully.

"Is Mr. Border secretly interested in the occult, do you think?"

"I should imagine not."

"Has he shown himself at all interested in this matter of THE INEXPLICABLE?" Runder asked.

"Well—"

"We think it rather strange," Touchcord said quietly, "that *he* did not take part in the search for a creature that had destroyed a human life in his own garden."

It was strange. Yet till now, remembering Vin's difficult nature, Terry had not considered it strange; but, come to think of it, from the personal point-of-view, the personal menace involved, one would have thought . . . Quite unexpectedly Terry thought of Vin's description of his father. He glanced at Touchcord. What had this strange, powerful man discovered in Vin to make him put these very personal, probing questions?

"I'm in rather a difficult position, gentlemen. I cannot supply information about a neighbour's private . . ."

Runder held up his hand.

"We will assure you solemnly, Mr. Cliffe, that every word of this interview will be confidential . . ."

"I am seeking light upon deeply dark matters, my young friend," Touchcord said softly; "not information to be used in our book. Please accept that as simple truth . . ."

"Naturally—from you gentlemen."

"I think, perhaps, you have remembered something that has bearing on my question: Is Mr. Border secretly interested in the occult?"

"He told me his father was a close student of and believer in the occult. I think I can recall his actual words. 'But father was a strange being . . . He believed in mystery, forbidden mystery; the hidden and dreadful secrets . . . He believed absolutely in vampires and had a religion founded upon the undead . . . He swore by . . . by his dark world he'd still live after he was dead! . . .'"

During this effort of memory Touchcord leaned slowly farther and farther forward, his gaze fixed unblinkingly upon Terry.

"Those were his actual words?"

"I daresay I've misplaced or altered some words; but it's near enough to be called his actual words."

"And does he *believe* his father still lives?"

Terry stared. The question that twenty minutes ago would have seemed absurd and have challenged the scoffer in him—now filled him with wonder; for had not Mary told him that Vin had annoyed Aunt Charlotte by jesting about THE INEXPLICABLE, who, he had said, was his father . . . Good lord alive! Of all the fried rot!

Placing his hands on his powerful knees, Touchcord leaned so far forward that his breath played upon Terry's face.

"Don't keep anything back, Mr. Cliffe, because it seems to you outlandish and absurd. You have thought of something else?"

"Well, the fact is, I've come to wonder if Border is quite responsible . . . He says and does things at times that alarm me . . . He did in the trenches. There's this stuff about his father. Is it some sign of mania?"

"Why do you ask that, Mr. Cliffe?" Touchcord demanded in a way that suggested his determination to know the truth was inexorable.

"Well . . . Of course, it may be mere nonsense on Border's part, but, when he heard about the freak's escape, he declared it to be his father."

"IIc said that?"

Terry sensed vast excitement beneath the occultist's seeming monumental calm and thought of volcanic violence boiling beneath a mountain's still crust. He glanced at Runder, who was smiling.

"I think, Mr. Cliffe, your neighbour is perhaps a little too sane . . . An exceedingly sharp-witted party, with a watchful eye, always ready to snatch at floating chances. A flamboyant creature, a little of the clown and always trying to create effects. A jackdaw who loves to dress up in peacock's feathers and strut. But, if he's a poser, he is one, I should imagine, who always poses to procure some definite advantage for himself. I should not believe that because he dribbled all that rot over you, Mr. Cliffe, he did it without some practical reason. He *wished* to create an occult atmosphere, but, of course, he's no more occult than my boot. This freak's escape appealed to the acquisitive mummer in him and I've no doubt that a little Paul Prying on my part would reveal the motive."

There ensued a curious, stony silence. These two men, each in his own way a magnificent mentality, were, Terry felt, at once firm friends and sworn enemies, who lost no chance to bombard each other's ideology. Touchcord, by far the more massive and physically imposing, rose and stood back to the fire. He turned his steady, concentrated gaze upon Terry, who asked himself: "What do these two mental detectives think of *me*? Uncomfortable companions!"

"Well, Mr. Cliffe, you see how utterly diverse our opinions are," Touchcord said, but without a trace of rancour.

"*You* entirely differ from Professor Runder's conception of Mr. Border?" Terry asked.

"Oh, yes! Absolutely. My friend is supreme in the world of exact science and no one has a more comprehensive knowledge of the human brain. Therefore we must unconditionally accept his affirmation that your young neighbour is sane. But I do not dispute that. On the other hand I unhesitatingly, and after as much profound research as the professor has put into robbing science of its secrets, declare that everybody, more or less— some much more, some infinitely less—has occult powers; but those who neither study nor develop them naturally ascribe what they fail to understand to material sources . . . Sceptics seem to expect occultists to prance on stages and perform like conjurers, produce phenomena at will. True occultism is a silent, secret communion, peculiar to the privacy of a being's silent journey along secret, silent paths. It is the *few* that voice their doubts. Millions believe and are silent . . . It is not necessary to have ocular, aural or tactile demonstration to know that profound 'Influences' exist for which we have no suitable names. Upon some of us the knowledge is forced. And I would even dare to say that there is no man, no woman unaware of them as death slowly approaches.

"I am interested in your neighbour's aura-waves. They communicate strange things to me . . . Evil 'Personality' exists, though it does not work directly or in positive form. Now and again, however, errors occur, as they occur in the natural processes, and into our normal creeps the a-normal—a touch of that which man is intended not to see, know or guess; an invasion from the *dark world* whose myrmidons catch men unaware, use them for purposes incomprehensible even to seekers like myself, but never appear in concrete shape so that men may say 'This and that exists.' But the *whole* of mankind has an instinct that gropingly knows the 'this-and-that' exists and in desperate confession cries Devil, Demon, Vampire, Un-dead—while the empirics jeer . . . because they are never seen, cannot be dissected; as if one had never heard of rationalization."

"Do you suggest," Terry asked almost irritably, "that Mr. Border is actively related to vampires and demons?"

He glanced from one man to the other and was aware of Runder's quiet smile.

But Touchcord still continued to survey him gravely.

"I do not suggest anything extravagant, or what we term supernatural, Mr. Cliffe . . . I think your neighbour is conscious of unusual forces and inclinations in himself and that he is in alliance with, or possibly in alliance with, what we should term malign powers. At the same time we might pronounce him more victim than free agent. It is probable he fights hard against urges which he himself hardly understands."

Suddenly Terry found himself telling the whole story of Vin and Mary, to which both men listened intently and without uttering a word. At the conclusion of this tale, however, Touchcord turned to his collaborator and asked:

"*You* see nothing significant in:

"One. Border's declaration regarding his father's beliefs and pursuits?

"Two. His claim to blood relationship with this so-called freak?

"Three. The freak's coming to this town, his unexplainable escape, his lurking in the Border garden, his appearance to the mother of Border's child—and lastly, Border's fit?"

"I see a chain of events fully capable of commonsense explanation. I agree with Border, evidently concerned for the welfare of his child, that Mrs. Border, having brooded to an unhealthy degree over this monster, and clearly affected by a phenomenal storm, imagined she saw what she did not. As for the young fellow's fit, having formed a definite opinion about his play-acting propensities—well, there you are!"

"Why," Touchcord asked slowly, "has the monster not been apprehended, if merely, as you believe, a degraded mixture of human and animal life?"

"It will be, my friend."

"It—will—*never*—be."

Terry turned to the speaker.

"*You* believe THE INEXPLICABLE to be supernatural?"

Touchcord paused, then asked:

"During your service in the trenches—were you able to explain everything you saw and heard in terms of natural science?"

The question staggered Terry, for he, like innumerable others of his fellow soldiers, had found himself in touch with incidents—often of little importance—that puzzled him and frightened others less controlled by will and mind.

"THE INEXPLICABLE has magically vanished?" Runder whispered with a quizzical tilt to one eyebrow. It was too charmingly suggested, this question, to cause offence, had Touchcord been one easily offended, which, Terry thought, he was not.

"THE INEXPLICABLE is—*buried*," the occultist replied as softly.

"You are suggesting common murder?"

"I am suggesting what is definitely best left to the oblivion to which it has been committed."

~ ~ ~ ~ ~

His two extremely interesting and certainly unexpected visitors left Terry in a puzzled frame of mind.

"Good lord," he thought, "I'm more in two minds about Vincent Border now than when they came!"

Both men had so well-supported their theories, and if the prosaicness, the literalness of life, in which one so easily finds explanations for apparent mystery inclined him to accept Runder's infinitely more probably conclusions, Terry had to acknowledge much evidence in favour of Touchcord's improbabilities, not least of which was that "oblique" aspect of Vin's mental and physical behaviour.

According to Runder, Vincent Border was what police and other evidence bore him out to be, a plausible rogue, out for the softest spot he could wrest from life, and a little too sane. According to Touchcord, he was dark-ridden, a victim of phantoms more elusive than the shadows of ghosts; a creature to some extent aware of being curiously cursed and secretly rebellious. In either case certainly no husband for a lovely and dear creature like Mary . . .

Which of these two men was right, the child would sooner or later prove. If in due course it showed itself a normal and decent human soul, triumph for Runder.

Meanwhile Mary was safely with his mother and the only problem remaining at present was where THE INEXPLICABLE was hiding. Strange if it never was found, as Touchcord predicted. Strange, too, that its keeper had vanished. Was the man a rogue? Had he been foisting a fraud upon the public, a doctored, faked-up wolf, and now feared the consequences of exposure?

Time would show.

Time did show. THE INEXPLICABLE was never seen again by mortal eye.

Writing to Mary, Terry said:

" . . . Things are still quiet and orderly in our little sphere. Everybody now takes it definitely for granted that the freak creature is gone for good. It would hardly be an exaggeration to say every leaf has been separately examined; and after all this time there seems little likelihood of its showing up.

"All's perfectly in order next door. Vin seems to be exercising an extraordinary control upon himself and is as quiet as the

Rev. Mr. James. So far as it is possible to tell he no longer drinks at all. He's been shutting himself up at nights with hefty-looking books.

"Personally, I imagine he's pulled up his socks because . . ."

In another letter he wrote:

" . . . Would you believe it: Vin's won £700 in a football pool and for the moment is a local celebrity . . .?"

And in another:

" . . . When I called on Aunt Charlotte to-day, she told me she had made up her mind to go home. She looks rather feeble and I imagine is truly homesick . . . No doubt you have heard direct . . .

"Mrs. T. has seen Dr. Grove and made the arrangements; but she wrote to you, Mother tells me, by the same post.

"Mum tells me we won't see her for the event after all and that her next brief visit will be her last for a considerable time. She's going to America as a member of some fantastical committee. Personally, I think she misses Dad dreadfully and is trying to occupy her mind with work . . .

"Incidentally, *how* I miss you . . ."

CHAPTER IX

IT WAS QUITE BY ACCIDENT that Vincent Border met Holly Chambers. The meeting took place in the public library, where Vin, in his new rôle of bookworm, had gone one lunch hour to change his books: a volume of Poe's poems and the other a history of alchemy.

There was an affinity between these two that each immediately recognized and did not try to retard. Holly was tall, with wide shoulders, pronounced breasts, big, long, well-curved thighs, a head of natural chestnut curls and seductive, heavy, provocative blue eyes. Added to these charms, she could boast an unflawed, creamy skin.

Vin liked her physically, but it was, despite this liking, something in her mentality that attracted and bound him to her from the first instant of meeting. The attraction was quite mutual. In Vin Holly saw not only the most dangerously handsome man of her career, but also recognized, unconsciously perhaps, another of her own kind.

There was a flash of the eyes between them—and the fates smiled.

In turning he had knocked her book to the floor.

"Dreadfully sorry," he said languidly, before he'd seen her face and met her gaze. Then he darted for the book.

"These aisles are very narrow," he suggested, returning the book.

"Yes, they are," she agreed, returning his smile.

"The whole place is stuffy and out-of-date, like most public libraries."

"Well, museum would be the right name for most of them."

"You've said it! You seem to have a pretty close acquaintance with them—various ones, I mean."

"Oh, I've traveled about England and Scotland pretty extensively. I'm a nurse."

"Oh, are you nursing in this little burg temporarily?"

"Not exactly, though I don't know how long I may stay. I'm attached to Dr. Grove's Nursing Home."

"Really! He's our doctor."

"Well, that doesn't tell me much," she murmured with a smile, looking at him closely.

"My name's Border."

"Vincent Border, who won that £700 in the coupon business—football wasn't it?"

"Yes, I'm that celebrity."

"Then your wife's going to be a patient before long, I think."

"D'you mean *you* may be the nurse?"

"I *might* be. I daresay I could be by a little manipulation."

They were eyeing each other under lowered lids.

"I say," he exclaimed suddenly, noting her pretty and tasteful mufti, "are you off duty?"

"For the day."

"Well, I'm just going to have lunch. What about a spot?"

"That would be delightful!" She turned, then added, "My name is Holly Chambers."

"Holly! That name suits you, somehow."

They began to flirt. Vin felt blazing inside. This girl was just his sort. And he agreed with the implication when she said that during her probationary days she had been known as Jolly.

"Sometimes it was Jolly-Holly," she told him.

She spoke well, which pleased him. Uneducated himself, he yet managed to pass as a polished person; and Holly, it was evident, shared this gift; for she had known no greater initial advantages than he. Her father, it appeared—and this struck Vin as a strange coincidence—had been a showman, had made sufficient with exhibiting novelties at fairs to retire and live quietly in Cornwall.

"He's a wonderful man!" she exclaimed. "At fifty-two you'd think he was forty; and he's as strong as a horse."

"You're very fond of him?"

"We get on well together; we're excellent friends; but I don't know about *very* fond. I don't believe in getting so attached to a person that you can't live without him—or her."

He shot her a glance. Yes, she *was* just his sort. That was his sentiment. Life had suddenly blossomed. Since that night of the storm he had rigidly forsworn drink and, therefore, things hadn't been too bright. Life threatened to become boring—which, to his temperament, was dangerous—but now!

She was, he could see, as interested in the main chance as he himself. And wary! Yes, she was wary. Before lunch was over he contemplated a liaison and knew perfectly well she reciprocated his desire. There'd be little obtainable in life she'd deny herself; but she'd help herself secretly; always with an eye to number one.

They met again and again, becoming more and more friendly.

And then the opportunity occurred for their liaison to begin. She could get away from the home, could pass the night with him—an easy thing to do undiscovered in his empty house. But she did not jump at the idea. He had not expected she would; for Holly knew her own value.

"I've kept clear of silly risks, young man," she told him.

He reassured her.

"Oh, yes; I've heard all that before. But even the smartest of us make mistakes. Even Lily."

"Lily?"

"My sister. She thought she was smart, but she wasn't quite smart enough and now . . . Well, bless my soul . . . She'll have *her* baby practically at the same time as your wife'll have hers. Strange!"

"I don't see it . . ." He began to argue, knowing full well that she was not really afraid, that she, of all women, knew how to take care of herself, even protect herself, for she was exceedingly strong, stronger than he.

"Is your sister a nurse, too?"

"No. She's married. Her husband's an Indian civil servant. He's coming home next summer to a job here . . . Lily couldn't stand the climate out there and's been home some months . . .

She's pretty desperate. He'll know it's not his child, of
course . . ."

"What'll she do?"

Holly laughed; there was, Vin thought, rather a sinister quality in her laugh and this drew him even closer to her. He comprehended that laugh intimately and all kinds of cruel little ex-
citements within sprang from nowhere to dance a second upon
the floor of his mind.

"She's offered me a fairly large sum—what folks in our position call large sums—to help her."

"Well, can't you?"

"I can; but I won't. I'm taking no risks like that . . . She's
got herself into the mess, she must get herself out."

Holly was suddenly aware that Vin watched her with strange
attention. His ears, she saw, were pricked up in a way that
made her think of zoological creatures and she thought:

"Hello! What's *he* got on *his* mind? Something to his advantage—and against mine. He'll be disappointed."

Though she desired Vin and in her calculating way loved
him, she was not prepared to take the smallest risk for his
sake—unless a reward was offered greater than the risk.

But, whatever his thoughts were, he said nothing. Then. Instead he pressed his suit.

"You know there's no risk for us. You get *no* fun in this life
if you're *too* cautious."

This was true and she smiled. Vin need not have concerned
himself; she had no intentions of foregoing this particular lux-
ury.

~ ~ ~ ~ ~

Time swept on. Holly and Vin pursued their amour with discretion. He, on his part, derived profound material satisfaction
from their relationship and no longer craved for drink. He was
deeply preoccupied with this admirable new companion.

Even Terry and the women of his household failed to discover the truth of what was happening next door.

"It certainly *looks*, Mr. Terry, as if he's turned over a new leaf."

"Yes, it does."

"And maybe he'll be a good father."

"Let's hope so."

It was with infinite surprise that Vin one day received a letter from Mary announcing her imminent return. So the time was at hand.

"Our meetings will have to cease when she does come, Holly."

"Without question. I can't afford the slightest suspicion of scandal . . ." She paused and looked at Vin through narrowed eyes. "By the way, Dr. Grove told me to-day that I'm to attend Mrs. Border."

They both stared a while, then laughed.

"We'll have to make the most of what time's left, old thing," Vin said. "What about to-night?"

"I shan't be seeing you to-night."

"Why ever not?"

"I'm going to see Lily and won't be back till to-morrow morning."

She saw the strange, dark look that so often warned her to take care in judging this man. Suddenly he was remote, miles from her; lost in some black jungle of thought. But she had the invaluable gift of being able to wait. She waited; and presently he asked:

"Does your father ever take jobs?"

The question was so unexpected and startling that she stared—used as she was to his non-àpropos remarks.

"In his own line d'you mean?"

"Not necessarily."

"He *hasn't* done, although he still hankers after the show business . . ." She stole another inquisitive glance at her companion. "But he might be tempted if the pay was good. Why? Have you a job for him?"

"There's the possibility of a really good job for him—if he's the right man."

"What d'you mean, 'The right man'?"

Vin stared at his finger-nails, a sly smile flitting about his lips.

"What sort of man *is* your father?"

"Tall, handsome like me."

"I don't mean in appearance . . . Is he a Bible sort?"

"Oh, I get you! You mean, is he unscrupulous . . . Well, I'll tell you: he's me all over again."

Vin grinned.

"A thoroughly bad lot?"

There was a moment's horseplay between them; but presently Vin became profoundly serious, so serious that he impressed Holly and for the first time she felt fear of him. More than once she had suspected sinister depths in his nature, but never till now had she believed him dangerous and that his debonair exterior masked potent evil.

"I might find a job for your father . . . A curious piece of work . . ."

"Not criminal?"

He laughed. "Do you associate me with criminality?"

"We've agreed we're both unscrupulous. We are. But I'm careful, too."

"Take heart, sister. This job's not one of common crime. It is indeed practically without risk, but it'll be lucrative if he's the sort of man who's not squeamish . . . and can hold his tongue."

"Do *I* play a part in it?"

"A big part."

"H'm, I thought so. Well?"

"As a matter of fact we can be mutually useful . . ."

"Hedging on the offer of payment?"

"Certainly not. I mean that by helping me you help yourselves."

"You thinking of Lily?"

"Well that's your trouble, isn't it?"

It was now Holly's turn to sit very still. She began to see light.

Speaking softly and with precision, Vin reconstructed the events of Mary's gestation thus far. She listened carefully and when he paused said:

"You're afraid that your wife's mental torment over that freak, her brooding and definite fright when she saw the thing . . ."

"When she thought she saw the thing . . ." he murmured.

Holly glanced at him. Vin was watching her from under lowered lids.

"When she thought she saw the thing," she repeated carefully, "may result in a . . ."

"Quite . . . Well, you're exceedingly quick in the up-take, Hol . . . You're already on to my plan."

"You suggest substituting Lily's baby for . . ."

"Exactly."

"But supposing your child's born normal?"

For a fleeting instant his face, she thought, changed unrecognizably. A spasm passed through his entire body and distorted his features. It might have been either mental agony or rage. He leaned forward and his lips dithered before utterance came.

"It won't be," he said harshly.

A bold, downright person, Holly wanted to contradict, ask, How *can* you be sure? But something stayed her . . . And from that instant a conviction settled in her mind that Mary Border's child would come into the world a monster.

"Well, you may be right," she agreed; "but even so, what you suggest sounds practically impossible . . . It's all very well in books and plays to outwit the law, but extremely difficult in everyday life; especially where infants are concerned. Birth is the prerogative of *all* the nosey-parkers. Then there's the doctor . . ."

"The doctor would not be present."

"What, you propose to tap him on the head with a hammer, or something?" she asked derisively.

He ignored her mockery, merely repeated very quietly, "The doctor would not be present. Only you would be present at the birth."

"Huh! . . . Well, I couldn't be present at the birth of Lily's child. And how are you going to fix the authorities in regard to that?"

"The authorities would never *know* of its birth. According to what you've told me, your sister's baby is due to be born . . ."

"Almost to the hour at the same time as your wife's according to the data we have in both cases. Of course an examination in each instance will . . ."

Suddenly Border sprang up with a velocity that checked Holly's calculations and held wide both her gaze and mouth. Again he seemed hardly recognizable; and there crept into her mind a suspicion of his sanity, a suspicion his words were not suited to allay.

"Has it never dawned upon you, Holly, that I am psychic? Are you dull, like most people, regarding the exceptional in human mentality? The two births will take place in the same hour."

He stared at her with a steadiness that bore down her own usually dauntless gaze.

"Anyhow, an examination will show whether he's right or wrong," she told herself practically. "The fortunate thing is both Lily and Vin know the exact dates of conception . . . And one can always help things along."

Nevertheless, after this she found herself accepting the fact that both births would approximate, not because she knew the dates of conception, or because subsequent examinations fully suggested that they would be practically simultaneous, but because Vin's pronouncement had established itself—unknown to Holly—in her mind as an irrefutable fact.

"Well, providing that the two births come together or as near as needs be, how are you going to conceal Lily's condition and the ultimate birth of her child?"

"That's where your father comes in. Your sister is quite an obscure person, with few friends. No one knows of her condition. I understand your father still has his touring caravan. He picks her up and goes on a definite tour of isolated districts, returning to our vicinity at the prescribed time . . . The only ugly part of my plan is who would superintend Lily's confine-ment? That means chancing a stranger."

"Not at all. Dad's had every experience in the world, includ-ing the birth of children. He's a better doctor than most practi-tioners and has gipsy blood in him. She'd be safe in his care."

"Then, do you think he'd undertake the job?"

Holly's hard mouth tautened, a crafty expression crept into her eyes. But beyond the craft lurked a soupçon of fear; an in-stinctive rather than a conscious fear. The gipsy in her had, perhaps, uttered some warning against the secrets of Vin's na-ture. Nevertheless, since her four-square, practical courage was at any instant prepared to face the traditional image of evil himself, she did not shirk her present determination.

"Well, as to that, what are the terms you suggest?"

There was silence, then Vin said:

"They will be as generous as I am *able* to make them. I've already told you I'm not well off." Again a considerable pause; and once more: "I'll pay your father a pound a week for his life and continue it to you should your father pre-decease you."

Holly grinned to herself. Her crafty, scheming brain saw dis-tant possibilities in Vin's proposal that had nothing to do with his pocket. A pound a week was contemptible in view of what her father and possibly herself were supposed to saddle them-selves with.

"What's your income?" she asked curtly.

He hesitated then answered:

"I earn a fiver a week."

"Five pounds. Then you can afford to make your offer thirty shillings. You have your wage to yourself, that I know."

He smiled coldly, his eyes dilated and, she observed with a touch of almost superstitious awe, gleamed as if from some in-ward source—though she knew very well the true source was a reflection from the actual fire leaping and spitting in the grate.

"You're not contemplating any future advances?" he asked smoothly.

The implication left Holly cold.

"We're not blackmailers."

"I can take care of myself," he whispered, his fire-lit gaze flickering over her. "I'll make it thirty shillings per week; never more."

"Okay, Mr. Poe. Now about myself . . ."

"You!"

"Yes. I'm the one who takes most risk; I'm the most important actor in your little drama. Think it over."

"And what do *you* want?"

"Five hundred pounds; and cheap at that."

They wrangled; but he agreed.

"And, if your wife's baby is born normal and Lily's is left on our hands, we get two hundred, to help us place it."

His laughter, she thought, sounded like oil falling onto velvet. "If it's born normal, I'll pay you a million."

Despite all her cool self-assurance, Holly shuddered.

Never, she determined, should there, from now on, be any but formal business relations between Vin and herself. She had reckoned up her man wrong. She knew when it was time to get off. Moreover, despite her new repulsion, Holly was conscious of intense excitement. Both the showman and the gipsy in her responded to possibilities as yet hardly adumbrated in her mind; the first because her inherited judgment whispered that a source of considerable profit was coming her way, the second because always she had desired to see the world, tour all the picturesque towns and townlets that her father knew so well; and here was her immaterial wish assuming corporeal proportions before her secret vision. Given the right monstrosity, one could travel the whole world over on a fast, deep stream of profit. And how she had always hated the humdrum! How sick she was of nursing!

The arrangement suggested by Vin was, from her point of view, admirable in every way. It disposed of Lily's unpleasant problem. It ensured what she knew would prove a most welcome addition of income for her father. It provided her with a solid lump of capital, which would be necessary if her foreshadowed plan was to eventuate. She would set about arrangements without delay. That very night she'd fix things with Lily and she'd send her father a wire immediately.

~ ~ ~ ~ ~

This meeting between the retired showman and Vin was a momentous one. A tall, lean, wolf of a man, the former clearly revealed traces of gipsy ancestry. One thought of great waterways, plains, heights, forests and gorges when one looked in his eyes—restless, haughty, lawless; and one understood why this man had on his retirement chosen the rugged coast of Cornwall as his sanctuary. It was astonishing to Holly, a witness of the meeting, that Vin should show to so little advantage in her father's presence. His beauty seemed less, his stature less, his personality less. Added to which, she observed an odd uneasiness about his manner of approaching the older man, who, on his part, revealed to Holly—an expert in weighing-up her father's reactions—a curious and humanly fastidious hostility. Presently, too, she realized he was reluctant to conclude the bargain, a very surprising change in his attitude to this affair, since till now he had, in agreement with his daughter, seen remarkable possibilities in the acquisition of an exhibit that should appeal powerfully to the millions of morbid minds throughout the world. Certainly he not only agreed at last, but even signed a contract of sorts, yet, it was plain, under protest by his silent judgment.

"If you had not been so set upon the matter, girl," he told Holly afterwards, "I'd have taken the train back to Cornwall *without* this sheet of paper."

Seldom had she seen her father so fundamentally disturbed.

"Why?" she demanded.

"No good will come of this bargain." He was silent for a while. Lore, occultism, prophecy—these were gifts from his lineage. Presently he added: "Reason and judgment are acquired products, acquired by slow process. Instinct lies, often tongueless, behind both. Instinct, a knowledge not so clearly defined as the artificial one of civilization, but actually more subtle, more accurate, obedient to more precise laws. Men have all but smothered instinct. Events have ignored it. To an enormous extent it is an atrophied asset. But it is there, in man's nature. It plays its part in world affairs—a more powerful part than many realize. It seldom raises its voice, so its part passes unobserved. I am one of those who recognize its infallibility. My instinct advises you to have nothing to do with this birth, with this bargain, with that bi-man. I know places where he'd be instantly destroyed by the so-called ignorant . . . And what's about to be born should be burnt . . ."

He paused, then added:

"You are my child. You have your way to go as I had mine. Your will is free. I shall stand by my word, if you wish; but not one penny of that man's money will I touch, nor will I handle the—the—the issue. It will not belong to life as we know it. It should go back—to the dark."

Holly shrugged and eyed her father coldly.

"Nonsense! You get word-drunk. Some of your utterances are absolutely meaningless. And probably the child will be born normal. If not, it'll be just another freak."

Father and daughter both somewhat alike in nature as well as in looks, both compounded of knowledge and ignorance, both prone as much to superstition as to clear-sighted science, and both reticent, authoritative, brief, characteristically turned to the consideration of practical details of their undertaking. Both agreed that the first thing that must happen was for the old showman to put his caravan into commission and collect Lily.

~ ~ ~ ~ ~

Terry, observing Vin during the days immediately preceding Mary's return, thought him strange. He seemed exalted by some odd excitement and at the same time, wildly anxious; yet what he was anxious about, Terry could not guess, but noticed that his neighbour often smiled as if immensely amused, and at other times muttered furiously and to all seeming senselessly.

" 'Pon my soul," Terry reflected, "if I didn't know that Runder's one of the world's authorities on mental matters, I'd begin to doubt his assurance that Border's sane."

CHAPTER X

RETURNING AFTER her long absence to old familiar scenes, Mary felt a rush of sentiment sweep into her heart. Her home! Her garden! Her shining windows! Her waving trees! Those sturdy chimney stacks, hers! Those mossy walls, here golden, there grey, hers!

And that window up there, catching the sun from the south, catching it from the west—in which ever direction it might be—hers and the little girl's; for surely all her prayers to that great Negative, Fate, must result in a whole and healthy teeny, tiny Mary the Second, heiress to this teeny, tiny estate, to that ruddy, warm, friendly house, to that smiling, damelike, bright and happy garden; and to the sunny nursery whose window she gazed upon.

The dreadful brooding had long since departed. Her morbid acceptance that her earlier state of mind and the appalling shock she had sustained must inevitably record itself in what was then a sensitive embryo had given place to a sunny optimism, so that she was even prepared to meet Vin in happier mood; especially in view of the fact that Terry said he, Vin, no longer drank. Granted that fear finally removed, granted a healthy, perfect baby girl, she could still find a full happiness in life. Mary's experience at Vin's hands of sexual relations had shocked her own generative impulses into latency. Love henceforth would represent her child and Terry, whom she now cared for consciously but without passion. He was to her a refuge for the spirit, just as the old home of her childhood's days was a refuge for her body.

Somewhat in advance of Terry and Ruth, Mary slowly walked round her quaint little red-gravelled drive to the rather worn, shallow, wide steps on the top of which both Mrs. Thatcher and Anne stood in smiling welcome. But, as she advanced in the full glare of a jolly noon sun and in an entirely composed state of mind, the most astounding experience of her short life came to her. As certainly as if a black mist had swept up from the unemotional gravel upon which she stood, invaded and possessed her entire being, she *knew* that the grossest evil not only impended, but actually lived within her, she had a swift recurrence of what Vin had previously declared a mere phenomenal vision and, as at the first "seeing" she had fainted, so she fainted now.

And thus she was carried into her friendly, sheltering home. Nor was it Terry who accorded her renewed peace of mind and soul, but him whom she had associated only with strife and horror—Vin. He knelt beside her when her eyes opened. His eyes, she saw, were entirely without the old askance oddity, his lips were gentle instead of faunish, and from his brow there seemed to emanate a wave of peace, as if from his mind to hers; a message of peace which his lips immediately made audible in authoritative tones.

His eyes held her. Even had she wished to remove her gaze she could not, Mary felt, have done so. Perhaps because her will just then was weak, his stare imposed complete subjection upon her mind and slowly all horror faded. A calm, enduring content took its place.

Presently Vin leaned down and whispered in her ear.

"Don't worry. It will be a little girl and like you."

Now that was what she had been repeating to herself for months, "It will be a little girl and just like me."

She whispered back.

"Yes, just like me."

"Fix it—on your mind. A little girl; like you."

She nodded emphatically. Almost immediately he rose, turned and, without a glance at the others, went away.

"Well, did you ever?" Mrs. Thatcher muttered.

Her astonishment was shared by Anne, who murmured back: "More like a saint than a devil!"

And the only rage obtaining in that still room troubled Terry's heart; for a confounding red jealousy suddenly flourished there. His resentment expressed itself in spite.

"I'm *sure* that bird's batty," he told himself. "Kneeling like a Romeo at the side of a woman whom he's pasted like the loser in a fly-weight competition! He's a disgusting piece of work!"

And yet he was bound to admit presently, in calmer mood, that Vin had strangely comforted Mary, who hardly seemed to know now why she had cried out suddenly in horror and as suddenly fainted at Terry's feet.

Nevertheless, Vin's behaviour had impressed itself upon Terry's mind unpleasantly.

"More of his uncanny acting," he told himself.

What was it a prelude to? Did it mean that, now Mary had come home, they might expect more outbursts, more violence? Beautiful behaviour in habitual drunkards invariably makes me think of the calm before the storm, he thought.

Yet it was clearly not of Vin that Mary was thinking when, in Terry's company, she wandered round her fairly spacious home, admiring it in the way home-lovers do admire their partly forgotten possessions after long absence. She liked its mellow shabbiness, which had an intrinsic value of its own, and, while admitting that much of her furniture was both clumsy and out of date, she thought all of it suited her home and that many were really beautiful pieces—which they were, in one or two cases actually articles of virtu. Though the carpets were worn, they had been costly carpets and were beautiful still.

"This is going to be the baby's room," she told Terry when they came at last to those windows upon which the sun had seemed, to the home-comer's eyes, to shed a golden blessing.

He glanced at her, wondering if she knew how her words wrung his heart . . . Mary's eyes were rapt. In that moment he realized that her entire happiness depended upon the expected little girl. A feeling of panic startled him . . . If some dreadful termination, some gross termination, to her pregnancy blasted these bright hopes, it might easily wreck a mentality unused to the greater abominations of life and unsuited to face them. She must be vigilantly guarded, but, with Anne permanently established in her home, with Mrs. Thatcher ever on the alert, with himself prepared to tackle any fresh misbehaviour of Vin's, she should be as safe as was, in the circumstances, possible.

"You are adhering to our arrangement regarding Ruth?" he asked her a little anxiously over a cup of tea welcomed by both.

"Oh, yes. Anne will stay. Ruth will take her place in your house, as you suggested. She would not dare to live here now."

"And you, Mary?"

"I have a feeling that the child's going to make up for everything; and it makes all the difference your being next door."

A rush of emotion surged over him. Vehement declarations filled his mouth; but fortunately so many demanded to be heard at once that he had regained control before any had established right of precedence. Nothing could be plainer than that her trust in him was blind, complete and gloriously selfish. Let it be so! Everything else might be left to time and destiny.

~ ~ ~ ~ ~

Two days later Holly rang Vin up.

"Everything's in order," she told him. "Lily's on the road. Dr. Grove's going to call on your wife and will arrange for me to make an examination in due course."

But when this took place, the result was unhappy, for Mary took an abrupt dislike to Holly and expressed this dislike quite clearly.

However, Dr. Grove laughed at her.

"This is a woman's time of likes and dislikes," he told her. "As a matter of fact you've my most competent nurse, the coolest head in a crisis among my staff. Moreover, she holds certificates in midwifery as well as in all other branches of nursing. I'd not let mere prejudice interfere with your child's chance of a successful birth."

Here was an argument to which even instinct had no answer and Mary withdrew her objection.

"As far as I can see, everything is perfectly normal," Holly told Vin. "It lies correctly and if anything's wrong it'll not be in the birth, which I imagine will be an easy one."

~ ~ ~ ~ ~

Day by day Terry anxiously awaited some violent demonstration from Vin as a signal that his old habit had triumphed over
his present control; but he waited vainly. The culprit's conduct
was exemplary. Day followed day without his even seeing
Mary, who now had her breakfast in bed.

"He might not be in the house," she told Terry. "His com-
ings and goings are quieter than a thief's."

Terry welcomed her news as much as he disliked her simile.

"It all depends," Vin told Holly at a meeting, "upon the two
births coinciding. You think they will?"

"Everything points that way," she assured him. "Dr. Grove
agrees with me about your wife; and dad agrees with me about
Lily; and his opinion's as dependable as Grove's, you take my
word."

"I hope this weather holds," Mary said when her time was
very near.

But it did not. Clear skies grew leaden and very slowly the
conditions patterned themselves upon that tragic time when
THE INEXPLICABLE appeared, as it seemed, in answer to
Mary's curse.

Three days before that upon which, according to all calculations, her child should be born, Vin paid what Mary afterwards
described to Terry as a formal visit.

"I might have been Queen Victoria and he Prince Albert."

But she did not recount the actual conversation that followed. The interview took place in her own sitting-room, now
littered with articles advertising the expected event. He tapped
quietly at the door and Mary, thinking this was Anne or maybe
Mrs. Thatcher, who was almost as much in the house as Anne,
said 'come in' absent-mindedly, but looked up in somewhat
startled surprise to see Vin hesitating in the manner of one un-
sure of welcome.

"Oh, it's you, Vin. Won't you sit down?"

However, though he came further into the room, he did not
sit down. Mary was struck, as Holly had not long since been
struck, by a depth in his personality to which his usual flip-

pancy seemed utterly opposed. Power. Yes, she saw there was that in him. Mystery. Of this she was exceedingly aware. Inscrutability. It was impossible to judge the nature of his mysteriousness, which might be either good or bad.

But the change was there. And it was profound. He might have called into activity a second nature that had lurked behind the first. What had been sinisterly faunish had vanished, temporarily at least; or was strongly held in abeyance.

And yet, strangely enough, he had lost in attraction. A light had left his beauty, which, to some degree, seemed leaden. Gravity did not suit his delicate features. She had a powerful impression that his purpose here was exceedingly important to him; that he was deeply in earnest.

"How are you, Mary?"

The question brought rushing upon her a flood of realizations. Prominent among these, that it was hard in this weighted atmosphere to breathe; that with the atmosphere's oppression had come depression; and fear. She had fought the fear; vainly. She realized this now.

"You look distressed, Mary."

"It's this sultriness . . . It's like—like—before . . ."

He looked at her sharply, licked his lips and said:

"You're not imagining things?"

She paused, then:

"Perhaps . . . unconsciously."

"What is it you fear?"

She *knew*. She had not known, but, now, she knew.

"I think . . . it's the similarity of weather . . . I think I'm afraid that thing, you know . . ." Her voice faltered. " . . . Never found—was it? Perhaps it may come back."

"It won't come back."

"If only I felt sure."

"It can't come back."

"Why not?"

"It—no longer exists."

Something awesome in his tone silenced her. She stared. His face was livid. His eyes were enormous. Lips—taut. And his entire body rigid.

So!

He had killed that thing.

Why had she not known before? That was why he had lied, said she had not seen it.

Cold horror overcame her. A killer! This father. The father of her child . . . soon to be born . . . Then sense said, but think what he killed. Yes, but that *was* it. *What* had he killed? A man? A beast? A "Thing?" One could not justly call him a murderer. In fairness one should say, Deliverer . . . And all men of her generation, all of her father's, were killers; all hands bloodstained. If not in fact, by consent.

His lips were moving, rapidly. His eyes glowed, dully. She could not catch the words . . . till, suddenly, quite clear and strong, came two words.

" . . . The stake."

He was not looking at her now and not, she felt very sure, thinking of her, or even aware of her; for his glazed stare was looking into—what? . . .

Then she heard:

"And may I not have buried half of myself, too?"

Drops of sweat appeared on his brow; his lips twisted in a tortured way.

Whatever it was he came to tell her, he left unsaid and, as abruptly as he had come, turned and went.

~ ~ ~ ~ ~

Agony endured in clement weather is no one's envy, but agony borne when the sky is like flowing blood, when at any instant it may shower the earth with all its violence; when the air is like the stagnant breath of death—then agony is trebled. And such were the conditions when Mary's labour began . . . at midnight.

~ ~ ~ ~ ~

Anne, like Mary, did not take to the nurse by whom Dr. Grove swore; but, being a just creature, admired her businesslike efficiency. Nor was there anything in Holly's manner of address to which Anne—or Mrs. Thatcher, so often in Mary's house—could take exception. Moreover, when, as she so often did, Anne endured one of her appalling heads, it was not to Holly and her rapidly relieving remedies that she owed surcease.

So, on this night, when Mary's first sharp pang heralded the coming of her child and Anne, distraught with, it seemed, a cleaving head, paced her room, this way, that, it was with almost frantic joy she heard Nurse Chambers' voice simultaneously with a quiet tapping on her door.

"Anne!"

Anne ran to and threw open the door, disclosing Holly with a wineglass in which was a small but familiar draught.

"I heard you walking about and guessed your head had come on worse; so I brought you this."

"Well, it's exceedingly kind of you, nurse."

She almost snatched the glass from Holly's hand and drained its contents.

"Is *she* all right?"

"Oh, quite!"

"No sign?"

Holly laughed.

"Not yet. Probably to-morrow morning."

"Well, thank heaven, then, I can sleep. I promised to let Mrs. Thatcher know if her pains start in the night . . . *If* they do, you'll wake me?"

"But they won't."

"I hope not . . . Though heaven knows, I want the poor thing to be over it."

She yawned heavily.

"You go and lie down, Anne. You'll be asleep in ten minutes."

And she was.

~ ~ ~ ~ ~

Vin stood in his open doorway as Holly approached with an unmistakable question in his eyes.

"It's begun."

"What about Anne?"

"I've given her a dose. She's asleep. Safe for hours."

"When will it actually be?"

"Not for three or four hours."

~ ~ ~ ~ ~

Dr. Grove did not recognize the voice.

"Who is speaking?"

"I'm John Brotherton, Tennyson Farm. My wife's dying. Fell from top to bottom of the front stairs. Please come at once—or it may be too late!"

"How long will it take to get there?"

"Forty minutes."

"By car?"

"Might be less. I don't know. I'm out of my head. Can't think. Are you coming?"

"Of course. How do I get there?"

"Dighton Road. Seldon Road. Then first to left. Keep on till you come to a black and white gate with a stile beside it. You'll have to leave the car, climb the stile and follow the footpath right up to the farm gates."

"Right! I've jotted those directions down. I'll come at once."

A conscientious and a kindly man, Dr. Grove did put his best leg forward. Though well able to do so, he employed no chauffeur. Big, hale and hearty, he liked nothing better than using his hands, fiddling with engines and discovering faults to be repaired. The only job he left to another was the cleaning.

Night work held no grumbles for him. He was a man who needed little sleep and possessed the power to sleep where and when he pleased.

Nevertheless, even his cheery nature was somewhat daunted by this night when the sky seemed to be converging upon the earth and annihilation easy to imagine. He found it hard to fill his lungs. But it took a lot to impair either Dr. Grove's efficiency or his optimism. A few moments of rapid preparation and he was on his way, headlights blazing. Without them, he would have been puzzled, so deep the dark, to find his way.

" 'Pon my word," he told himself, "the smell of petrol's absolutely welcome for once. Attar of roses in this atmosphere."

Dighton Road. Seldon Road. First to left . . . Damn car running queerly; smell of petrol strangely strong. Anyhow, here was the stile, next to a black and white gate.

The road was narrow, going had been slow . . . Woman might be dead by now . . . Anyhow he'd wasted no time. Climbing the stile, he made his way, aided by a powerful torch, yet with some difficulty, along an uncertain track. He could see no light ahead. P'raps the farm was in a dip. Fellow'd been so full of emotion that he had most likely left out some important detail.

Presently, however, it became clear he was lost in a wilderness of fields, that there was no farmhouse within many miles. Yet he had followed his instructions faultlessly . . . If fault there were, it lay with the anxious being who . . . Surely it could not have been a hoax? Why? Besides, who'd be so wicked as to hoax a medical man?

However, there was nothing for it but to return. His watch told him he had wasted well over an hour and a half. Approaching his car the smell of petrol struck him afresh . . . The tank, he hoped, wasn't leaking . . . But the tank *was* leaking.

The doctor raised his massive frame.

"Heavens alive, the tank's been bored!"

Moreover it was all but empty . . . There was merely one outlook, shanks' pony, send for car to-morrow.

Worried, he set out. Why this trick? Burglary? Well, no use anticipating trouble; besides, no burglar'd make a haul from his place of any value . . . P'raps it was some trick to get him out of the way and rifle his drugs. But such an opportunity often occurred without all this elaborate preparation . . . It was to be hoped no serious call had come in during his absence . . . Would have been away at the very least five hours when he got back . . .

~ ~ ~ ~ ~

"I've phoned for the doctor," Vin's clear whisper said, as he came up the stairs to Holly, looking down. "He's gone out on a call. Some farm in the country, they say . . . No one seems to have the foggiest notion when he'll be back . . . You'd better let Mary know . . ."

"She's past worrying . . . Funny," she said with a choked giggle, "you prophesied the doctor'd not be present at the birth . . ."

Any reply he might have made was checked by the fierce shrilling of the phone.

"Doctor?" Holly whispered.

"Impossible . . . I'll see . . ."

A long wail directed their eyes towards Mary's all but closed door. Silently Holly glided away and as silently Vin glided down.

~ ~ ~ ~ ~

And now began *la danse macabre* of the heavens. As Holly slipped into Mary's stifling room, there greeted her through the gaping windows raucous bursts of giant laughter, followed immediately by violent scurries, fierce glints, gusts of gargantuan passion all at a faster and faster measure . . .

The jagged flashes showed Mary's pang-arched body glistening . . . Her scream was one partly of fear, partly of pain . . . Her wild eyes sought the open window and into them darted a determination as fierce as supernatural temper.

Holly's spring was in time, but only that. The struggle waxed fierce; yet was short; Holly's physical power equaled most men's. Her hypnotic murmuring began again and, as the pang passed, Mary grew calmer; but every hair dripped water and lay dankly flat, a component of this or that tangled mass . . . It was dangerous to leave her, but that phone call could only be either the doctor or her father. And it *must* be the latter; or their plans would fail. Here, in this torment-pit of a chamber, birth was imminent.

"I think the doctor has phoned," she whispered to Mary; but no answer came.

"She's exhausted . . . doped with exhaustion . . . I'll risk it!" Holly stole out.

~ ~ ~ ~ ~

Vin—up and down, up and down, up and down, like a wolf in a cage. So many paces, one swift, graceful turn making a continuous movement of the parade . . . so, on, on, on . . .

He looked up fiercely as Holly stole out, his whole attitude inquiry.

"It was your father . . . Lily's child's born . . . He's on his way . . . Go back!"

~ ~ ~ ~ ~

Vulpine, with something cruel in its precision, the parade began again, very, very faintly growing faster—as if symbolizing the process of birth . . .

A piercing scream, loudest yet . . .

The parade checked sharply. He waited, watching that door. Holly's face showed ghostlike in the unearthly light; she shook her head.

The parade went on.

~ ~ ~ ~ ~

Gaunt, silent, swift, the old showman, gipsy now in every gesture, opened the bag and took out its par-boiled burden, wrapped lightly in a cashmere shawl, and laid it on a cushion. Vin, picking up the bag, nodded. Neither man spoke . . . and the younger glided out.

~ ~ ~ ~ ~

Holly stared down in grim amusement at this second birth . . . Had Vin thought of this? And then a vague nausea drove back wonder, mirth, excitement. Like a little spew-forth from some noisome pit of horror. Even in this instant of birth the tiny eyes glinted. There'd be fleas soon in that thick pelt. One hand as gentle as its sister's, the other—claws . . . Slender, human feet . . .

She must act. Mother's coma was bad . . .

~ ~ ~ ~ ~

"Well?"

"Twins!"

Vin growled. Anger? Surprise? Both?

"Girl—boy. Girl normal. Boy—what you said."

He shuddered, dashing sweat from his brow.

"Quick, then!"

~ ~ ~ ~ ~

Dark, unseen Intelligence, warm, haunting evil, does not one feel it? Dark, unseen . . . Omni-present at night . . . Odour, to the soul . . . Like savage, unseen rats . . .

He stared down with tortured eyes at the obscene bundle, threw it in the bag, snapped to the catch and ran lightly down the stairs.

"Here!" He handed the bag to Chambers whose real name must surely end with -sky, or -ski.

Without comment the gipsy showman placed the other child in Border's arms.

"Boy or girl?"

"Boy."

"Splendid!"

About to turn away, Border laid a finger on the bag that Chambers held.

"If I were you," he whispered, his voice containing a snarl, "I'd run a skewer into its heart."

The gipsy's brooding eyes flickered. Surreptitiously he crossed himself as Vin went out.

"I'm going for the doctor personally," the latter told Holly as he handed her Lily's child. "This is a boy. Marvelous thing, isn't it? I'm going to rave at the doctor . . ."

~ ~ ~ ~ ~

"Is it a boy or a girl, nurse?" Mary asked faintly. Holly laughed pleasantly as she came to the bedside.

"Both, Mrs. Border."

"Both!"

"Boy and girl."

"Twins? Well!"

"Are you glad?"

"I . . . I . . . don't know. It depends . . . Are they . . . all right . . . Perfectly normal?"

"Perfectly. Two beautiful babies. Mr. Border's gone to Dr. Grove's . . . He was very angry. But I'm sure the doctor'll have some good reason for his absence. He's the most conscientious man I ever met."

"What does it matter now? You've been very skillful and efficient, nurse," Mary said faintly.

"And now you must take this and sleep. Then you can see your babies."

~ ~ ~ ~ ~

"Fancy twins, eh, Mary?"

"Yes, isn't it awful, Terry?"

He glanced at her happy, absorbed eyes. Awful? Never had he seen such serenity in any eyes before. All horror was past, for Mary. All woe. She was like some new arrival stepping ashore in a new, lovely land. She was going to live in these children and would never have a fully conscious thought for any other living creature. She'd want and appreciate him, Terry, as the years went by, in the same manner she'd want and appreciate the sun; but she'd never look up and worship the sun as one lover looks up and worships another.

Well . . . thank God this benign ending to her dreads had been vouchsafed her.

"And the doctor wasn't there, eh, Mary?"

"No. He's still terribly upset. But who can possibly blame *him*?"

"No one in their right senses . . . Exceedingly odd, though, that mysterious call."

~ ~ ~ ~ ~

"Feel like a game of cards, Mary?" he asked a few weeks later. "Or what price pictures?"

And then he was aware of Vin, walking to and fro, one of the babies in his arms.

He made a little moue and Mary smiled; but Vin seemed unaware of his presence.

"Well, if you're so unsociably-minded," Terry grumbled, "may I get a book? I've run out."

"Yes, do, Terry. There's a boxload come to-day."

"Which prodigy is that?" he asked nodding at Vin's burden.

"Faith."

Faith—always Faith.

"And where's my godson?"

"Where his sister should be, in bed."

"Can I go and steal a peep?"

"Of course, Terry."

He smiled and was gone.

. . . He was a fine boy. Both fine children.

Murray, their nurse, approved of his godfatherly devotion and stood nodding her head as if she were responsible for the virtues of all human beings.

"Seem wonderfully healthy kids, Nurse."

"They are, sir."

"Mr. Border's got the little girl downstairs, I see."

"Yes. I've never known a father so devoted to his baby daughter, I . . ."

Mary's entrance cut short her confidences.

"S'sh! She's asleep. You must go, Terry."

"Yes, Ma-ma. I'll get my book."

He grinned as he ran downstairs and turned towards the library door. Who ever'd have expected such domestic harmony in *this* house.

The door was ajar. Through the aperture he caught a glimpse of Border, posed before the huge, out-dated overmantel, into whose mirror he stared grimacing and excitedly laughing at his own reflection.

But almost immediately the fantastic gaiety left his face and he gazed with infinite sadness into the polished glass, whispering; but his words were inaudible to Terry, who stole away.

What was this odd being? Mad, surely? If not, then who else was sane?

~ ~ ~ ~ ~

Years slipping by. Like the rattling of dice, events, Terry thought, were shaken up and thrown down before him, swept away—forgotten. New faces. Old ones vanished—among them his mother's, Mrs. Thatcher's . . . And he alone in his unsuitably big house; getting each year richer, watching Mary get poorer—but afraid to help.

Like many others, Mary's income had depreciated considerably during these post-war years; but, despite Vin's offers and Terry's protests, she would not accept her husband's help. What he earned he kept to spend upon himself or on toys for the children. This was not only a matter of pride: Mary declined to form any fresh link between herself and a man she still could not trust. The great link—common parenthood—already binding them was unhappy enough, in Mary's sight. Her struggle therefore was considerable and, when education loomed in sight, it became obvious she must either sell stock or find some other medium of raising the wind.

"I shall have to get a paying guest, Terry," she told her adviser.

He swung round, his eyes alight.

"And I know the very chap."

Relief flooded her face.

"Oh, good! But I hardly know what to charge."

"For full board and all home comforts you must ask five pounds, laundry extra."

"That seems a tremendous lot! It's as much as Vin earns in salary."

"It's not out of the way for a home such as he'll get here."

"Do I know him?"

"You've known him all your life."

"*You*, Terry?"

"Yes, me, Mary. And don't begin accusing me of charitable intentions . . . It's you who has to show charity to me. I'll confess now, old thing, that I've honestly been meditating a change, giving up the house in favour of rooms . . . What do I want with a barn of a place like that? One man. If you'll accept me as a lodger, Mary, you'll do me a signal favour. Besides, after all I am the kids' godfather. So, what about it?"

She glanced up, soft-eyed. It would make her happy to have her old friend constantly with her and the terms he offered would certainly solve her problem. How could she, in face of his sincere pleading, refuse?

"What'll you do with your own house, Terry? Let it?"

"I'll either let or sell. But I imagine it'll be a difficult house to let with all these modern flats and estates springing up. Mine's too big for people who wish to live in a moderate way and not swanky enough for the mushroom class. Time will show."

So it came to pass that Terry achieved what had long been his heart's desire, real membership of Mary's household. His motive in wishing this was far from merely selfish. Like Mary, he had acquired no greater confidence in Vin's stability, even after all these years during which the one-time drunkard had lived a model life of sober and excellent fatherhood—an effect often spoilt by outbursts of behaviour which, while harming none, certainly differentiated him from his kind.

It was partly on account of these periods that Terry felt increasingly thankful to be at hand so he could watch over Mary and her children. Never could he eliminate from his mind a sense of living over a powder magazine that might explode at any instant. Again and again as the years passed he had reason to doubt Border's sanity and twice took ingenious precautions to reassure himself—if that were possible. For this purpose he arranged that experienced mental experts should observe Vin and spent, unknown to Mary, large sums in a vain desire to know the best or worst. Unfortunately, however, he obtained little, if any, satisfaction. One specialist merely contradicted another. On the first occasion he heard that Vin's was a subtle and extraordinary case, that the subject was unquestionably an incipient maniac, who would die raving. And this opinion was endorsed by the great man's young but brilliant protégé. Yet, two or three years later, a celebrated French alienist laughed at these opinions and pronounced Vin completely sane. After a further lapse of time Julius Von Hermann, the Prussian psychiatrist, who spent three weeks as Terry's guest studying Vin, plainly considered him deranged, but in a way difficult to explain in words.

"If I believed in definite influences of which we have and can have no knowledge, I should be inclined to say that your friend has somehow or other got his abstract self entangled."

"Do you predict future violence?"

"I can do no less than put you on your guard. He may die raving."

Nevertheless, Vin caused no actual unhappiness. On the contrary, he seemed to be a pattern father, whose devotion to Faith, Von Hermann declared, went beyond the limits of healthy parental love; was morbid and even alarming. True, Vin could not bear the child out of his sight, fussed over her strangely and suffered to a strange degree if she acquired even a common cold; but it was also true that at times he told her queer fables, propounded impossible doctrines of eternal life. And these tales of future existence were far from being founded upon orthodox principles of religious people, but were odd, outré, grotesque. Mankind in the bulk died—but there were those who *need not die*. The secret was vouchsafed to few; but he, Vin, possessed it. He would live forever and Faith should share his eternity.

"But won't Mummy and Uncle Terry and Don (the boy) live forever, too?"

"No," Vin would whisper. "Only you and I . . .Think of it. You and I—always together."

Faith *did* think of it and cried bitterly; for, though bound by strange ties to Vin, all her impulsive childish love was Mary's.

BOOK TWO

CHAPTER I

YEARS PASS so quickly now. With the speeding up of engines, with the intensifying of the rate at which we live life, with the crowding one upon another of major events, one easily gets the illusion that time, our greatest illusion, has speeded up.

Certainly it seemed so to Terry and Mary when, at breakfast and before Vin joined them, they both realized that ten years had passed since the first-named became a permanent paying-guest in Mary's home. Ten years. The children grown up. An enormous deal had happened and yet nothing seemed to have happened. We both, Terry thought, appear to have been expecting some tremendous event, some enormous fulfilment, and yet, when I examine my life and Mary's too, we might both have been flies in treacle for all that life's brought us. And that, he supposed, was the most common experience of all who suddenly cease looking ahead and—look back.

Surreptitiously they examined each other. Mary, Terry thought, was improved by time. In some way she had subtly altered and had a spiritual air that determined her claims to beauty. The passing years had granted her grace of both feature and form together with a strange, fascinating dignity. But Terry had altered. He had aged. Mary saw that. His face was rather gaunt, his hair was greyish. He had lines.

It was, perhaps, because she felt in an examining mood that her mind concentrated upon Vin, who at this instant, with his arm round Faith, entered in his usual rather spectacular fashion

... Of course, Mary told herself, that was what she had been trying to comprehend for all these years. Everything he did was to some extent spectacular. He was like some one cast for the part of a human being. And yet, immediately, it was plain to her clear and special seeing that he was deeply preoccupied, not with his effect upon others, but with some trouble in his mind. His eyes were full of alarm. It was seldom she thought of Vin, seldom, for that matter, she saw him; and, therefore, it seemed curious even to herself at this moment that she should know that something of enormous import troubled the strange being whom once she had loved, in whose arms she had slept and whose children she had borne.

Suddenly, because in this considering mood, she contrasted the two men, Terry, Vin; and, in doing so, realized all that she owed to her one faithful friend; the service, both material and spiritual; the immense encouragement; the never-failing comfort; the admirable counsel of a skilled, trained mind; the almost unbelievable loyalty. Love. She had been living beside a love so immense that surely it could have few counterparts! And what had she given in exchange? Nothing . . . Or very little. She had merely accepted all these years. Yet she had something to give. Yes. Love, with time, had not only grown within her, but had changed. Preoccupation with her children had always come first; but now, suddenly, astoundingly, Terry came before everybody. In one instant. One flashing instant. What would it be like to be Terry's wife? What would it have been like all these years? A sharp pang pierced her heart. What fools humans were! How they neglected the present for an empty future; made the mistake of feeling the colder years with the ardour of youth's hot blood. Believing joys then would seem as urgent as joys now . . . Whereas . . . whereas . . . Oh!

But Vin had changed—with a vivid difference. His alteration came from within and had left its mark mysteriously, for she searched in vain to find objective evidence of this change. He looked hardly any older—yet had aged profoundly. His hair was unstreaked. His lips remained red. Where was there a line on his smooth skin?

Her gaze wandered to Faith. Ah! Now here was true human loveliness. The girl was so beautiful that Mary thought it strange such a face should have escaped publicity. Thank God it had! Such a shrinking, dreaming creature was not made for public stares.

Strange how Faith had captured all their hearts! It fell to the lot of few human creatures, surely, to be so loved. Don—nice boy. Wholesome. Clever. Go-ahead. But curiously detached from them all. And not, in his thin, gipsyish saturninity, like either herself or Vin. Satisfactory son—yes. Good to her. Hard worker. Terry said he would make a sound, perhaps a brilliant, lawyer—if, after obtaining his articles, he was still content to be merely a lawyer. There was a hard determination in Don; Terry suspected a hard ambition. He would go away, make a name, forget them, become relatively forgotten. His very absence from this breakfast table, because he chose on rising to snatch a frugal bite and study alone, showed that. Every warm impulse was shriveled by Don's cold self-sufficiency. Work, that was his love. But no one had ever suggested that Faith should work; no one ever would. Her rôle was loveliness.

Mary's preoccupation grew deeper. They were all preoccupied; Mary with this survey, Terry with some office problem, Faith with her insubstantial dreams, and Vin—with the cutting in his vest pocket.

Already it was imprinted on his mind, word for word.

"Marburg, Styria, Austria has been the venue of a remarkable drama. A curious and, according to description, exceedingly unpleasant freak which was being exhibited to astonished crowds, has disappeared after killing its entrepreneur, believed to be an English-woman, whom it tore literally to pieces. The creature, whose nature cannot be determined, is still at large, despite the most exhaustive efforts to recapture it. Described as an indeterminable mixture of wolf, man and ape, it has been popularly stigmatized a supernatural embodiment."

As a sun-spot eventually returns to tantalize observers, as certain tides eventually return after long years to astonish the ignorant, and as shadows slowly creep round a dial to symbolize inevitability, so this dark event had gradually been completing its cycle before menacing the clear prospect that they all—Mary, Terry, he, the children—had for so long enjoyed. Deep in the mysteries of his nature the knowledge had always lurked since that torrid night when into the gipsy's bag he had flung that matted little body, which was tainted with hyperphysical virus.

And now, as surely as the padding of paws in stilly night heralds a wolf's approach, so surely did each fleeting moment herald the coming of his son.

He glanced at the absorbed faces round him. What would they say if he suddenly shouted, it's coming, INEXPLICABLE Number Two is on its way? They'd pity him. Cool-brained Terry would be more than ever convinced that madness explained everything that was unusual in the conduct of his rightless landlord.

What, indeed, would the metaphysicians say? What did any of them know about *black-animism*? Or of any hyper-force, the deadly, stealing, undetectable hyper-forces? How did they think the foulness of Man *was* to be explained? How did the sceptics imagine their Good was to be explained? If any one of them could lie still in evil physical circumstances, in thick darkness, and open the subtlety of himself for those black forces to creep in and possess, he'd know. They were chains, those dark bonds. And there was only one surcease from torment, surrender, total surrender. Disaster to stand half in the light, half out. Obliteration—the one salvation. But who could take it, while those inexorable tugs were pulling one powerfully, surely, gradually nearer and nearer the foul eternity?

Disaster was inevitable. No action of any kind could stave it off. Better far to let them bask in their apparent sunshine until the last moment. Their ignorance was their bliss indeed!

Improbable any of them would see the item for themselves. It had not been in the local paper, only in the *County News*, apart from *The London Daily Journal*, which everybody called some opprobrious name. Terry took the *Times* and *Telegraph*. Mary seldom bothered about the papers. Don, even if he saw the item, would see no special significance; and that applied to Faith as well.

He would destroy the cutting . . . And live in fear. Fear, not of the Thing approaching, *but of himself*; of the unaccountable part of him and how it would react to his son's arrival.

He rose, rousing the others from their thoughts. It was generally like this, Vin quietly rising and quietly going, as if he were the guest and Terry the host. Faith, too, rose; and this was also a rule. Always she saw her father off.

"Good morning, Mary. Bye-bye, Terry."

They watched them go, Vin's arm round Faith's shoulders.

"Do you know, Terry," Mary said when the door was closed once more, "I've just been marveling that Faith is not famous for her beauty?"

Terry smiled. He agreed about the beauty, but in secret considered that the girl lacked the other qualities necessary to make mere beauty appeal.

"Well, it's strange you should bring up Faith's name, Mary, for I was just going to speak about her myself. I don't think she's looking well."

A worried expression dawned in Mary's eyes. She, herself, considered the girl looked run down and had been meditating tonics.

"She wants a change," Terry suggested. "You've always taken your holidays about now. What about it?"

Mary flushed.

"We shall have to postpone them a little. I've got behind with the rates and shall have to wait for my dividends."

"When it'll be little benefit your taking a holiday at all . . . Mary, let me . . ."

"Please, Terry!" For this question of financial help was an old bone of contention between them. For some reason, which, probably, had a psychological explanation, Mary's objection to accepting any financial aid from her old friend was little short of an obsession. Maybe it was due to her dumb, repressed caring and as secret a striving against convention. Whatever the reason, nothing would have made her accept help from Terry; and she dreaded debt.

But, as the morning progressed, she pondered over his words. Something would have to be done. Faith at least must have a change. It was Anne who unconsciously suggested a solution.

"What about lunch, Anne?" Mary asked, as every day for all these years she had invariably asked.

And as inevitably Anne answered, "What d'you think yourself, M'm?"

"Is there any of the cold lamb left?"

"Yes. Sufficient for rissoles . . . Oh, the butcher's been and I ordered the meat for to-morrow, as you said. By the way, he tells me Mrs. Clifford's got another paying guest . . ."

"Has she? I wish I could get another."

"Why don't you advertise, M'm?"

"I did, Anne."

"In the local papers, M'm. Tom Godley tells me Mrs. Clifford advertised in the London papers."

"I never thought of that."

"She's made a splash about the local golf courses, the Luston fishing and the historical associations."

"Well! I certainly have been slow!"

Anne smiled. She was a woman now of over sixty and deeply attached to Mary, whose soundest adviser she considered herself.

"It's never too late, M'm. Why don't you write out an advert *now*? I'll post it when I go down about the fish."

"I will, Anne, I will!"

She told Terry what Anne had suggested when he came home for lunch, for which he, unlike Vin, who still kept to his old habits, invariably returned. Terry was a man who liked home life—and Anne's cooking.

"Is this let of Mrs. Clifford's a permanency?"

"No, just for the summer months. If I could get someone for the summer, I'd be able to send Faith away."

"Would she care to go by herself?"

"Well, she'd not mind Mrs. Hampson's farm. It's just like home to her and she's very fond of Muriel Hampson . . . I might manage a few week-ends myself."

"What Mrs. Clifford's achieved, you might easily repeat," he said encouragingly, to hide his chagrin. It galled Terry to see

Mary strive. The day would come when he'd finally put his foot down. There'd be a regular rough-house, but he'd have his way.

~ ~ ~ ~ ~

There was a letter for Faith by the midday post.

"It's from Mrs. Lessingham, Mum," Faith said, turning the envelope over and over again—a habit of hers whenever she received a letter and a habit that Terry thought illustrative of her indeterminate nature.

"Well, why not see what she says?"

"Yes . . ." Faith opened the envelope with what to frayed nerves might have been excessive precision and read its contents.

"Oh, Mum, she wants me to go and stay at Feathersdale!"

Mary laughed.

"Why do you laugh, Mum?"

"Well, I was only saying to Uncle Terry this morning that you needed a change and here's the chance."

She did not add that her advertisement had already gone and now, in view of this altogether unexpected suggestion, it need not have gone at all . . . However, perhaps it was just as well. If, by good chance, she did get a reply and made arrangements for the summer months, the money thus obtained could be put by for future contingencies. She disliked the idea of strangers in her home quite as much as Terry, if, perhaps, for different reasons; but the war had put many such women as herself in similar positions. The only thing to do was carry on and be thankful.

And three days later a reply did come.

It was from a firm of solicitors in Gray's Inn.

"Bless my soul, I know Josh Wray," Terry told Mary. "I met him in Paris during the war and I've had dealings with him since; more than once, too. The last time was regarding that Crayley property; you remember, Mary?"

"Oh, yes."

"What does he say?"

"DEAR MADAM,

"A client of ours has seen your advertisement in the *Daily Telegraph* and would like to arrange for a visit of two months. In these circumstances perhaps you would be so good as to quote your terms to us so that we may advise our client.

"It is, however, necessary to explain that the gentleman who has consulted us is a foreigner and has recently been the victim of fire which not only injured his sight, but also inflicted other severe damage, especially to the mouth, which he has to keep covered.

"It is because he is exceedingly sensitive regarding these disabilities of appearance that Mr. Govina has asked us to conduct these negotiations.

"Apart from his misfortune, Mr. Govina is a very pleasant person, exceedingly well read, a linguist and by profession an author.

"It is because he is writing a book upon the cathedrals of the world, their history and architectural features, that he proposes to visit your town, whose cathedral he considers will prove of particular interest to him.

"If the unhappy matter of Mr. Govina's appearance proves no bar, we can doubtless come to terms. Our client would require his own apartments and all meals served privately.

"Perhaps you will be so good . . ."

"What do you think, Terry?"

"Sounds all right, Mary. Josh Wray'd not deal with anyone who's not desirable. And, if he's so sensitive, you'd not see too much of him; and that's all for the best, eh?"

"Then you'd write?"

"I would."

"Help me to . . ."

"Look here, old thing, since a lawyer's written to you, let a lawyer reply. Leave it to me."

"Oh, bless you! I'd not know how to word it."

"Then that's all right."

"Vin won't mind, do you think?"

"How can he, Mary?"

For an instant she did not reply, but said at last:

"We were talking this morning again about how the years have flown."

"Yes."

"Have you *realized* how long it is since those horrible times . . ."

"Vin, you mean?"

"Yes . . . And how . . ."

"Different he's been?"

"Without us really being aware of it."

"Whereas we should have a permanent sense of surprise."

"I . . . suppose I've been quite fair to him?"

"In keeping him so utterly at arm's length?"

"Yes."

"That's a matter I can hardly comment on, Mary."

"Why, Terry?"

"You know why, Mary."

Sudden, almost overpowering emotion showed in his face and, startling her, a corresponding surge rushed through her entire being.

Both realized the impossibility of discussing this subject further. But Mary said:

"I think I will speak to Vin."

"About this guest business?"

"Yes."

"Well, it's not a matter to delay, why not get him on the phone?"

"Very well."

She returned in less than three minutes, her eyes wide.

"Did you get him?"

"Yes."

"What did he say?"

"He . . . was most extraordinary . . . He said, terribly loudly, in the funniest voice . . . It seemed to burn my ear . . . 'Oh, he's come!' And groaned . . . It was a terrible sound, Terry. I said,

'Do you mind, Vin? Because if you do, I'll decline the offer?'
But he answered, 'No. Nothing can avert the inevitable.' And
then he rang off . . ."

She looked inquiringly at Terry; but he said nothing.

"He is such an incomprehensible man, Terry. There's always something frightening about him . . . Even now when his
conduct's so perfect . . . I sometimes wonder . . ."

"Yes?"

"If he's sane."

"My dear!"

"Have *you* wondered that, too, Terry?"

"Darling! (Neither was consciously aware of the endear-
ment) I can't discuss it . . . What shall you do about the letter?"

"Oh, send it . . . Terry, tell me . . ."

"Yes?"

"What could he possibly have meant—sensibly, I mean?"

"Heaven knows, old soger! Vin has said and done some very
curious things during all these years . . . But it's too late to try
and explain them now, don't you think?"

~ ~ ~ ~ ~

Josh Wray's letter of acknowledgment and confirmation duly
arrived. Mr. Govina would himself arrive in two days' time and
his firm had pleasure in forwarding their client's cheque for a
substantial deposit. When told of the confirmation and shown
the cheque, Vin refrained from comment; nor did he offer any
explanation of his strange words over the phone. Mary had
long since recognized that she and her husband were separated
as widely as if situated on opposite poles. Between them existed an unbridgeable gulf. Though they stood face to face, it
was impossible for either to touch upon each other's affairs.
They were two strangers, bearing a common name by right of
marriage, sharing equally in the love of their children, but less
in touch than Mary was with her trades-people. None more
aloof than Vin since the days of his sobriety, could, Mary
thought, possibly exist. In temperament and behaviour he
seemed to have no relationship to that other Vin, Vin the

drunkard. Her warmest emotion was a cold, compelled respect for a will that could abjure an evil and abstain year after year. Mary explained this seemingly miraculous change in Vin not by any powerful and inherent virtue suddenly manifesting itself and controlling her husband's morbid desire, not by any sudden contrition, and not in any way on her account, but simply by the abrupt springing to life of his violent adoration of Faith, a gift from the bountifulness of life that he had not expected. For Vin had supposed the coming child would be a boy. And now, at the moment of telling her husband of Mr. Govina's advent, she really and truly looked consciously at him for the first time since the start of their neutrality—a period, the calendar told her, of a length almost impossible to believe.

She thought he looked extremely ill; then said so, offering advice, suggesting a doctor.

"I'm not ill," he told her coldly. "If I felt in need of medical advice, I should have it."

In view of such a rebuff, what more, Mary asked herself, could she do? Nevertheless, an impression remained with her that Vin's rebuff was artificial and intended to hide both fear and suffering; but of what he could be afraid of and why he should be mentally suffering, she failed to comprehend. Did it not seem absurdly impossible, she would believe that his concern and distress were both occasioned by her announcement . . . Unless he was *not* mentally stable. That would account for much. But it was a horrible thought—remembering her two children, who were his two children.

But despite this temporary concern about Vin and his incomprehensibility, Mary felt uplifted that day, without realizing how little it needed to uplift her now, or how narrow her range of interests had become, a state of things for which Vin was responsible. Had he been the man of means Mary first believed, her present horizon would have been wide indeed, her range of interests great.

As it was, some little relief from her perpetual money-strivings provided her richest treat and the concentration needed to arrange for a new guest's arrival her only type of interest.

Mary and Faith had for some years now shared two rooms on the first floor, one leading out of another; the first being furnished as a sitting-room, the second as a bedroom possessing two single beds.

She would relinquish these two rooms for the expected guest's convenience and herself move into the two corresponding rooms on the floor above. During Faith's absence, she'd get Anne to sleep with her; for now she was accustomed to company at night and would have found loneliness disturbing. She was content and composed in her arranging and re-arranging. To-morrow Faith would be off for her holiday, from which she should return shining of eye and rosy of cheek. This thought alone was a source of optimism. And then, on the next day, their visitor would arrive. She and Anne would look after him, thus ensuring him as much privacy for his afflicted condition as was possible. With a little tact they should soon put him at his ease.

She hummed as she worked. This incident was like an omen of good fortune . . . And she was happy about Terry. Happy to know that deeply hidden she had discovered a little precious spring of love.

~ ~ ~ ~ ~

Next day Faith set off on her visit to the Lessinghams.

Her farewell to Vin was in some respects extraordinary and would, had they witnessed it, have still further perplexed both Terry and Mary.

The emotion with which Vin said good-bye, the despair pictured on his haggard face, the struggle with which at last he let her go—these things seemed out of all proportion to the occasion's needs.

Still more extraordinary was his display of despair when at last she and Mary had entered the taxi and driven off. Naturally a silent girl, deeply respecting of confidences, Faith said nothing of her father's strange good-bye to Mary; but she was deeply distressed, even unnerved nevertheless.

There was much about the relationship existing between herself and Vin that puzzled Faith. At times it almost horrified her. There was something devouring in Vin's love, something absorbing. It was not the ordinary calm love of any father for any daughter. It was, she instinctively felt, hardly the love of a human being. It was a love that frightened . . . But she was afraid to express her fear. Did she let her father realize the horror with which his transports and occasional mysterious hints filled her, there was no imagining what might happen. She invariably denied to herself the possibility that such an exposure might rouse up in him certain latent furies of which she had seen glimpses, but never more.

His attitude to her Faith, perhaps rather absurdly, had always felt was that of Abraham towards his beloved son whom he was required to sacrifice.

Often at night she had lain awake in deadly fear: because in these dark hours the certainty came to her that Vin was waiting for something, but that always her life was never really safe at his hands. Morning light dissipated these fears, revealed their grotesquerie; however, there were exceptions to these daylight reliefs, exceptions when her fear persisted, but, under the scrutiny of reason, took a less morbid shape. And on these occasions her opinion was at one with those of Terry and Mary: Vin was not truly rational, but at times stepped into an odd land of fantasia of his own.

It was therefore to her a blessed relief to be setting forth, free and alone, to enjoy what should be a delightful change of several weeks. And this despite the wrench she always endured on leaving her mother behind.

~ ~ ~ ~ ~

The train was not a very good one; it had to stop at various semi-important stations before arrival. At the first of these an odd-looking man climbed into her carriage and took the corner facing her.

~ ~ ~ ~ ~

Next day Mary received a letter, posted on arrival, announcing Faith's reception by Mrs. Lessingham and her family and the immediate plans for excursions, entertainment in general, which, it seemed, would include a few visits to the sea by car.

"Excellent," Terry agreed. "It'll do the girl a world of good and is a load off your mind."

~ ~ ~ ~ ~

For both Mary's peace of mind and Terry's it was, perhaps, fortunate that on the night of Faith's departure they each slept peacefully and in ignorance, throughout that sleep, of Vin's behaviour; otherwise their growing suspicion of his mental instability might have received confirmation.

For, while they slept at peace in their beds, he lay nude on his back in Mary's unused cellar; unused because so damp and inclined to smell.

The only light—noisome, phosphorized fungi and gleams from the eyes of awe-filled rats, which, after The Black Commune had begun, crept from this hole, from that, reported prey and scurried in light-footed, light-hearted scampers to attack and, with luck, feed. Yet not a rat reached destination. Instead, one an all slunk slowly back to the shelter of their holes, where they lurked—as might untouchable pilgrims shrink back from a priest of high caste. Their eyes gleamed like tiny, fierce, warmthless jewels.

Thus began The Black Commune.

Stretched on his back and his mind full of an inverted faith, Vincent Border, whether madman or fanatic, surrendered his being to the unimaginable, inviting not possession, but repossession; seeking once more power long since abandoned. Opening his mind so that the forbidden might enter . . . A spine-chilling ritual. A Hogarthian orgy . . .

The rats grew uneasy and squealed . . . Vague light shed a ghostly radiance. It came—from Border's eyes? Or from a huge fat rat that now perched upon his brow? . . .

When the first faltering approach of light weakly threatened the profound dark, Vin rose, and staggered silently up the cellar steps.

In his own room he stole, wearing an odd, faunish smile, to his dressing-table and stared into the mirror. Either self-hypnotism can be profoundly potent, or in every truth he could not see his image in the glass.

CHAPTER II

MR. GOVINA was due to arrive at eleven a.m. on the morning after Faith's departure; but Terry, all expectant, returned to lunch and yet he had not come.

"P'raps he's changed his mind," Mary said, moodily.

"Whether he has or not, the deposit is not returnable," Terry replied grimly.

"This is the only real bit of good fortune that's come to me for years, Terry . . . and of course it *must* go wrong."

Terry glanced at her surprised; it was unlike Mary to be fretful . . . He began, as upon many a previous occasion, casting about in his mind to discover some undetectable fashion of helping her financially. He'd simply have to and risk discovery, with its subsequent anger. It was impossible to let her be plagued by these shifts and debts and lackings . . . P'raps in a way it might be a good thing if this visit fell through; then he'd have an excuse for putting his foot down. It was because of these thoughts that he left again for his office in a more than usually buoyant mood—buoyant even after several vain attempts to cheer up Mary.

On her part she gave way to despondency and was deep in arithmetic, with her mind empty of all thought of her visitor—when he came.

"He's come, M'm," Anne announced in a hoarse whisper.

Mary shrugged nonchalantly, as if his coming or his not coming were of no consequence; but her heart secretly gave a bound of joy.

"I thought I heard the bell," she said with a further assumption of indifference.

But Anne grinned. She knew Mary; and she knew human nature.

"I've put him in the drawing-room. Oh, M'm, he *is* queer."

Anne, usually the most sedate of domestic aids, giggled.

"I'd better go along," Mary said in sudden and unexpected nervousness. "Oh dear!" she sighed as she somewhat slowly descended to her unfamiliar interview, "after all Terry was right; it's something to have one's home to one's self."

She felt an absurd inclination to knock at her own drawing-room door; would have given much could she have run away. All this, she supposed, was due to Josh Wray's explanations of Mr. Govina's accident and its unhappy consequences.

She opened the door.

An odd figure awaited her. Tall. Drooping. Gaunt—in so far as one could judge; for, despite the time of year, the visitor was swathed in wrappings. Immediately Mary had a strong revulsion from her guest, who stood strangely still, strangely impersonal. Round his mouth was woven a muffler of soft, fine material. His head was bare, revealing a tough-looking black thatch, which was almost too coarse for human hair and resembled nothing so much as what is known in theatrical circles as a scratch wig. Perhaps, Mary thought, it is a wig. He may have lost his hair. With his mouth definitely concealed and his eyes masked by special dark glasses, which had side-flaps to prevent all hurtful rays reaching his eyes, the stranger's face reminded Mary of a carving rather than of a human head. One hand, she observed was gloved, the other not. There seemed, for an instant, something baleful in his stillness. It was impossible to determine the newcomer's age.

Suddenly a strange thought disturbed Mary's serenity . . . There was something familiar, something amazingly elusive, yet powerfully familiar in his attitude. A vague suggestion of grace? A singularity of pose? A matter of line? She could not determine . . . And, of course, the idea was absurd.

"Good afternoon."

"Good afternoon, madame."

His voice sounded far away, due, naturally, to the muffling of his mouth. Possibly due also to his injuries. Yet she heard him distinctly, which seemed to Mary strange, considering how wrapped about his mouth was. Though noticing the continental Madame, she was yet surprised at the perfection of his English.

His voice, perhaps, was guttural; but then his nationality doubtless accounted for that. She disliked his voice, not because of
its throaty notes, but because of its harsh quality. It was an inimical voice.

"I hope you . . ."

Mary had hardly opened her mouth, when he stopped her.

"I beg you not to stand on ceremony with me, Madame, nor
to talk more than is actually necessary to learn my require-
ments. This is not rudeness. It makes me unhappy to talk.
Kindly instruct your servants so. I will go to my rooms, if you
please. I eat hardly anything and will be no trouble. Is there a
means of summoning attention in my rooms?"

"Oh, yes, an electric push-bell."

"Well, may it be understood that I am not disturbed unless I
ring?"

"Certainly. You may be sure we shall be as discreet and tactful as you wish."

Her own voice, Mary thought, sounded a little dry. But she
definitely did not like this odd creature and resented his high-
handed commands. Nevertheless, he was, she felt sure, best
obeyed and obeyed implicitly. A nasty person to cross.

"If you will come with me, please."

"If he had not come so fully vouched for, I'd be uneasy at
having this man in my house," she thought, as she led the way.
"Heaven knows why, but I feel positively uneasy at his gliding
behind me . . . As if . . . as if . . . Oh, I don't know what. Mary
Border, you're a fool!"

In his room she turned and noticed his soft, swift approach
and disliked his curious, slouching, loping movements.

"Like the movements of something wild," she half-
consciously decided. "Do you require any food now, Mr. Govina?"

In spite of her better judgment she could not prevent her
voice from sounding curt.

"Not now, I thank you. These rooms are very nice. I shall
be . . . quite at home; that I think is the idiom. I will ring if I
need attention."

It was nothing more nor less than a dismissal.

"Exactly as if I were a servant!" she told herself as she hurried from the room. And then added irrationally: "I'm glad Faith's away."

Anyhow he was here. The money was secure. And since the terms were exceptionally generous that was something to be thankful for, something that made a little inconvenience and brusque manners worth enduring.

Suddenly she wondered about his luggage. It was still down in the hall. She should have asked at the recent interview . . . Better go back, since obviously such heavy stuff couldn't stay where it was. For an instant, so great was her reluctance, Mary played with the idea of sending Anne, instead of going herself; but cowardly shirking of obvious duties was repugnant to her forthright nature.

Back she went.

She knocked sharply. No immediate answer came and she was about to rap a second time when the door flew open. Mr. Govina had discarded his voluminous wraps and presented himself as a study in black, made the more marked on account of the tiny portion of putty-hued face that was visible, together with his one uncovered hand. From halfway down his nose a black apron depended, so that the lower half of his face could not be seen. A sinister, forbidding figure, well calculated to fill ordinary people with vague apprehensions. Mary, suddenly confronted with him now, fully realized his craving for as much privacy as was humanly possible and his irascibility. He must have been appallingly burnt. However, the most uncomfortable impression arose from the blanking out of his eyes. It was rather dreadful, Mary thought, to have someone in your house whose face, good or evil, you had never seen.

"It's just as if he's invisible," she told herself. "Or negative."

There was a stillness about him, an immovability when he was not speaking or engaged in necessary action, that affected Mary profoundly . . . And yet, was there not in this very stillness, in its very excessiveness, a suggestion of controlled violence? His voice, his lines, even, somehow, his horrid, tow-like hair—each seemed to her unaccountably excited imagination prophetic of dammed-down power, terrible physical power obeying the will of still greater mental power.

She explained about the luggage and he said:

"Let it be put here, in the sitting-room. I will then arrange it myself."

~ ~ ~ ~ ~

Terry returned that night somewhat late, for his firm had been engaged to prepare evidence of an extensive and important nature for a local commission of a public character. Nevertheless, he was in a happy mood, for his determination of an earlier hour still held good: Mary *should* accept his help. He was also keen for a report upon the new arrival, and, instead of going up to his room immediately, he decided to see Mary first and hear her opinion.

"Oh, hello, Terry! He's come!"

"Good egg! Well?"

"I'm sorry, now, he has come."

This was what Terry had hoped to hear. Providing this experiment turned out unpleasant and consequently a failure, his approaching task would be easier.

"What's the matter, then?"

"He's somehow frightening, Terry . . . And brusque to the point of rudeness." She explained at some length what had taken place between the visitor and her, then added: "And since, it's struck me, Terry, it's a bit risky having a peculiar creature like that in the house: all muffled up. It's like living with a masked man on the premises. You can't possibly find one point by which, at any future time, you could identify him."

"H'm! That's a shrewd thought, Mary."

"He has one glove on continually, I imagine. The right glove. So you see he could commit all kinds of criminal acts without incriminating himself."

"Yes, there's quite a nasty sound to all that. However, on the other hand, Josh Wray would not have undertaken the arrangement had he not been fully acquainted with the fellow's bona fides . . . Should I see him and have a talk?"

"Oh, no! He'd never stand for that. I feel sure he'd be tremendously angry and would go."

"Still . . . I'll tell you what, Mary, after dinner I'll slip back to the office and ring up Josh . . ."

"Oh, not to-night; the morning . . ."

"Well, I've got to go out, in any case. It's the guild night . . ."

"Oh, lord yes! What are you going to ask Mr. Wray?"

"Exactly what grounds he has for accepting this merchant as okay."

"Well, I'd be really glad if you would."

"On the other hand, if you feel uneasy, why not chuck him out to-morrow? We can hand back the deposit."

"It wouldn't be right to do that because of mere prejudice, which, I suppose, is due to his misfortune. No doubt, if we could see him as nature originally made him, we'd find him charming. But I'd like you to satisfy yourself that your friend had solid grounds for his recommendation."

"Very well, old lady. But if it's necessary—out he goes."

"Will you be able to get him so late?"

"Who, Wray? Oh yes. They're posh folks the Wrays; never dine before eight-thirty . . . I'll get through to him all right."

~ ~ ~ ~ ~

Terry was now determined at all cost to catch Josh on the phone, even if he had to keep on till every one else had gone to bed. For some reason Mary's rather vague uneasiness had awakened doubts in his own mind. After all, one should be careful before bringing complete strangers into one's home; and Mary's description of Mr. Govina certainly made the visitor sound a dubious proposition.

If Josh could not completely satisfy him, he'd give up the guild dinner and return to look after Mary. Vin was seldom in before midnight; often not then. He suspected at times that Vin was away all night. Still, that was nobody's business; not even Mary's in the circumstances.

However, rather to his relief, Josh Wray was able to satisfy him fully, was prepared to vouch for Mr. Govina in every way.

"His credentials are first class, old man. I had a letter from Zimmern, for one thing."

"Oh, well, that should be enough in itself . . ."

"But I even had references from two of our own consuls and Lord Portage. I really think you have no cause for concern."

"Right ho! You quite understand . . ."

"Oh, rather. As you say he's got it all cut and dried for a first-class, unsolvable murder. Only, he's merely unfortunate, not criminal."

Terry went to his banquet with a lighter heart. Indeed, not for years had he felt so gay. This was partly on account of his determination to enter more fully into Mary's life and partly because he knew that a spark, smouldering beneath her immediate cognizance, had gained in strength, might even become a flame. Long years ago he had hoped for this, deploring the waste of two human lives; but had learned with some bitterness that high regard, though it may in time produce the purest, the most covetable love, does not induce women to burn their boats. But now, as he walked briskly through a dark yet pleasant night, he felt compelled to admit that seen from this long, clear perspective he would not change the love that he thought had developed in Mary's heart for that fiercer love he had one desired. Rewards delayed are often the greater, he told himself. A little revolution had begun inside him. Granted that he could be sure of his facts—and what lover isn't?—he would, even at this belated period, fight for a little autumnal romance. Reconstitute this home, with himself as its directive head. Never had he known a stronger case for divorce than this . . . Vin could be bought, no doubt, even if he was well-satisfied with his present mode of life. But what was that mode of life? What now was the source of Border's joy—if he had any?

One light burned—Don's room—as he sauntered homeward, seeing both his and Mary's properties softly suggested by night's vague refraction. If he'd any sense, he'd put that old dump of his up to auction. Been empty far too long; far too long for such old property. Bad enough when new property stands empty for any considerable period, but old, really old, buildings deteriorate seriously when unoccupied. Damn place had only *been* let that once! Never likely to be let again. Yes. He'd sell, at any price . . . But—there was sentiment, still profoundly strong in the breast of man, as it would always be. Few men, few Englishmen, at any rate, care, Terry thought, to put up their old homes, homes that have housed their blood for generations, for sale by auction. And that even when the home is a mere house, not some palatial pile. And at least they'd always had the benefit of its garden. Since it adjoined Mary's, they'd had a truly tremendous garden to ramble in. The gardens to both houses were separately very large, but considered as one were uncommon both in size and picturesque effects. He ought really to inspect the place more often. He'd have a trot over it this week-end . . . As for selling, well . . . no. He'd put the place in complete repair and let it absurdly cheap, if he could get really nice people for neighbours. One day it might make a nice wedding-present for Faith—or, of course, Don. But Terry, strangely enough, never took Don's future into his mental account; nor had he that paternal affection for Don that he had for Faith. Don was so utterly capable of carving his own way, so fenced round with odd bigotries, so insular. He hardly seemed to belong. While Faith was nothing if not dependent.

He let himself in, pausing on the mat to listen, a thing he'd never done before. Everything seemed peaceful. But so it should be at this hour of night. What had he expected?

He began, soundlessly, to mount the thickly carpeted stairs. His room, by his own choice, was on the same floor as Mary's and possessed a lovely view of the two gardens and of distant hills, with fields adding to their variety of colour.

On the first floor were the rooms Mary's bizarre guest now occupied and these were faced by two rooms which Vin had claimed as his own. Facing the head of the staircase was an attractive and fairly large room: Don's bedroom-den. And, as he softly mounted, Terry became aware that there peeped out from Don's door a still, watching face. It was Don himself. Without speaking the young man beckoned Terry to come in. Wondering and somewhat alarmed, the latter obeyed, waiting in perturbation while Don carefully closed the door. What did this mean? Sensationalism was the last thing he expected from solid, silent, wise, materialistic Don. But he waited.

"Uncle Terry, what sort of guy is this lodger chap of mother's?" Don whispered.

"I don't quite understand, Don. You heard, he's a foreigner who's been injured by fire and is writing a book."

Terry, despite all he had heard from Josh Wray and despite his own calm, legal mind, looked at his godson with apprehension. Something had got under Don's stolidity and, temporarily at any rate, shattered it. Here was fear and intense mystification. Was it his imagination, or did the boy tremble?

"What's up, Don?"

"Listen . . . Just about five minutes before you came in—it might have been less, for all I know—I opened my door to slip out to the bathroom and I saw an odd figure half in, half out of the visitor's room . . ."

"Oh, I see. All in black and his face half covered by a black, silk fall and two huge, dark glasses. I know and . . ."

"It wasn't that. Mother told me how queer he looked . . . It was his eyes . . ."

"Eyes? You can't see his eyes. They're . . ."

"*I* saw them . . ."

"But how could you with those goggles on? It . . ."

"He had no goggles on . . . His eyes were uncovered. They shone like a wild beast's."

"Don't talk too wet, Don, old pal . . . You've been taken in by some illusion. To begin with, you can't *see* on that landing. There's only the faintest light coming through the window and . . ."

"I'm not talking wet, Uncle; I've seen no illusion. There was a tall, black-clad figure there. That I could just vaguely discern; but his eyes shone. They were a beast's eyes. I'm no funk. I didn't turn tail and bang my door to. I immediately thought of an illusion. I stayed where I was. And you can just take it as fact, I saw two, bright, gleaming, feline eyes. I spoke. I said:

Hello! And, call me a fool, start splitting differences about the degrees and peculiarities of nightmare if you like, but it's just plain gospel when I say—THAT THING VANISHED as I spoke."

Terry frowned. For some reason his mind was carried back years . . . The cat in Mary's garden . . . Gleaming eyes . . . Dead child.

He shuddered.

The sense of uneasiness that had prevailed earlier came back. Yet commonsense rebuked it. Undoubtedly Don had imagined what he saw, or had been the victim of some unaccountable vision such as does come to all of us seemingly without cause or purpose. It was easy, really, to rationalize these things; and, sometimes, as hard to accept one's own abstract solutions.

Anyhow, life had taught him nothing is more foolish than to try and convince others of their folly. Quite clearly Don was satisfied, hence the wise thing to do was—nothing.

"Even if you did see what you describe, Don, what do you propose?"

"To-night, nothing, Uncle; but I think you, or I, or Dad, or all of us together pay this merchant a visit. And early."

"Just tell me what you suspect: that he's something supernatural?"

"Not necessarily; but perfectly good material magic has been used before now for criminal purposes."

The quiet sense of this sobered Terry.

"We'll not trouble either your mother or your father with these—er—unpleasant fantasies, Don. What? P'raps we two to-morrow can call on Mr. Govina . . . When I feel sure you'll come away feeling . . ."

"A fool, eh, Uncle? But we'll call that a bargain. I certainly feel I'd like to satisfy myself that everything's above board."

"Very well. Stick around after breakfast and I'm your man. However, I think I should explain that I felt, because of your mother's misgivings, a little doubt regarding Mr. Govina, so I rang up Wray and Wray and Tableman, the Gray's Inn solicitors who conducted the negotiations, and they assure me that

Mr. Govina is vouched for by two consuls, various firms, and
Lord Portage."

"Oh yes . . . all that . . . It wouldn't alter my feelings if he
had brought testimonials from the Archangel Gabriel. We'll
make that call, Uncle."

"Okay, young Daniel. How much wiser you may be! Good
night!" As he turned away, the wish welled up in his mind with
imperative force that this stranger had never crossed Mary's
threshold. Already nothing but perplexity and doubt had accompanied his advent. At the best, he was a bird of ill omen.

However, the one thing necessary was to retain a sense of
proportion.

~ ~ ~ ~ ~

Terry opened the door quietly and slipped out; but checked
with a gasp . . . A muffled figure, seeming a black ensemble
darker than the prevailing gloom; and two gleaming eyes . . .

And at the same time he became aware of an extraordinary
oppression, of being in an atmosphere wherein human will,
human strength has no defenses. His brain whirled, his heart
clamoured, his blood boiled, his skin burst into uncountable
particles of fire. He was afraid; understanding fully what means
the hyperbole, his blood turned to water. In war he had been
brave. All its dangers and foulness he had endured and met
with inscrutable visage. But, if the means and the strength had
remained to him so that he might, at this instant, flee—he'd
have been gone like dust before the wind.

But he was trapped.

Yet the eyes of fire, those gleaming points, were not turned
upon him, but were gazing in an oblique direction. It was an
agony to turn his own gaze, as if this slight and silent gesture
were a tortuous and turbulent proceeding, involving crashes,
grindings, outcries; but, while not fully turning his eyeballs in
their sockets, he so far glanced askance to bring, if dimly,
within his vision a second shadowy figure. Unable to distin-
guish this second figure, Terry nevertheless knew it was Border . . . and that some extraordinary conflict was in process be-

tween the being to his left and the being to his right; and that, thus far, his own emergence had not broken what his excited mind felt to be an interlocking between those two shadowy opponents: an interlocking in enmity.

But what his mind deplored, his subconscious perpetrated: his *fear* grasped. As if he had blown upon dust, the oppression lifted . . . He was gazing into two luminous pools . . . Gone! One blinding, terrible glare . . . And he was alone, as if no sinister shadows had occupied his attention; as if there had been no gleaming eyes or sense of combat.

Trembling and fumbling in his pockets, he found a box of matches and struck one. Stillness. Emptiness, save for the usual furnishings to which, through custom, he paid no attention.

Mr. Govina's door was closed. Border's door was closed. Nothing moved.

Half eternity seemed to have elapsed since he had stepped out of Don's bedroom door; but truly little more than a second had passed.

Could reason explain this phenomenon? Was the picture Don had so graphically portrayed impressed upon his mind to a degree sufficient to carry it almost visually with him from Don's room into this deep darkness? Yes, there might be some such explanation. But how explain his fear? His deadly fear.

Oh yes . . . common sense, a bit of logic might explain everything, but for the first time in his life he crept timidly up to bed wondering if the little we *know* of life is not the merest sublimation of its profundity.

And also, for the first time in his life, he kept the light on till dawn.

CHAPTER III

According to rule, morning light brought to Terry a renewal of scepticism and an inclination to self-mockery. But it also brought a grim determination to see this peace-disturber and form his own impressions.

Whereas, in opposition to custom, Vin absented himself from breakfast, Don, to Terry and Mary's surprise joined them. It was plain, Terry thought, that the young man was as determined as himself to obtain some first-hand knowledge of his mother's strange guest.

"However, I'm glad," Terry decided; "now I won't have to report the result of my phone to Josh."

He saw the unquestionable advantage of delaying this report until he had personally satisfied himself as to Govina's desirability. It was no use allaying Mary's fears, merely, a little later, to resurrect them in uglier shape.

"Nevertheless," he ruminated, "I expect to find the party quite normal and politely resentful of my pushfulness. Luminous eyes! Extra-to-nature, emanations! Oh, Mr. Lawyer!"

Curious, though, how that impression of last night persisted, how clear it remained. Curious, too, how, when a man deliberately began to ask of how much he was sure (*que sais-je?*), reason failed to satisfy some underlying sense of knowledge, rather than knowledge itself; failed to still a curious uncertainty. Even the most cut-and-dried scientist must have these instants of doubt; must say: "All this rationalization of mine, all this accurate assumption, all this splitting and re-splitting, all these mathematical analogies apply to life as we know it, as we presume it. And if we could proceed to split to an infinitesimal nth, it would still apply to this life as we know it; to this life in relationship to the planets as we know them, to the entire all-embracing systemization as we know it. But that does not prove there exists no other form of existence totally unrelated to our own, with its methods simple and its methods subtle; its laws plain and its laws complex."

"Personally," Terry told himself, "I always do, always did, have the feeling that something lives cheek by jowl with me, that I *serve*, that all-life serves. Whose amusement I, we, may even be . . . We're such a spot . . . Infinitude—eternity, we cannot adjust our minute mentality to them and of necessity all our thinking is local and ridiculously personal. Swedenborg had some conception of the fluid total—but he got mixed up in dreams."

He determined to finish when Don finished, leave the room with him.

And presently the younger man rose abruptly, brushed his mother's cheek and glanced with sharp inquiry at Terry, who also rose.

Rather to his consternation Terry experienced a degree of nervousness as he and Don, by silent consent, turned towards the stairs—though, ordinarily, Don would make for the hat-rack, grab his hat and coat and be off as if making his escape from pursuing hordes.

Now Terry had every intention of approaching this interview in a polite, friendly, tactful manner; but he counted without the stern impetuosity of youth; and Don, mounting the stairs in strides that even the fit and athletic Terry found hard to equal, merely slung himself at and opened the door of Govina's sanctum—to find it empty. Then, before the elder could lay a restraining hand upon him, Don sprang at the second door, behind which, since it was his bedroom door, Govina might have considered himself safe from intrusion. This suffered a similar fate . . .

And the intruders found themselves faced by him whom they each had expected to see—feared to see. A Something—which no words in the vocabulary of either could name, or describe. An animal-human face, eyes pools of fire, carnivorous jaws agape showing them fangs easily able to tear out their throats. And, in its human aspect, a face contorted with terrifying fury.

Both men stared aghast. Held. Helpless . . .

Yet as this paralysis fastened upon them, the extraordinary vision—as upon the previous night—faded, and they saw *a man*. A man plainly mutilated by fire; but a man. A man with filmy, injured eyes, whose sight could only be seriously impaired; a man whose jaw had been contorted, puckered by fierce flames, and which was now sparsely covered with a newly grown beard. Moreover, the *Man* smiled courteously, if with inquiry.

Apart from his injured face, uncovered for toilet attentions, Govina was dressed as Mary had described and was, even thus, a sufficiently impressive figure.

Terry made a grab at his whirling control, strove to clear his mind and turn this dreadful *faux pas* to good account.

It was possible, he thought, to see in that mutilated face evidence of primary good looks; and it was not difficult to understand Mr. Govina's sensitive reluctance to have his misfortune viewed by others. And here were two seeming busybodies bursting in on an apparently groundless errand. It was a cutting rebuke that the disfigured man very quietly, with easy dignity and quite without ostentation, assumed his black silk fall and put on his masking goggles.

Anyhow, from now on they did know that the unjustly suspected visitor had mutilations, seemed inoffensive and might easily be a very scholarly man.

"We really must apologize most profoundly," Terry said with the easy aplomb that his legal training had enabled him to assume at will. "We heard a crash . . . And couldn't determine where it came from."

There was an instant's very uncomfortable pause; then Mr. Govina said quietly:

"It did not come from here."

"Well—we wondered . . . Looks as if we're very intrusive; but it sounded like a fall; so we just came along to see if you were all right."

"It was most extraordinarily kind of you. However, I did not fall."

He had an accent, Terry noticed, but his English sounded fluent, yet it was a disagreeable voice, containing some mysterious quality that grated. Once, in the night, across a humid bog, Terry had heard just such another timbre—and had kept his gun to hand.

"This is Mrs. Border's son, Don," he explained, laying a hand on his young companion's shoulder. "My name's Cliffe. I'm by way of being Don's god-father and self-appointed uncle."

"I am deeply interested to meet Mrs. Border's son," Govina said foreignly. And added the inexplicable remark: "It is an astonishing performance."

"P'raps," Terry thought, "his English is not so good as I assumed. That's a perfectly pointless remark."

"I must be going, Uncle," Don said curtly.

"Master Don don't like our pal here," Terry decided with a grin. "And I must say, he's not immensely prepossessing. There's a contemptuous satire behind his remarks." But aloud: "All right, Don. I've got to put my best foot forward, too." He turned to the black-clad, sombre figure. "I trust you're quite comfortable, Mr. Govina?"

"Thank you, yes."

"You must not run away with the idea that we're an intrusive bunch, or that you won't get the privacy for which you bargained. It was . . ."

"The fall you heard," Govina said gravely.

Terry flushed. There was a faintly malign ring to these soft sarcasms uttered with so much polished dignity.

"Hell!" Terry growled inwardly. "I wish more than I've ever before wished anything in my life that the fellow'd never set foot in this house. Bless my soul, is what Mary's getting worth the unpleasantness?"

He and Don withdrew and descended to the hall in silence. Arrived there, however, they both involuntarily paused and remained an instant each deep in thought. Then Don jerked his head impatiently and turned to Terry.

"Well?"

"Well, what?"

"What about it?"

"What about *what*?"

"That human adenoid."

"For God's sake speak plainly, boy!"

Don glanced at Terry in surprise. It was unlike his uncle to be irritable.

"What decision have *you* come to about him, Uncle Terry?"

The latter gave his godson a sly, sideways look.

"Well, we made fools of ourselves, didn't we, old man?"

Don opened his mouth to speak, closed it, fumbled with a raincoat, then burst out:

"When we first went in, what did you see?"

Terry now hesitated. Then his overwhelming honesty urged him to be frank.

"I thought I saw a phenomenon similar to what you described last night."

"Worse!" Don snapped urgently. "If you saw what I saw . . . Fangs."

Terry nodded. They were silent a while, eyeing each other uncertainly, wondering, in the manner of self-conscious Englishmen, how to put their thoughts into words that would not sound emotional or suggest mental disturbance.

"But there were no glinting eyes, Don; no fangs."

"Yet we both *saw* them!"

"I wonder . . . We went there with a fixed idea in our minds, formed during the night when odd things do happen to human minds—even if they're only the result of lobster or crab . . . And then there's telepathy. Nothing very metaphysical or extra to nature about that. Less mysterious than the electric waves our voices ride on. How long did your impression of headlights and bone-grinders last?"

"Hardly a second, I suppose."

"Same here. So we both saw the bogey business simultaneously and it vanished simultaneously, which rather supports my theory of a fixed idea possibly made mutual by telepathy."

"I suppose so . . ."

"We've got to suppose so, Don," Terry said gravely.

The younger looked up in a sharp, startled manner.

"Just *think* if we don't keep our heads and allow our imaginations run away with us, what we'd let ourselves in for. I think it's safe to say we saw nothing but the actuality: a sadly disfigured human being upon whose privacy we had intruded in a most unwarrantable fashion. Life is prosaic, Don. More may exist than we wot of, but that more's not, definitely not, shown to human creatures."

"Yes, I know, Uncle; all the same I feel oddly disturbed . . . And I think you'll admit I'm not morbid or given to this sort of thing."

This was only too true . . . Moreover, Terry had, secretly, to admit that he, too, was oddly disturbed.

"I'll tell you what, Don, I'll try, when I come home to-night, to persuade your mother to fire the blighter out."

"Good. If needing support, I'm your man."

~ ~ ~ ~ ~

This interview had curious results, the first of which was the descent upon Terry of an unfamiliar bad temper. Customarily he was an exception to his kind, for year followed year without one seeing even a frown on his forehead. Blessed with an equable liver, an astonishing sense of humour and a strong will, he seldom experienced a desire to snap and on the rare occasions when a degree of irritability did win through it was either laughed away or suppressed. But now he felt, to quote his own words, "Damned savage."

He hurried from the house with a guilty feeling, well aware he should see Mary and compose her mind; but for once he failed her and deliberately turned his back on what he felt to be a duty. It would be truly the worst outcome of this unpleasant affair if he should speak rudely to the person whose esteem he valued more than any other on earth.

He wanted solitude. Though Terry was sufficiently gregarious as a rule, at this moment to be alone seemed suddenly urgent. Yet it was not easy for one so well-known locally to *find* solitude. When walking to his office, he mostly met friends or clients who wanted his pleasant company and a chat.

And that wouldn't do. He wanted no inept remarks, was he queer, had he got out of the wrong side of the bed, or one of those clumsy income tax jokes.

Hamlet! Yes. He'd hop into his house and inspect it as only last night it had seemed urgent he should do.

Right!

He slipped in through the big wooden gates, which, he told himself, should really be kept padlocked, and marveled at the ruin of a once well-kept and attractive garden. How could he expect either to let or sell? A sense of shame invaded his mind and he determined to have a man in, a couple of men, to remedy all this waste and decay. The house, too, he'd have done up. And this determination grew stronger during his tramp from room to room. His examination was more comprehensive than he had intended, because from the instant of entering he was pursued by an uneasy feeling of something wrong. So strong, indeed, was this impression that he stopped halfway up the stairs, after examining the ground floor room by room, and considered just what his uneasiness amounted to. Was it a ridiculous feeling of not being alone? Or something more undefinable? Or a mixture of—of . . .

Oh, he did not know what!

It was absurd, all this fantastical surrender to impressions, first in Mary's house, now in his. He stumped impatiently upstairs.

Here was the room that his grandfather (and, early in his independent career, his father) had used as an office, with the dressing-room, shelf-lined, steel-doored, converted into a strong-room in which grandfather had kept confidential documents, family records, secret wills, hush-hush agreements, collateral securities, bonds, stocks and money. No getting out of that, once you got shut in. The door opened to a combination, which had last been set at *Grandfather*.

Mechanically he moved to the door and worked the combination, half expecting that the massive door would remain stuck . . . But then the lock and hinges had always been elaborately oiled. He had oiled it himself before the recent tenant took possession . . . He wished now that he'd had it reconverted into an ordinary dressing-room. That had been his idea when letting the house, but the incoming tenant had been intrigued by a strong-room actually to hand. He, of course, had used his own combination, and it had not been altered back to *Grandfather* until the house once more stood empty. The almost airless chamber exuded a stifling clamminess and an offensive, dead sort of smell. Much better to do away with the room. It struck him, now, as dangerous. Anyone might get stuck in there, if he or she chanced on the combination, which, however, was all but impossible. Mary knew it. And, Vin, he knew it. He'd shown him the room long ago—in the days of that uncertain early friendship when Mary had invited them to spend their leave with her. He had shown Vin his home then, had worked the combination, opened the door, exhibited the strong room . . . But after all these years Vin couldn't remember the word . . . and he'd not alter it now, in case he himself forgot the new word he might choose, or lost it even if he wrote it down.

He secured the door. And went up to the attics . . . Still accompanied by that odd impression of not being alone . . . Though, for that matter, the feeling was not so strong as it had been on the ground floor. And this idea was confirmed when he presently descended. What rot it was! He swore angrily at himself. An entirely empty house and going on about impressions as if he were some half-cracked spiritualist . . . He'd been through the place like a valuer. And his best plan was to get out, make for the office and work this silly stuff out of him. Urged by this impulse, he was halfway down his wide, semicircular steps when he realized he'd not examined the cellar . . .

And quite definitely he was not going back. For one thing, the cellars were unpleasant places, his worse even than Mary's. Besides, they'd always been kept shut up, even in the recent tenant's time. He was going to the office to get to work.

But to have examined his cellars just then would have been worth to him many days of work, could he have known it.

~ ~ ~ ~ ~

Hauntings . . . .Could it be, he asked himself when he sat in the profoundly materialistic corporation tram, that hauntings were not all rumour? Was it possible that *minds* were haunted? Was *his* mind haunted by that INEXPLICABLE of long ago? Had his mind's unsuspected repression become suddenly disturbed; and had it infected Don . . . Or . . . or . . . Oh, there was no end to the "ors."

~ ~ ~ ~ ~

At the time when Terry and Don made their somewhat dramatic entry into Govina's rooms, an old man of striking appearance rang the bell at Anne's back door. He was tall, certainly over eighty, silver-haired, hawk-faced, and, despite his apparent age, possessed two alert, glittering black eyes. Though not distinguished in speech, he was distinguished in appearance and Anne had every excuse for wondering why such a "personage" should be ringing at her back door.

"A foreigner," she thought. "Another of them! As if one at a time isn't enough!"

The old man presented a scrap cut from some newspaper.

"I called in respect to this," he said slowly.

It was Mary's advertisement for a paying guest.

"I meant to call before, but illness prevented me."

"The rooms to which that advertisement refers are let," Anne explained a little tartly.

"Oh, I am sorry. I like this neighbourhood and the garden attracts me. Perhaps there are other rooms. One would . . ."

"Excuse me, we have no other rooms to let."

"Perhaps if I could see your mistress . . ."

"My mistress is engaged." Anne's tone was sharp. She felt annoyed.

"If I were to wait . . ."

"It wouldn't be any use." Her quick temper flamed. "And one foreigner in the house is enough."

"You are a little rude," the old man said quietly. "I am not a foreigner. I will bid you good morning."

He vanished quickly down the flagged path leading to the tradesman's gate, leaving Anne a little ashamed of her irritability.

At the gate the old man paused, gazing up—at a difficult angle—trying to see the back windows, but with little success.

"Foreigner!" he muttered.

"Well, we have no other rooms to let," Anne grumbled to herself, returning to her duties. "And what in the world did he want to come to the *back* for? He was very old . . . but, I don't know, there was something queer about him . . . I don't believe he did want rooms; and one can't be too careful these days . . . Not that we've got much to steal in this house. But one never knows . . ."

She decided to say nothing to Mary; perhaps because she had a sneaking sense of guilt. After all, it was not for her to dismiss applicants for rooms; and with a little trouble another guest could be managed.

Anyhow, best left as it was.

At this instant Mary bustled into the big, stone-flagged, back kitchen, looking gay and hopeful.

"Has Mr. Govina had his breakfast, Anne?"

"Oh yes, M'm."

"What happened? Did you see him?"

"No. I tapped and then went in. The sitting-room was empty, but I heard him moving in his bedroom, so I just put everything on the table, tapped on his bedroom door and said, 'Your breakfast is on the table, sir.' And came away. I shouldn't think it was ten minutes later when his bell rang. I went up. The room was empty again; but the food was all gone, so I cleared away. What about his bedroom?"

"I will go up and see."

Mary hurried away to implement this intention, but in crossing the hall paused on impulse by the telephone.

"I'll just ring Terry," she thought. "It was queer his going off without saying a word about his phone message to Josh."

She got through to Terry's office and asked for him.

"That you, Terry."

"Yes. Mary speaking?"

"Yes. Why didn't you wait to tell me about your phone message to Mr. Wray?"

"I'm sorry, Mary. Don and I got talking and then made a bolt for it. Wray's message was quite reassuring, but I want to talk with you. Shall you be going out this morning?"

"Yes, in about half-an-hour to do some shopping; but can't you talk to me over the phone?"

"No. Take too long; be a lad and pop in when your shopping's done."

"Oh, all right. There's nothing wrong, is there?"

"No. It's just an idea I want to talk over at some length."

"All right."

She rang off and continued on her way upstairs. At her knock, the harsh voice of Govina bade her enter. To her immense relief she found him muffled up as on his arrival.

"Good morning, Mr. Govina. You are going out?"

"To the cathedral, madame."

"Will it be all right if the maid makes your bed and straightens the room, while you're out?"

"I was about to suggest it."

"You have everything you want?"

"Thank you."

"Lunch is at one-thirty."

He did not reply and she withdrew feeling curiously awkward and at a loss. Moreover that vague suggestion of familiarity troubled her.

"How *can* he remind me of anyone, in that odd get-up?"

Five minutes later from her own bedroom window she saw him go, grotesque, yet impressive.

"How strangely he glides."

For no reasonable cause she immediately thought of Russian steppes and wolves on the hunt, monotonously gliding with swift, mechanically perfect, motion over a seemingly limitless expanse of snow.

"I seem," she told herself, "to have been doing nothing but image outlandish things since this man came . . . Great heavens! *That's how Vin walks . . . And he stands as Vin stands!*"

That was where she got her sense of familiarity. But it was absurd. Mere imagination, or some accidental resemblance, as one has so often occasion to say, 'Doesn't so and so remind you of so and so, the way he, she walks, stands, tilts the head . . .' And so on . . .

Anyhow, Anne could do his room now and she herself would hurry over the shopping, then call on Terry.

"It's a funny thing," she pondered, as she hastened her preparations, "I thought it was such a splendid thing getting this guest and now I'm more worried than ever. There's something about the creature that's inimical and offends one . . . A feeling of not being properly safe with him in the house. I believe I wish he'd never come."

Wrapped closely in her own thoughts, Mary was oblivious of a tall man who stood exactly between her gate and Terry's and exactly in the direction towards which she must turn. She did not, in fact, observe him until he stood right in her path.

"Excuse me, madam."

"Oh, how you startled me!"

"I am sorry. You are Mrs. Border?"

"Yes."

"Well, I'm going to ask for your indulgence. I'm from *The Weekly Report* . . ."

"*The Weekly Report* . . . Gracious, am I in the news?" Mary asked with a smile.

She could see this rather remarkable old man was deeply anxious and felt disarmed.

"Well, yes, madam, you are—in a small way. News is scarce in this town and the spryest of us find it hard to keep our jobs. Unfortunately I am not among the spryest, as you can see; so any bit of exclusive news that comes my way is worth its weight in gold to me. Is it true, madam, that a distinguished foreign writer is staying with you?"

"Oh . . . I see! . . . Well, I hardly know whether it's right to describe him in such glowing terms. *I* didn't know he was distinguished. But he's a writer, I believe."

"It seems to have got round that he's a writer and you know how local gossips exaggerate. I saw a rather remarkable-looking man leave the house a while back; but didn't presume to approach him without your consent."

"I'm very glad you didn't," Mary ejaculated. "He'd have been terribly annoyed. He's extremely sensitive ... Please don't put it in the paper, but he's been seriously injured in a fire and that, I think, has made him morbid."

"Is it because of his injuries he wears those extraordinary goggles?"

"Yes. His eyes have been damaged and his mouth's dreadfully disfigured, I understand."

"Thank you very much, madam. You may depend upon my discretion."

But Mary suddenly didn't care whether Mr. Govina took offense and left or not. If he did go, well, what after all did it matter? Faith had got her holiday. With a few smiling words of farewell, she left the tall old reporter making notes and hurried on towards the trams.

It was little more than half an hour later that she hurried into Terry's office.

"Hello, Mary!"

"Well, I'm here, Terry. What is it you want to see me about so particularly?"

"Sit down, my dear."

She did sit, but Terry rose, plunged his hands in his pockets and began an erratic parade, from which symptom Mary judged he was not only in a fighting mood, but intended to have his own way regarding something or other. And she was the more sure of this because, before speaking, he produced and lit his old briar pipe.

"Look here, Mary, I want you to send that blighter away."

"What blighter?"

"Your Govina."

"But I thought you said Mr. Wray had ..."

"So he did. Wray vouches for him utterly, even has illustrious names on his list of guarantors; but I've got it in my noddle he's a fraud."

"But is that fair, Terry, when Mr. Wray ..."

"Great continental swindlers are quite capable of pulling the wool over even distinguished people's eyes."

"But, Terry, dear, supposing that he is a crook, which hardly seems likely, what on earth should he be doing in *my* house? I've nothing to steal."

Terry was checked, in danger, he knew, of checkmate—unless he played a risky move; but he had begun a fight to gain all or lose all and at no cost could he afford to abandon it. Nor would he.

"I have discovered things about this man that make him an undesirable inmate of your house, Mary," he said gravely.

"What things?"

"Things I cannot name."

"That doesn't sound very convincing, Terry."

He paused, took his pipe from his mouth and stared at it blindly.

"Mary, it was Don who first drew my attention to these nameless things."

"Don!" She rose.

"I must be told," she added sharply.

"You can't be told, Mary; and you won't be."

A rush of hot, angry words filler her mouth, but she restrained them in time. Terry meant too much in her life for her to risk a serious quarrel. She knew his level-headedness, his unswerving love for herself . . . But it was that love which now filled her with doubt. It was all too possible that it unduly influenced his judgment at times and might be doing so now.

"You'll simply have to be a little clearer with me, Terry. I can't afford to do anything rash in regard to Mr. Govina."

She had quite forgotten that only a short time back she herself had been wishing the undesirable guest away; but now, faced with the putting into practice of what had been merely a wish, she felt confounded.

"You don't seem to realize," she added feebly, "that I've got to do something."

He paused abruptly, just in front of her, staring down at the woman he loved with an expression at once charming and stern.

"That's just what I don't forget, Mary. Something has to be done. The time has come to do it and . . ."

She looked up at him in deep distress; he was going to offer financial assistance once more; but nothing would make her accept it.

"Mary, do you remember that night when I first went to France and we left Dad and Mum on the platform and walked to the end and back on our own?"

"Of course I remember it, Terry."

"You know, Mary, I've often thought since that, had I asked you then to by my wife, you'd have said yes. Even though you didn't love me in a passionate way."

"How I wish you had!" burst from her.

His eyes lit, his whole face shone.

"You'd have said yes, eh?"

"I should. Something came over me then. Realization that you were at last going from me."

"Well, it was just a matter of principle with me, dear. I felt chaps had no right to—to tie lovely women to corpses . . . And, if you were free now, Mary, would your answer still be yes?"

She moved over to the window with a little cry. "Don't let's speak of impossibilities, Terry."

He came behind her and laid his hands on her shoulders.

"It isn't an impossibility, old lady. You know it isn't."

Suddenly Mary found herself struggling with uncontrollable emotion, with desire such as in all her life before she had not known and with the urge to cry Yes, yes, yes.

"I am married to Vin," she whispered.

"You are tied to Vin, not married to him, and knots can be undone."

"This one can't. There are no grounds."

"That is a matter of Vin's willingness to meet us and I imagine his willingness can be bought."

She turned slowly, her eyes streaming with tears.

"I'm afraid you're wrong, Terry. You're thinking of the old Vin and can't grasp how long it is since we saw him. You judge the matter merely as one concerning him and me; but it also concerns him and Faith. If I agreed to surrender Faith to him . . ."

Terry broke in.

"Faith would not go and she's of an age to please herself. She'd choose you."

"Are you certain of that, Terry?"

"Faith loves you in the purest, simplest way."

"But Vin holds her—somehow. There is a tie between them that does *not* exist between her and me. She may not be as bound to him by love as she is bound to me, but his bond is stronger." She paused and added: "And happiness bought at the price of justice must always have a worm at its roots."

"Justice?"

"Why yes. What have we against Vin all these years? He's kept his bargain. More than kept it. And what little share he's been allowed in the children's up-bringing he's done well, if quietly. Would he not have the right to say, 'Why wait until I'm beginning to be old before . . .?"

"Old, Vin?" Terry said wonderingly. "Great Scott, yes; he's over fifty . . . It doesn't seem possible. He seems still the same age to me."

"So you see . . ."

"I see you've made out a wonderful case for him and against us . . . You'd make a fine K.C., Mary . . . but why not let me sound Vin?"

"Are you not reckoning without the sordidness of the human mind? Wouldn't his reaction be immediately to suspect us, Terry? Wouldn't he say, 'Oh, so you two have been secretly in love all these years? No wonder Terry was so anxious to live under our roof.' "

The eager light faded from Terry's eyes.

"You make my determination sound hopeless," he said sadly.

She said nothing, because she had known all the time his secret intention was and always had been hopeless, unless a free and barrierless road presented unexpected access to that happiness they now both saw clearly at hand—even if forbidden.

Mary took out her compact and began to remove all signs of recent tears; and Terry by force of habit fiddled with deeds lying on his desk.

"What about Govina?" he asked dully.

She hesitated, then rose sick of her nays.

"I'll do as you wish, Terry. I'll explain on Saturday that I find the arrangement inconvenient and ask him to go. I can suggest Mrs. Clifford."

He looked up suddenly and smiled. Again a rush of mingled fondness and desire, sweet because so strangely like the return of spring in autumn, swept over her. Did she not indeed owe a debt to Terry that was greater than the debt she owed to Vin?

~ ~ ~ ~ ~

She did not see the old reporter crossing the road towards the doorway she had just passed through. Wrapt in her thoughts, alternately uplifting and depressing, she had sight only for the visions of her own mind.

However, the old reporter saw Mary and hesitated until it was clear her attention was not directed to immediate things; then with a faint smile he passed on, up to Terry's office, gaining almost immediate admission.

Terry stared at this gaunt, white-haired stranger, made aristocrat by age, without being able to place him. What was his nationality? What was his standing?

Then the old man said:

"My name is Chambers."

Terry raised his brows; the name conveyed nothing to him.

"What can I do for you, Mr. Chambers?"

For answer the old man leaned forward and laid a cutting on Terry's desk. It was similar to that which had not long since troubled Vin at Mary's breakfast table. And as its contents penetrated Terry's understanding a gloomy premonition enveloped his mind. What the special significance in all their lives that little cutting might have Terry was quite unable to determine, yet without any pretensions to second sight he felt very sure that it and this old man had *some* deplorable concern with his, with Mary's, with Faith's, with Don's, with Vincent Border's immediate fates. A show woman, an incomprehensible freak, part man, part wolf, part ape and a killer. Was it the long lost INEXPLICABLE?

He glanced up to find his visitor's keen gaze fixed on him with a sort of fierce interrogation.

"What has this to do with me?" Terry asked quietly.

"A very great deal."

There was both power and authority in the old man's voice.

"A tough type," Terry thought. "Likely to be hale at a hundred." Aloud he said: "Perhaps you'll be good enough to explain."

The other leaned forward and tapped the cutting with a long, dark finger.

"That means something to you."

"Well?"

"It is here . . . in this town."

Terry's heart, war-toughened, missed a beat. He felt a huge, dark shadow approach, chilling his blood: coming events. Already prescient knowledge was tapping for admission.

"I think it would help a lot," he said tersely, "if you'd be plain. You say this creature is in this town? Where?"

"In Mrs. Border's house."

That black prescience had expected this; but Terry's heart seemed to sink—into icy water, into viscid, chilly mud, where it froze.

He was about to say, "You're talking rubbish!" when a sudden vision checked the words. Gleaming eyes. Fangs. Two men, commonplace, healthy-minded, literal creatures, seeing luminous eyes, fangs. A strange certainty of crisis sobered him, driving away his impulse to irritability. Love. Mary. Marriage. How remote—now. Instead, battle, war with an enemy to him and his, ten times more subtle, ten times more dangerous than that the ingredients of which he knew so well.

"I think you have a tale to tell; and it seems to me, Mr. Chambers, you'd better tell it without preamble."

The old man nodded abruptly. He was a curt, tart, brief being, too; one, it was plain, completely divorced from verbiage and fairy tales.

"The 'man' to whom Mrs. Border has let her rooms is the thing referred to in that cutting." He leaned abruptly forward and spoke in a hoarse whisper. "But it's *no* man. Nor is it merely a beast. *It's something to which this earth should not give shelter.*"

"Are you English?" Terry rapped suddenly.

"Cornish."

"English by extraction?"

"Hungarian gipsy stock."

"Quite. Go on."

The old man's eyes flashed. His hawklike face tautened.

"My daughter," he said, in angry, deep tones as if to a disbeliever, "was the nurse who delivered from Vincent Border's wife . . . (He suddenly shouted) . . . that thing which has killed the same woman who brought it into this world."

The full implication of this hit Terry like a blow. All sorts of issues belonging to this cataclysmic statement seemed to float in and out of his mind. He caught sudden clear glimpses of facts that, seen, swam out of vision . . . Don—alien. Don—strangely like this old man . . . The storm—Mary's curse . . . The mystery of Dr. Grove's hoax-call.

He put his hands over his face.

"Tell me the whole tale," he muttered.

He was obeyed, in graphic, bitting phrases; and Terry listened, now in amazement, now in consternation, now in anger, now in derision. Yes, this man was a truth-teller. But was above all a lore-monger. Had been born saturated in superstition and credulity. Apparently he believed Vin "touched" with forbidden attributes, that THE INEXPLICABLE had been of the were-wolf order and that Mary's son was something out of the foul, forbidden world which Chambers believed to ride parallel with ours and which was inseparable from the unimaginable vast in whose enormity we are lost. Because he was filled with some indefinable horror that strove with his everyday mentality he felt a wild anger against the teller of this mon-

strous tale . . . His facts were true; his surmises false. That creature in Mary's house, ghoul in appearance only, might have
luminous eyes, might have fangs, might have some exceptional—natural to itself—hypnotic power; but these were details belonging to a freak; their possession certainly did not require any sane man to believe it hyperphysical. It could be shut
up. It could be destroyed . . . And that, of course, was a matter
for the authorities . . . Mary had certainly given birth to an unnatural being, a monster—call it; but the explanation was clear:
that other freak bursting in upon her at the dramatic moment
that it did, with all the circumstances as they were, she laying
her hands upon her hidden embryo at that vital instant, there
was only nature's own magic in all that, and it was no more
marvelous than a birthmark.

"What is your object in coming with this tale to me?" he
asked suddenly.

A tremor passed through the old man's being, his face
twitched.

"I did very, very wrong in countenancing Holly's deception.
I protested against it at the time . . . And now I've lived to see
the consequences of my own folly and Holly's greed . . . I'm an
old man. I don't want to end my days in prison . . ."

"You realize, then, the public enormity of what you did?"

"Yes. I came to you, knowing you to be a life-long friend of
Mrs. Border's. Friendship, it seems to me, is needed in dealing
with the situation that has arisen. There is much that you
would, I take it, wish to conceal. You, being a legal man, will
know how to approach the authorities, without making bad
worse. As for me, I have said, I'm old . . . I want a chance, having told the truth of my share in an act that was meant to be
merciful, I want a chance to get away."

"That, even if I consented, would not be easy. The police
will be after you with a warrant . . ."

"Spare all your explanations. You're telling me nothing I do
not know. But you may trust me to take care of myself. The
police won't get me." He paused, looked keenly at Terry, then
said: "Will you act, in my place?"

The younger stared up at the now risen elder with indetermination showing in his eyes and manner for the first time since the interview began . . . Was there no way of dealing with the affair without full exposure, with all its incumbent disgrace and suffering for Mary?

"It will be kinder to her for you to take on the job; but, if you're doubtful, say the word and I'll go now to the police station. It'll start killing, then things will be too late. I don't want more blood and innocent blood on my conscience."

Kill! Terry's face froze. Mary, Anne alone with . . .

Both men faced each other. Chamber's eyes were wild and concerned with his own soul.

"You must ask yourself *why* it has come here," he said in a low, harsh voice. "Not in love. Of that you may be certain. And, if it hates, whom does it hate? Not Border. He is of the thing's own kind. It has turned against the womb that conceived it in its present shape. It has considerable intelligence. My daughter wrote to me; so far as I can remember she said something like this: 'It is half human, half animal. Both human and animal mentalities are above the average. It picks up foreign languages with ease and can converse with considerable ability; but in the middle of a perfectly rational conversation its intellect is apt to fail, when it will growl or snarl. I have done my best to educate the human side, because that would be fine for show work; but I've not dared to let it hold long conversations in public, in case it suddenly reverts.' Another time she said: 'To tell you the truth, Father, I am afraid of it. I have discovered it has powers denied to ordinary beings; just as you said. How I wish I'd listened to your advice . . . It hypnotizes people. Suppose it tried that on me. I shall have to cage it. Yet I'm afraid to do this because it talks. THE INEXPLICABLE was silent . . .' " Chambers gave a gesture of despair. "Evidently she took too great a risk and left the caging till too late . . . Or maybe the creature knew her intention and slew her. Holly, one supposes, told it the truth about its birth, or it may have overheard some conversation . . . Again, it could read. Holly and I corresponded unguardedly . . ." He broke off and was silent once more. But before Terry could speak he burst out: "So, you see, action must be taken. Maybe it's my duty to go to the police . . . Yet the thought of a cell galls my wild streak . . . I'd rather die by my own hand." He looked sternly, almost accusingly at Terry, as if it were he who had erred in the past and was now culpable. "What shall you do?"

Terry frowned and rose, moved to the window, as Mary had done a little earlier, and stared out unseeingly. What should he do? He felt the need to think, to comprehend fully all he had heard and its exact relation to Mary . . .

He suddenly understood the urge to crime that comes upon quite good, but threatened, people . . . A shot would settle this . . . But no, not while this old man lived to tell his tale. Moreover, if he, Terry, were arraigned for an apparently motiveless crime, that would still ensure suffering for Mary.

There was so much! That thing Mary's son, Faith's brother! And Don? Not even of Mary's blood. No wonder he seemed alien!

Hate of Vin flamed in his heart, mind, brain, blood. He'd see and confront him with this dreadful revelation. Meanwhile here was this old man expecting some definite assurance. But how could he say, 'Yes, I'll make a public exposure of the woman I love, and . . .'

He turned to Chambers.

"All this is utterly strange to me, while you have had the circumstances in your mind for years. I must have time for reflection."

"Delay is dangerous."

"I do not take your extreme view, you know. It's in your blood to accept contra-to-reason points-of-view. Give me till to-night. Meet me here at eight and I'll tell you my decision."

"It is too long, but I'll agree."

He rose, put on his hat and again turned.

"It is the dark that is the dangerous time. It is dark at eight. I will wait here from six onwards. Reflection may hasten you decision."

Leaving Terry no chance to reply, he marched out like—the lawyer commented to the closed door—some imperious emperor.

Terry strode about wildly. While reason must dispute Chambers' far-fetched suppositions, it could not deny that there was acute danger in harbouring such a being in one's house. The danger to Mary must be profound. Nevertheless, anything but exposure . . . How proclaim to her that this man-beast was her son, how tell Faith it was her brother, how rob Don of a home and parentage that he had fully accepted as his own; and how deluge Mary, the most innocent of all, in public shame?

How serious was the danger? How immediate? Why had the thing not already struck? Vin might know. And without question Vin must be confronted with this rotten tale.

He strode to the telephone . . . and learnt that Vin was not in the Institute, being away on some business or other; would probably not be back till five.

"When he comes in, please ask him to step over to Mr. Cliffe's office on a matter of the utmost urgency."

"Mr. Govina went out this morning, Terry," Mary told him at lunch, "and has not come in. Anne's taken his food up and left it as instructed. I promised yesterday to take Anne with me to that New Home Exhibition at the Round Hall. Do you think it'll be all right?"

"Good lord, yes! Govina's told you not to fuss about him. It's not your fault if he's out for lunch. It's cold, anyway. Just leave his grub, in case he comes in unexpectedly."

Terry was infinitely relieved at this news. It at least meant some hours of surcease from absolute concern. The exhibition, he knew, was not over until five and, since there were several important demonstrations, it was unlikely that Mary, at least, would leave before that hour. Tea at home, he knew, was usually about five-thirty. Perhaps by that time he'd have had his interview with Vin and decided on his course of action; and that seemed, inevitably, the police. The creature must be removed and kept in safe custody.

He saw Mary and Anne to the exhibition before returning to his office, where he spent the most profitless, the most restless, afternoon of his life thus far. He counted the moments and had to exert considerable will power to resist phoning the Institute to ask whether or not Vin had returned.

Periods of profound revulsion seized him. Typically an Englishman and a natural, irrevocable opponent of unhealthy doctrines, this position, with its whispered suggestion of devilry, nauseated Terry. Nor did he relish the forthcoming interview with Vin, far from a natural, typical Englishman. Nevertheless, he was steeled to it.

~ ~ ~ ~ ~

Vin's step. He came in. The clerks had gone. They were quite alone.

Already dusk was gathering and the mingled glows of twilight quarreled violently with the artificial glare from a great street-standard that shed its somewhat ghostly rays through Terry's window.

Within the office it was as yet too light to justify electricity and Terry was glad of the vaguely gathering dusk, since it is an insular impulse to hide from the exotic.

The visitor came tiptoeing in, as if afraid of being overheard, and looked, Terry thought, even in this slightly uncertain light, desperately ill. His cheeks were hollow, his flesh sallow . . . But how those eyes danced! Yet what inscrutability! The mincing had returned to his step. Here was surely the old Vin. But no! Something towered over and subdued the old Vin. Behind the smirk there was pain. This was no mere sadistic clown, this was plainly a being torn two ways, manipulated by two profound inward forces, each, maybe, trying to possess and use secret potentialities for entirely different ends.

Terry, seated back to the great arc light without, faced Vin, who had perforce to sit in its full flood. Terry felt startled by the restlessness of the other's eyes.

Suddenly—because about to speak of him—Terry remembered Chambers and rose, glancing down at the entrance to these offices. A tall, dark figure lurked in the portal. The old gipsy, he supposed.

He sat again.

"Border, an old man named Chambers visited me to-day."

Terry paused; but observed no reaction to the sharply uttered name.

"He showed me a cutting from a newspaper."

With a swift, deft movement Vin produced a slip of paper which he flipped onto the desk in front of Terry, who immediately saw it was just such another cutting as had been shown him earlier in the day.

"Then you knew?"

"I saw that."

"Chambers told me of the conspiracy between him, his daughter and you."

"Yes?"

"He told me who Mr. Govina is. *You* knew?"

"Yes."

"You see the outcome of your conspiracy. You have brought not only terror into Mary's life—to which, perhaps, you're indifferent—but also into Faith's life, and presented us with a problem impossible to assess."

Vin sat opposite this accuser, his face a mask.

"What especially do you wish—that I had let Mary see her monster and all these years suffer degradation?"

"She has to suffer it now."

"Maybe not."

"In what way can you prevent it?"

"That will be my concern."

"No!"

"*You* intend to take action?"

"Yes."

"Public action?"

"This is no occasion for private consciences."

"Nor private loves?"

"What d'you mean?"

"I know you love Mary."

"If so, then why have you not given her freedom?"

"Faith."

To some extent this was unanswerable. Vin was not the man one associated with unconditional renunciations and his calm revelation of full knowledge of Terry's love had nonplussed the latter.

"You could have let Faith choose," he said, for him a little uncertainly.

"Faith *belongs* to me." Terry felt there was something more meant in these four words than their mere apparent meaning. And was proved right by the other's insane-sounding complement: "HE has come for *her*, but she belongs to me."

Vin laughed. Terry glanced sharply at him. Surely all the ingredients of unreason were in this mirthless laugh. That was it. The man had come in *looking* insane. Undoubtedly he'd have to depend upon the police and not expect rational help from this at least dangerously disturbed creature, who, as if he had read Terry's mind, leaned forward and said with extraordinary, quiet force:

"There is only one person on earth who can deal with— Govina."

"You?"

"Yes."

"I venture to suggest," Terry said a little superciliously, "that the police will prove as effective."

"Were they effective before?"

Again Terry felt silenced . . . But he was silenced by more than his companion's words; by Vin's manner, too. It grew increasingly strange. Maybe, Terry felt, the odd, elusive and deepening light produced the unpleasant features of Vin's physical behaviour; yet it filled him with uneasiness . . . And, to disturb him more, a sense of uncanny danger crept into his mind. His flesh tingled. A curious chilliness flowed like a vapour over his body.

He gripped his chair and admonished his failing commonsense, cleared his throat and, a little stiltedly, said:

"They were unable to lay their hands on THE INEXPLICABLE . . ."

"Exactly, they will be unable to lay their hands on his successor."

"Why?"

"Do you not know?"

"You mean all that rubbish Chambers frothed?"

Border's eyes, Terry saw, grew bigger and brighter until it seemed to the watcher they would burst into flame.

Vin rose, looking unusually tall.

"You will be of some use in this crisis, Terry, when you realize that other, THE INEXPLICABLE, was more than just a man . . ."

Terry leaned abruptly forward. Border, he thought, was about to become impossible, make a fantastic claims that could only offend reason. He had not forgotten that Vin once told Aunt Charlotte and Mary that THE INEXPLICABLE was his father . . . And yet there was mystery concerning that monstrosity and Border; mystery of which Terry had always been aware.

"Border, what happened to THE INEXPLICABLE that night? You swore Mary didn't see it . . . Then why were you so concerned about her child? Why did you tell Holly Chambers that it would be born a monster?"

Vin swept his hands wide in an extravagant gesture.

"If I told you, you would not believe me . . . But if I took you to, and showed you, its grave, you would believe I killed it?"

"You! . . . How?"

"I wish you'd been there, my sceptic . . . As Mary fell, I put my arm round its shoulders and led it away. It trusted me completely. And I had power over it that no other being walking this earth possessed." He wrung his hands with a wail. Terry looked away from his companion's contorted face—looked away in fear. "It trusted me—and I killed it."

"How?"

"I shot it with my service revolver . . ." Suddenly Vin laughed. "Its bones lie not a thousand yards from where we sleep . . . There is a stake through its heart . . . I could show you *that*."

For the moment, Terry felt his judgment wilt, his mind cloud and reason surrender to the other's spell. The power behind Vin's assertions, his complete indifference to confession did, in that instant, subjugate Terry's norm and convince him that there might be something more than any *man* could explain in this unholy matter. At the same time he was more and more convinced that this was an affair beyond any individual jurisdiction, that despite all the horrible consequences there was less danger, less prospect of misery in telling his story to the police than in trying to circumvent both present danger and unpleasant publicity. One had to be faced and publicity seemed the inevitable choice.

Vin came closer. His voice changed from shrill to guttural and there was menace in his chuckle.

"You think me mad, don't you?"

Notwithstanding his invincible courage, Terry shrank a little. In the other man's appearance there was every justification for an affirmative.

"If I *did*," Terry replied cautiously, "would it be wise to tell you so?"

But Vin ignored the question, seemed to have forgotten his own and began to walk rapidly about, to and fro, to and fro, at a speed that made his companion's eyes ache.

"You and Mary have wondered at the change in me . . . Do you not understand; in killing HIM, I killed something in myself—a something needed to fight this—offspring . . ."

"You mean that you now have not the power to . . . deal with . . . Govina?"

The effect of this question on Vin was extraordinary. He became profoundly still, drew himself absolutely erect, so that he stood like some high priest inspired by his own beliefs, and the tortured look came back to his eyes.

"Yes, I have received back the power," he said slowly, and as Terry in his early days had been wont to make his responses in church. Then he laughed quietly, triumphantly. "Yes, I have the power."

The telephone shrilled sacrilegiously. Terry snatched at the receiver with relief that so prosaic a medium had entered into a scene beginning, he realized, to get him down. He said "Hello" and hardly knew his voice.

"Is that you, Terry?"

"Yes. Mary speaking?"

"Yes, Terry. You remember the old man we talked about at lunch?"

"Who said he was a reporter? Yes."

"He's been killed, Terry. Torn open . . . Just like before . . . You know, THE INEXPLICABLE . . . His body's been found in Clayton's Waste."

She rang off. Why? The fact worried Terry . . . On a sudden impulse he moved to the window and looked down. The dark figure lurking in his doorway was still there.

CHAPTER IV

He turned to Vin, who now had shrunk into where the room was deeply shadowed; here he leaned against the wall; and, for the first time, Terry, as with Mary, was struck by a likeness in line, in attitude between this man and Govina; between this man *and the shadowy lurker below*.

"I'm going to the police, Border. That was Mary. Chambers has been torn open. Bang to the door when you leave."

The absurdity of speaking in these rational terms to one whom he believed a madman and who, his own incredible tale accepted, would be as little to be trusted with the security of an office as something from a zoo!

But at that instant Terry was as preoccupied with the crisis at hand, with the need for prompt and bellicose action, as when first these two had met in their slimy, blood-lined trench.

"See Mary first," Vin whispered softly.

Though he made no reply and though he did not consciously register the suggestion, Terry accepted it. Yes. See Mary first. Her sudden ringing off needed explanation.

He dashed out. Down . . .

Ah, the dark lurker . . . Attack? Well, it must be just met. Fortunately he was still active, still a terror with his fists, still fast on his feet, in either fight or flight, as ever.

But there was no dark lurker . . . He looked swiftly this way, that; no sign. P'raps he had imagined him. Some effect of shadow. His mind, just now, was inclined to turn solid things into shadows and shadows into solid things.

Strange that Mary should have rung off so abruptly. He'd be full of fear now until this business was not only settled but committed to the past.

He turned right. Came to the tram stop. No tram and a long queue waiting. He'd walk, or, rather, run. Left, left—straight ahead into his own long, at first light, then dim, road. When almost at his destination, Terry paused. He had an impression of being accompanied and paused to look, to listen. No one. Nothing. No sound. Not a soul in view. Quite, quite alone.

He turned and continued.

Something sprang and struck. Claws ripped his throat, caught in his breast-clothes and rent them to the waist, penetrating into the abdomen. The moving shadow growled, drew back the claws to strike again; but another hand touched its shoulder and a strange word floated on the air.

~ ~ ~ ~ ~

Mary had heard the news in the tram. A stout woman had told the conductor.

"I saw him," she said. "All ripped up, pieces lying about. And the blood . . ."

Mary leaned forward.

"Who?" she breathed, surprised at her own intrusiveness, since, she was by habit reticent.

"An old man."

"A local man?"

"I think not. He was a very tall, thin, white-haired old man, like a gipsy or a foreigner . . . It was terrible . . . As if some animal had attacked him . . ."

"Then they don't know who or what attacked him?"

"No."

"I see."

"Do you remember that INEXPLICABLE business years ago?"

Mary shuddered.

"Yes," she whispered.

In addition to its being a horrible crime that utterly revolted every decent instinct, it was to Mary an awesome murder from other aspects. One, she had actually spoken to the old man and liked him. Another, it seemed uncanny that after all these years such well-remembered killings should start again. And, again, it was with active fear she remembered how closely she and her hone had been associated with those all-but-forgotten, blood-thirsty attacks.

Suddenly and clearly her mind repictured that appalling apparition that had burst upon her at the instant of her curse . . .

She shuddered. A sense of gloom, of the dark, inevitable approach of fate, depressed her. Terry, Mary felt the need of her friend. Always it was so, she realized, when any crisis threatened her. Always Terry she wanted. Was he coming home early to-night? She hoped so . .

Would phone him and ask him to come as soon as he might.

She thought about Mr. Govina and the necessity to tell him he could not remain. Now that she was approaching home and, in all probability, an interview over this or that detail, she felt her courage ebb . . . He was a rather eerie sort of creature and honesty forced her to self-confession—she would never dare to face her self-sought guest in order to dismiss him. Perhaps Terry would take over this task . . . Or could she leave a note?

She hoped that Anne had taken up his tea and that he'd not been back for his lunch to feel offended by hers and Anne's absence . . .

She'd phone Terry immediately she got in; and in obedience to this determination she crossed without bothering to light up the now dim, almost dark, hall, running instead to snatch at the receiver.

"Is that you, Terry? . . . Yes, Terry . . . You remember the old man we talked about at lunch? . . . He's been killed, Terry. Torn open . . . Just like before . . . You know, THE INEXPLICABLE . . . His body's been found in Clayton's Waste."

"Mary!"

It was Terry's voice, softly behind her, from the stairs . . . But how was that possible? She'd heard Terry speak on the phone. But she banged down the receiver and turned, saying "Yes."

Then she heard her name again from the landing, or was it the passage off the landing?

"Where are you?" she called and ran lightly up.

But the landing was clothed in deep darkness, so she had to fumble a little for the switch and, when the light came, she could see no sign of anyone; nor, though she ran from room to room, could she find any living person from whom the voice might have come.

In a panic she ran again to the phone. Terry must come home. She must have some explanation why she could hear his voice in one place and almost simultaneously here in her own home.

But she got no answer to her ring. Lights! She plunged the hall into light harder than the glare of emotionless diamonds.

Where had that voice come from? No! It could *not* have been imagination . . .

She could not stay here in this empty hall alone. She must see and talk to someone. Anne! Crotchety in her advancing years, Anne hated to be disturbed when preparing meals; but, well, she'd just have to put up with it . . .

But Anne was for once as glad to have company even during her busy hour as Mary.

"I was just wishing you'd come in, M'm. I've fair got the hump to-night . . ." She looked round her uneasily. "I don't know why, but this house give me the creeps for once."

"Why, that's funny, Anne! I feel exactly the same. I came in for company . . . How's the dinner?"

"Oh, all set, as they say on the pictures. It'll look after itself for the next half-hour or so."

"Did you hear about that old man being killed?"

"What old man, M'm?"

"Well, when I was setting off on my shopping this morning, an old man stopped me and said he was a reporter and wanted to know if it was true that we had a distinguished writer staying with us? And . . ."

"What was he like?"

"Tall, lean, white-haired, rather foreign-looking."

"Well, that's a funny thing. He came to my back door and showed me your advert for rooms; said he wanted some. I told him we hadn't any to let."

"Well, that *is* a funny thing, indeed! How really, really mysterious!"

"Oh!"

"What, Anne?"

"D'you think he was a detective? That's it, M'm, you may depend! He was a detective in plain clothes and he was making inquires about that man upstairs."

The probability of this nonplussed Mary. It certainly did look as if Terry was justified in his strong warning.

"Well, he's dead, Anne. He was killed in Clayton's Waste. After you left the exhibition I only stayed ten minutes and then went to get that silk from Morgan's. Then I caught a tram and a woman was telling the conductor about this old man."

"Who killed him, M'm?"

"They don't know . . . He was ripped open . . ."

"Why, that's like . . ."

"Yes. THE INEXPLICABLE business."

"Oh lor, M'm, now I *have* got the creeps. I wish they was in for dinner."

"Hasn't Mr. Govina come in yet?"

"No . . . But I don't want him in without either Mr. Terry or Mr. Don."

The two women looked at each other with fear-widened eyes.

"Anne, let's go and walk in the garden. I'd rather be out than in."

"So'd I, M'm."

"What about the dinner?"

"It'll be all right for long enough yet."

"Very well . . . We'll go in the front, Anne, shall we? The back's too lonely."

"Yes, M'm. And then we can see Mr. Terry or Mr. Don come in. Mr. Terry's late."

"Well, that's not unusual. Some business at the last."

It was a pleasant night enough, though dark. Rain, Mary thought, was on the way. They walked about discussing the exhibition without either interest or concentration. Their minds were sufficiently alert, but not for clever domestic devices.

"Let's sit down," Mary said suddenly. Both had walked many miles that afternoon—or so, Mary thought, her limbs protested.

There was a seat in the shadows of the big beech tree, and here they could see the gate without being seen. The light from the hall, while illuminating most of their immediate surroundings, missed the tree. They were thankful for that light. It gave them a measure of confidence. However, the shrubs lining the far wall were, Mary noticed, in complete shadow . . .

She gave a start.

"Anne!"

"Yes, M'm?"

"Just look at that cat's eyes over there."

"Where, M'm?"

"Among those bushes by the gate."

"Oh, lor."

Both women fell silent. They stared at the gleaming eyes. Then they were gone—the eyes. Mary and Anne stirred uneasily.

"I believe I'm going to have a headache," Mary whispered presently.

"Maybe it's the weather, M'm. I'm feeling sluggish myself."

A sound attracted them. Someone was coming through the gate.

"It's Mr. Govina," Anne whispered.

In silence they watched his feline progress . . . until he vanished in the house.

"Ought one of us to go and see if he wants anything?" Mary whispered.

"Yes. But I'm not going—even if he explodes. And another thing. *You're* not."

"Look, he's up there, sitting by his window."

Anne, following her mistress's gaze, glanced up and saw the dark form of Govina, now divested of his voluminous outer garments, sitting by his window apparently reading. The radiance from the hall was sufficiently strong to make his black figure discernible. Now and again a ray caught the lens of his goggles so that they glinted.

"He don't look real," Anne muttered with a nervous giggle. And then she added. "Oh, why doesn't Mr. Terry come?"

"Look!" Mary exclaimed under her breath.

"What, M'm?" Anne demanded irritably.

"A policeman looked in at our gate."

"God be praised. I *like* policeman—all of a sudden."

Simultaneously they glanced up at the immovable figure at Govina's window.

"Still as a corpse," Anne breathed.

"Anne, be quiet! Or go in! Saying things like that!"

Anne sulked. But Mary ostentatiously began to talk about the domestic improvements they had seen that afternoon; and even death, crime, spooky forebodings were not proof against such fascinations. They actually forgot the dark figure up in Mr. Govina's window.

Both were jerked back to their immediate circumstances by the town hall clock striking seven. They listened to its sonorous announcement as if it were some supernatural message.

"Seven, Anne. You ought to look at that dinner."

"Oh, M'm!" the other squealed.

"Well. In ten minutes you'll *have* to."

The maid's mouth assumed an ugly, obstinate air. She was about to reply—something, maybe, that later she would bitterly regret—when a figure ran violently in at the gate and along the gravel drive.

Involuntarily Anne called out. The two women rose under a simultaneous impulse. Hearing the hail, yet unable to see from whom it came, the policeman stood puzzled, his face wearing an anxious, impatient expression. When Mary and Anne emerged from the deep shadow that had obscured them, he took two or three eager steps forward.

"You're Mrs. Border?" he asked sharply.

"Yes."

"Mr. Cliffe, the lawyer, lives with you?"

"Yes."

"Well, he's . . ." The policeman, a youngish, sharp-featured, intelligent-looking man, broke off abruptly, turned towards the

window in which Govina's dim figure still showed, dim, but
sufficiently distinct, "Who's that?"

"A guest staying with us."

"How long's he been there?"

"He came in just before you peeped through the gate . . ."

"Oh, you saw me?"

"Yes, we were sitting in the garden."

"Mr. Cliffe's been attacked," the policeman snapped.

A pain composed of surely a million different emotions
pierced Mary's heart and, causelessly, stupidly, it seemed, the
words *too late* sped like shooting stars into and from her mind.

"Badly?" she asked in the officer's curt tones.

"Yes. Hospital job. Will you phone the Borough Hill Hospital and arrange for an ambulance? I've administered first aid,
but he may start bleeding again and I want to stay by him till
the ambulance comes."

"Where is he?"

"Just a little down the road."

"Could we bring him in here?"

"It would be dangerous, I think, madam. I'm frightened of
starting a hæmorrhage. If you phone. Hospital and doctor.
There's Doctor Kane in Oakland Road. He could come right
away and be here in two minutes."

Without waiting for a reply, he ran off and vanished through
the gate. Taking example from his speed and efficiency, Mary
too turned and ran into the streaming hall.

~ ~ ~ ~ ~

Something silvery had awakened her . . . Mary had heard it in
her very sound sleep . . . And now she slowly roused to full
consciousness, to memory . . . sometimes more precious than a
handful of gems, sometimes more bitter than a handful of
herbs.

Terry, dangerously wounded, in hospital . . . They were to
phone her if he recovered consciousness, if she might go to
him; for already they knew, as she knew, that he might die.
Die—with all these years wasted; wasted by her.

She saw him, as she had seen him when, after phoning, she had run out . . . through the gate . . . Blood—a great dark pool . . . And the rent throat . . . Then the doctor, swift, precise, efficient . . . The ambulance . . . Her phone to the hospital . . .

"But he's my life-long friend, since we were little children . . ."

And the promise, if he recovered consciousness, she should know; if it was permissible, she should see him. They would phone.

And the police . . . Mystery . . . Absolute. Their questions about Mr. Govina . . . Sheer alibi. In before policeman peeped through the gate at ten to seven. Sitting in his window. Policeman on his beat: "To the top of the road, sir, and straight back. It was striking seven when I discovered the body. Not a soul in sight." The Superintendent's irrefutable logic: "A man can't be in two places at once."

Who had attacked him. What? How?

The fire Anne had lighted began to flicker. A long chapter of regrets opened in her mind . . . But upon this deep thinking there superimposed itself an unfamiliar condition that was not depression, but even more subtle. As if a door to impossibility had been opened and she was suddenly aware of a horror that she could not see, but which quickened, spread, impinged. All co-ordinated thought ceased in her mind. She merely lay inert, overpowered—and icy cold with fear. It was as if she were in a new element; on a new plane; over an eternal void . . . She was going to be killed. Of that her subdued mind was dully aware. Her head of its own accord seemed to turn . . . Quite clearly in the firelight she saw a tall form clad in black, a fanged beast-jaw, rapacious, wicked; eyes glowing with liquid hate. THE INEXPLICABLE! A dull but unbearable ache began in her womb. Knowledge of some sort, black knowledge was coming, coincident with death.

Then she saw the claws . . . Because they moved. The eyes grew, or seemed to grow, larger. Some foul effluvium, or what might not be an effluvium but a foulness of aura, began to creep about her, into her. She saw the black-clad loins tense and shake in the impulse of springing and a hand, a white hand, descend lightly onto the thing's shoulder . . . The face changed—TO VIN.

Now she screamed.

White, stark light blinded her, so that she blinked furiously . . . He was here, before her. Vin. He looked very ill. Terribly worn. Yes—old.

But he smiled . . . And strangely, it was a very beautiful smile. Protective.

"You were dreaming and cried out."

"Oh, no! I've been awake some minutes. Some sound roused me. A silvery, tinkling sound."

"That was the phone. You heard it in your sleep. You *thought* you awakened, but actually you were having a nightmare when I came in and switched on the light. I expect your dream changed suddenly. Anxiety-dreams do, you know."

The phone. Vin had said the phone had rung.

"What did they say . . . It *was* the hospital?"

He followed her thoughts.

"Yes, it was the hospital. Terry is conscious. His condition is serious and you can see him."

Her face drained of all colour. Terry was going to die. That was what the message meant. Her most urgent impulse was to rise and rush to Terry's side. But an inherent courtesy held her still, that and a more profound comprehension of the "newness" of this man, who, after all, shared her rights in the children. The children. To him, did that not mean merely Faith? Strange that Don should be so aloof. The politest boy under heaven's sun, but how impersonal. Both she and Vin had been forced into directing their love to Faith. She was a bridge that should, did indeed, span the chasm dividing mother from father—but there was a locked gate at each end. And yet, in this strange instant, he seemed positively benevolent and it was hard indeed to see in him the demented drunkard who had physically tortured her in the past and assaulted the now happily married little Ruth. Before actually rising, Mary, despite her anxiety about Terry, sought for the exact expression to nail down the elusive something she saw in Vin's eyes. And, just as she rose in despair, the term sprang to her lips. Martyr. That's what he put her in mind of: a man who had already suffered martyrdom, or who was about to suffer it. A man to whom earthly hates and loves were already dim memories, or so transcendent as to lift both hate and love into altitudes that gave each new significance.

But there never could be rapprochement between him and her. Had there, she now asked, ever been anything but a fleeting physical communion between them and that by reason of a fascination almost mesmeric in its quality? He had moved out of his orbit to dazzle her, then assumed his extra-terrestrial preoccupation. Even now she felt this. In an instant remarkable for its emotional content. He did not belong to mundane interests and never had. That inch out in mental adjustment would explain the phenomenon: the lack of contact with his kind.

~ ~ ~ ~ ~

If she weren't, like Terry—Mary thought in the taxi Vin had phoned for—the most practical materialist, she'd be inclined to ascribe ill-favoured powers to Mr. Govina, since only after his arrival had all this misfortune begun. What was it that Terry and Don had discovered about him that they each should demand his banishment? Were it not that now such an act would seem disloyal to Terry, she'd have a showdown with Don and demand to know what he had against their guest. Yet, what did it matter. Was not Terry going to die? And at long last she had learned that life without him would not be life at all. Strange, she thought, how so many of us need death to show us what life has offered and which we have so strangely undervalued.

There was a screen round Terry's bed and this alarmed her. Was he dead? She asked the night-sister, who smiled non-committally. But, of course, they never told one the truth in these places, where there were false conventions as there were throughout all life as we live it.

"Oh, no," the sister said, "he's not dead; but he's very ill."

"Hopelessly?"

"There's always hope while there's life—in a hospital."

He looked hopeless. The loss of blood had been extensive and his drained face showed it. Already the dark shadows showed in his eyes. Another precious human relationship seemed at breaking-point.

He was not unconscious, that was one thing. But how terribly unlike the vibrant, steel-strong Terry. Yet his pained eyes smiled when he saw her . . . and filled suddenly with tears as the love Mary's heart was so full of gushed into *her* eyes.

But the absurd part of it was that these two, at last united by the disunity of death, could not speak, had no words each for the other. They could only look.

He seemed so near to that final parting that nothing but this tragic severance filled her thoughts. And, all at once, she knew she could not bear it—and herself live.

She said so.

He was whispering. So she leaned near.

"Can I have you . . . if I live?"

"Yes. Altogether. In every way. Just how you like."

He smiled again . . . but differently, she thought. A faint flicker showed in his eyes, a reflex of the old Terry ready to face hopeless odds.

The nurse touched her and she left him, looking back once to see his eyes closed.

She felt, while the taxi sped her home, as if his frail hands, still warm with life, were round her heart. When it grew cold, her heart, he would be gone; and with him her own will to live. But they would cling now, unless forcibly dragged away by the inexorable selfishness of death. That little flicker had been his promise to her, than which, at such an instant, what could be more solemn? And if his fight were stout enough, if he came back—there was her promise to him. Her heart beat violently. And she began silently to say "Yes, yes, yes;" hardly knowing what it meant, but conscious of a vague symbolism in the words, which were, in their way, like a slow, glowing dawn.

She wished suddenly that life were simple, that she and Terry and Faith could live in gentle peace together; just letting the days slip by.

Never till now had she realized the little life had offered her; or, perhaps, it would be more just to say, the little she had accepted. She'd been too much a creature of domestic routine, with too little change and personal happiness. And that sort of thing did not make for fitness. Physical fitness. She was not fit. Her nervous system had been undermined. She was fretful, jumpy. Now with that murder, with Terry's wounding, with the curious sense of "imminence" in her essentially humdrum house, with the unpleasantness of having a weird person like Mr. Govina staying under her roof, she was ready to imagine even the most commonplace things had special signifi-cance . . . These black streets, these abruptly-contrasting stretches of brilliantly-lighted shops rasped her nerves. The stretches of darkness, the sudden glittering lights, reminded her of those gleaming eyes in her dim morning-room . . . And the stale odour of this old taxi brought back that curious creeping oppression when she had expected just such a death as Terry had so narrowly escaped—if he had escaped.

What was it that had struck him down? How odd that it should begin, this slaying, in the neighbourhood of her house—just as before.

Presently a thought that long since had found credence deep down in her mind sprang up, asserting itself as a live and unignorable identity. Govina was connected with this return, as it seemed, of THE INEXPLICABLE. And something to do with this was why Terry and Don had demanded his expulsion. All that muffling up . . . Oh God!

Till now she had demanded that the taxi break all regula-tions of speed; but now—oh let it crawl! She dreaded her re-turn. But in less than a minute they'd slow up at her gate . . .

And here they were.

She almost wished that Vin would come running down the steps to fuss and pay the driver. But he did not; and, for a brief instant, she toyed with the idiotic idea of asking the taxi-man to come in with her, have a drink, anything that would delay him, would prevent her from entering alone.

But he was a surly-looking man. Almost certainly he'd re-fuse . . . And there was Anne.

In the hall she hesitated, fighting an inclination to rush to Anne, as once, when scared of bogies, she used to run to her mother, to find reassurance in her sound commonsense and true devotion.

But she resisted the impulse stoutly. If she was going to give way to childish nerves like this, however, even with Anne's company, was she going to sleep another night under her own roof?

She crept on up three stairs . . . Voices . . . She listened . . . But she did not know whose they were . . . Yet she was almost sure they came from Mr. Govina's room. A wild impulse banished all her fear and all her wisdom. She would steal up, listen . . .

Now! . . .

She could not hear . . .

Carefully, very, very carefully, she opened the door . . .

CHAPTER V

APART FROM the impossibility of his having been the perpetra-
tor of this attack upon Terry—according to the constable's evidence—Superintendent Mann found Mr. Govina not only will-
ing in a very brief yet clear fashion to account for himself, but
courteous, honest in his manner and that most precious witness—a perfectly lucid being. More, Mr. Govina roused the
super's sympathy by a terse account of the fire that had afflicted him and sealed this sympathy with a display of his facial
injuries.

The Superintendent left not only in a very sympathetic frame
of mind but convinced that, whatever the explanation of this
mystery, it had no connection with Mrs. Border's recluse. In all
probability some wild thing had escaped from captivity. Mann
well-remembered THE INEXPLICABLE, but was inclined to
pooh-pooh any connection.

"Coincidence." That was his verdict.

Returning once more to the cherished privacy of his bedroom, Mr. Govina occupied himself in a fashion that would
have surprised both the Superintendent and Mary, could either
have seen him. For he was parcelling up quantities of food, all
the food, in fact, that had been provided him that day. Since it
was clear from this occupation that none of Mary's food had
passed his lips, it was also clear that he did not depend upon
her resources for his daily sustenance.

While putting the final touches to his task, he suddenly and
to all appearances without cause stopped and, paralytically still,
listened, then drew himself erect and, with his loping gait more
pronounced than usual, glided to the door. He opened it
abruptly and entered his sitting-room, once again to become
completely still.

Standing between Govina and the passage door was Vin, his eyes dazzlingly bright and wearing an air of curious authority that suggested some secret power. There was power not only in his unflinching gaze but also in his whole demeanour. It flowed from him like an aura.

So, for a while, they stood—like antagonists weighing each the other's strength, skill, resource.

Then, with a staccato movement, Vin turned towards, and locked the door, without knowing, however, that the bolt, since the wards were defective, could not reach its slot. But though he made this movement, his gaze did not leave Govina's face, nor fail to observe the latter in two swift movements snatch away both his obscuring goggles and black silk fall, thus giving ominous play to his curiously-endowed eyes. The face that to Superintendent Mann had appeared merely distorted and regrettably injured, to this intruder presented the same aspect as had alarmed Don and Terry; glaring, flaming eyes, fanged beast's mouth.

A third swift movement revealed the savage claws. If these actions were intended to alarm and unnerve Vin, they failed. He merely smiled. To him the eyes remained in their original seeming, the mouth did not change. The hypnotic regard affected his will no more than electric currents can affect glass.

"You see . . . my son . . ." Vin said softly, "you have not the power over me you have over others. We see each other as we are. We know each other for what we are . . . And let me remind you that though twice already you have obeyed me, you can never make me obey you. It will be always so."

A quiver passed through Govina's tense form. He snarled and bunched himself as if to spring . . . Yet, he did not. On the contrary his flexed frame relaxed.

Vin watched this surrender without interest, almost as if he failed to notice his own victory.

"The woman Chambers told you all?" he asked tonelessly.

He received a low, harsh affirmative.

"Well, how have you come to this house? In hate or love?"

"Both."

"Which for whom?"

"Hate for *her*; love for Faith."

"You realize the immeasurable difference between you and Faith?"

"Yes."

"And cannot let her alone?"

"I want Faith."

"Faith is mine."

Govina's wolflike jaws split in a hideous grin.

However, if he noticed, Vin responded in no way.

"How do you want her?" he asked quietly. "In human relationship, in life, in death?"

"In death in life."

"And—*her*?"

Govina quivered with a furious rage so ungovernable as to shake objects in his immediate vicinity.

"Give her to me and I will abandon Faith."

"I give nothing."

"And lose Faith."

"We cannot bargain about Faith . . . She is mine."

Govina began to laugh; it was a faint sound, but very intimidating.

"There is one person alone who can give Faith to you. The Woman Who Cursed Me . . . I will exchange Faith for *her*."

"You have not the power to impose such a bargain."

"Faith is my power, *I have got Faith*."

~ ~ ~ ~ ~

Faith, dreaming her own dreams, took little notice of her traveling companion, except to wish that he had chosen a seat in the far corner rather than just opposite her, seeing he was tall and so muffled up as to require more than a fair share of room. However, she tucked her feet away and forgot him. She was able easily to forget what was unpleasant. She lived largely in a series of pictures and, since they were of her own creation, they were invariably pleasant. She was glad for this change of scene, not because she liked excessively the friends to whom she was bound, or their house much better than she liked her home, but because it offered her new medias for her mind-pictures. And, too, she loved the flowers that grew in such abundance around Mrs. Lessingham's home.

Lost in reveries of such a nature, it is improbable that she would have given a second thought to the still creature opposite but for the tunnel; when no longer able to watch the lovely passing scenes she let her gaze wander, to find herself looking into the gleaming eyes that held hers still until they could not look away, or even falter.

She forgot Mrs. Lessingham, her dreams, the train, her home, her mother—everything.

~ ~ ~ ~ ~

She now entered into a state of bliss to which her sweetest dreams were in no way comparable. She existed and knew she existed, but was not wholly conscious. She was aware of her companion, but not clearly. She was infinitely content. Her mind had floated away, her will its captive; but she had a mind, the mind of him by whose side she moved in slow ecstasy. Whither they were bound she neither knew nor noticed. She saw objects without registering them, and might have been in Persia for all the significance England had for her. Individuality had no part in her state. Men and women were merely negatives. Even her companion whom she obeyed, of whom, in a way, she was the complement, had no actual individuality.

Her true self returned to her quite suddenly; and her coming to, was in fact, a shock.

She awoke, if that is the right term to use, in a cellar as dank, as horrible, as fumy, as fungus-ridden as her mother's cellar.

Her eyes opened slowly; and, for a time, she believed herself still staring into the eyes of the tunnel, the gleaming, overpowering eyes. But truly she was staring into the eyes of a rat, peering curiously with its quick-looking, sharp, corrupt stare. Always she had hated, dreaded rats.

She must, Faith knew, turn away her gaze, or she would lose control of herself and shriek in perpetual-seeming cascade—as once before she had done until silenced by exhaustion.

And then she had the urge to glance upward, at an oblique, painful angle. She did. Into the face of what she, for a wild instant, supposed was a monster rat. Here were the eyes of a gleaming rodent, its pointed jaw . . . only immense. A wild, sick rush of fear and horror seemed to tear her mind in two . . . But it suddenly eased as the eyes into which she looked changed to an opaque whiteness, and the pointed jaw became a pointed beard.

She sat up. Why was she here? By what extraordinary set of circumstances? Was this the cellar of Mrs. Lessingham's house . . .? And who was this strange, ugly being?

She saw him smile; and, though aware that the smile was hideous, she did not feel alarmed or even repulsed. Curiously she did not feel herself in danger.

She stared round about. Just a cellar, quite bare save for a packing-case and a gingerbeer box.

She was lying on blankets and a rug and was wearing a heavy man's coat—necessary in an atmosphere at once chill and damp. She felt alive and strangely intense, as if she had been fed on most invigorating sustenance.

The odd-looking man was clad entirely in black and only a livid patch of facial flesh, added to that of one ungloved hand, seemed to differentiate him from the surrounding heavy shadows, made the more uncertain because the wick of a lamp suspended from a beam, and which alone lent the cellar illumination, spluttered and yielded its meagre glow spasmodically—as if it were supplied with foul oil.

He came forward with a curious, loping gait and sat on the upturned gingerbeer box in a manner that Faith thought lupine rather than human. He began to speak and his voice, though harsh, held a tender, syrupy note. Now that he was near, she could detect a peculiar and, at first, unrecognizable odour.

"You are wondering who I am?" he asked.

"Have I been in an accident, or something?"

"Oh no!"

"Are we at Mrs. Lessingham's?"

"No. Mrs. Lessingham does not expect you."

"But she wrote."

"No."

"But . . . she *did*. I read the letter. It was in her writing."

"Hard as it is for you to comprehend the fact, Mrs. Lessingham did not write that letter, I wrote it. I was in the train. I was the muffled up stranger. I brought you here."

"But . . . How?" she asked in complete bewilderment.

"Look!"

Suddenly once again she was looking into those flaming eyes; once again she saw that wolflike face; once again she began to feel stealing over her that delicious langour. Then the eyes, the face, the pleasant stupor were gone. The man with the injured eyes and the puckered jaw covered almost completely by its ragged, pointed beard sat before her.

"You are not afraid of me, Faith."

And she was not. She, most nervous of girls, could consider this appalling abduction, these forbidding surroundings, this sinister man without a tremor.

"I have brought you here to tell you a very long and very strange story, one that I wish your absolute ego to understand. One which it is necessary that the eternal part of you should understand."

"Is there an eternal part of us?"

One half of her had always refused such beliefs; the other, Vin's half, had been filled with those fantastic tales of undead semi-beings of which he, Vin, in frightening moments when his mind seemed totally unrelated to the minds of earth-people as she knew them, told her such vivid, true-seeming tales.

And now this—this—this Stranger began to speak in similar language. There was, he said, in much the excited fashion of Vin's preaching, a state of undeadness. It was scoffed at by the vast majority. But supreme knowledge was granted not to majorities but to those who ruled them. Humanity, he explained, was ruled by secrets of which the matter-of-fact scientists had not the iota of information. She must understand that among all the teeming masses on earth it was not unnatural but natural, by the rule of exception, that there were beings, apparently ordinary humans, who in reality had more alliance with the invisible, secret essence of spirit of which we have no knowledge as a human race than with the merely corporeal creatures we call men and women. To these it was granted that they could retain immortality with, to offer a crude illustration, one leg in the human world and one leg in the immaterial world.

"My father has said all this," Faith admitted.

These arguments lay like lead on her soul and did not convince her reason . . . But, just now, neither her soul nor her reason was very active, though her ordinary faculties were sufficiently strong to impel her to ask:

"And did you abduct me just to convert me to father's theories? Or has father employed you to convert me by experiments or something?"

"I told you: I have brought you here to tell you a long and very strange story. It began at your birth—and at mine; for we two were born at one and the same time. But, indeed, it began before that; at our conception . . . And, to be more subtly exact, long before even that. It really begins with Him you call your father, who has a strain of the hyper-human in his composition—which incidentally has missed you, just as a germ in the blood will miss one twin and infect the other.

"This story begins really with His father, who became allied to the undead by uncommon means, by means illegal in the eyes of Our law, or the law of the Unseen; of The Silent Life; of The Nameless.

"What one might call Infra-immortality creates a link in the issue that has this strange aspect; if one corporeally related immortal destroys the immortality of another, he destroys at the same time his own immortality . . . In Him you call your father the hyper-influence was definitely subordinate to the human. He was more interested in his human relationships than in his Undead relationship; and this came to a vital point when he sowed his seed in your mother's womb. From then on he became overwhelmingly interested in his mortal aspect, because of the issue. His father, who, in his struggle to attain Undead endowment by forcing his way through the mortal limits, had become entangled with certain of his animal mediums, feared what he would have called his own son's treachery, that is his apostasy. He entered into an intrigue with a convert to Black

Animism and they came to this town, where your grandfather was shown publicly as THE INEXPLICABLE. Inexplicable, indeed, to the uninformed human mentality.

"So that I should be born in his image and possessing his immortality despite *his* son's possible renunciation, he visited your mother, our mother, at a vital moment and used his powers to ensure that his gift of Undeadness might, despite our father's renunciation, be perpetuated.

"Our father shot the mortal being of *his* father and then destroyed his immortality, thus losing his own, from thence concentrating his interest on normal human pursuits. He was aware, however, that the child his wife expected could not be born otherwise than a monster, that the coincidental happening of his wife's curse of her expected child and the appearance to her of a monster must have inevitable results.

"Since he had decided to live, in appearance only, with the woman he had married, and whose early infatuation had turned to loathing, he sought consolation and companionship elsewhere, meeting a nurse employed by the doctor in attendance on his wife. They became intimate, when he discovered that she had a sister who was due to deliver an inconvenient child approximately at the same time that is was reasonable to expect his own misshapen offspring.

"He bribed this nurse to change those babies. The plot was carried through with a success partly due to skill, partly due to luck. But fate, in its amazing way, had played a strange trick upon him. True, it had given him the monster son he anticipated, but it had, in addition, given him a normal daughter.

"Now the sister's child was also a boy. Hence to all seeming nothing untoward had occurred. Here, apparently, was a contented mother to whom had been vouchsafed the perfection of motherhood: a healthy boy and girl.

"I was the real son—you were the girl. But I was condemned to my grandfather's animal shape, my whole 'human' life spoilt, because of that woman's curse. From my father, from my grandfather, I inherited the gift of immortality as achieved by Black Animism; but of what use that gift to me in my human life when it had to be lived in animal shape?"

He stopped talking and to the already shocked girl's further dismay began to strip. Yet soon it was clear that her susceptibilities need not be ravaged. Here was no white skin, but the rough pelt of a wolf, the torso of an ape. His clothing shed, the thing that declared itself her brother, began to run softly here and there, seeming hardly to touch the ground.

But presently it stopped and crouched beside her.

"My mother by adoption was the daughter of a showman, partly gipsy, partly Cornish. He refused to share in the terms our father arranged as payment for this elaborate deception. But she, besides being considerably better off already for taking charge of the monster child, saw a future source of considerable profit in my misshapen body. She would show me at fairs on the Continent and in the East. She did so and prospered. In later years she took to drink and in drink talked. Slowly I learned the truth. I learned in hate and bitterness that I need not have been the foul thing I am to look upon, that I could not only have moved among humans as their equal, but as their infinite superior because of the secret powers beginning to manifest themselves.

"Eventually I killed her and came here; came with a desire to help and care for you and to avenge myself on *her*."

"On my mother?" Faith faltered.

She had listened to this—as her reason termed it—farrago of folly, deeming it entirely the product of a mind as twisted as its utterer's body was misshapen. A slow sickness of fear was welling up in her, growing in proportion to her abnormal companion's absorption in his tale. Where was she? How had she come here? In all this talk of magic there certainly was this much evidence in its support, that she was here, in this dreadful cellar, with this thing, and could not say in the smallest degree how she came to be there. She remembered clearly all details of her train journey up to the tunnel. Then, blank. Cogitation suggested that she had been overcome by fear, because she had been suddenly faced by those two glaring eyes; in all probability she had fainted. Yet commonsense told her that even this explanation left much that seemed incredible to be explained. But here she was: fast in the possession of this beast-creature, utterly ignorant of her whereabouts and as clearly destined to stay his prisoner. How had she been fed? For she was not only without a trace of hunger, but actually stronger than she ever remembered herself being before. She felt indescribably potent.

He looked up abruptly and for an instant it seemed to her she saw again the gleaming eyes, the fanged mouth, that so suitably completed his animal appearance. Yet, as soon as his gaze met hers, the phenomenon faded; she saw only his injured, blurred eyes and bearded, puckered mouth. And she saw a benign expression on his face, one of welcome, fondness and protection. The most powerful urge of instinct she had ever experienced bade her temporize, fall in with his exaggerations . . . But this, she told herself, was not possible in its entirety. Nothing would make her consciously agree to support his hate of Mary or to his criminal intentions towards the being she loved best on earth. And then she must, at all cost, know what his exact intentions were towards her. In addition to her reasonable, active fear, she felt a secondary fear: of something that lent countenance to his "otherness." A fear she had sometimes experienced when Vin had lectured her upon a mysterious immortality; something that went beyond the obvious lunacy lurking in Vin and active in this being. Could it *be* that their claims to render her Undead . . . Oh! Here was a pit of horror which it were folly even to glance into.

"What have you brought me here for? Just to tell me this tale?"

"Well, now that it is told, do you not wish us to be together? You realize I am your brother—even if I look like this?"

"Oh, yes, I understood all you said," she replied noncommittally. "But are you going to keep me here in this awful place?"

"For a while . . ."

"But . . ." There was such an incalculability to be said, such an immeasurability of remonstrance to be made that her tongue faltered at the start . . . "How am I to wash, change and . . . and . . . eat?"

He ignored the first questions, but answered the last.

"I have fed you," he said, "as I feed myself. It is not only a sure source of vitality, but a preparation for what is to follow."

"What *is* to follow?" she asked in a whisper.

And now he began to utter such unacceptable yet terrible folly that her stomach revolted and her understanding grew confused; but not so confused that it failed to grasp two outstanding facts: both she and Mary must die; for, however, two distinctly different reasons: Faith was to die with Govina himself, so that in Undeath they would be not only eternally free but eternally united; Mary was to die so that he could condemn her to suffering incalculable.

Without warning, Faith's control, never very powerful, gave way; she screamed—again and again.

Govina stared at her blankly, then miserably; and as if comprehending that here was a seriously bad subject for the rites he proposed; that Faith had not accepted his tale as true; that she believed him mad; and that to convince her he must not only supply witnesses to his statements, but also bring tangible proofs.

His life with Holly, though civilized to some extent, had hardly prepared him for the conventional obstinacy of minds accustomed to empirical facts alone, or to facts rationalized into practicability. He failed to grasp that what to his curious inward state was as clear as daylight was, to the average man and woman, blacker than night. His was, perhaps, the human reasoning mind braked by animal simplicity. He had never comprehended law, other than the law within him, which, despite some mental agility, was mainly based on instinct—and that cannot be admitted into any system of laws, for it is essentially irresponsible.

But he was not going to relinquish her because she was obtuse. There were other ways. He would employ them. After he had done so, she would turn to him as naturally as a child to its mother. There would be a mysterious, inviolable bond between them that would last, not for a day, a year, an age—but for always.

~ ~ ~ ~ ~

Again her free will was subjugated by the gleaming eyes. She sank back at peace, smiling contentedly.

But Govina sat regarding her in metallic fixity. He was thinking now, not of Faith, but of Mary. He had acted wrongly. He should have made sure of securing not only the daughter, but also the mother . . . This latter consummation was not going to be easy. He had a difficult foe in Vin, endowed, Govina believed, with powers more than equal to his own. It might be he'd have to surrender Faith to obtain Mary. And he would forego all other considerations to wreak his hate upon *her*.

But there was subtlety; there was guile. By some exercise of these qualities he might yet possess them both.

He rose and began to don his cast-off clothes. Presently, masked and goggled and muffled in his outdoor wear, he was ready to sally forth.

CHAPTER VI

"I HAVE FAITH," Govina repeated.

The contrast between father and son at this instant was startling indeed. Whereas Border faced Govina in an attitude of insousiant grace, with an air almost of nobility, Govina faced Border as if he had just risen from the mythological regions of Pluto. A veritable reproduction of THE INEXPLICABLE sustained by a greater virility.

It was thus that Mary, tottering in, saw him, her son, before she fell with a crash across the threshold.

For an instant she lay there with the eyes of both men upon her helpless form: Vin looking with oddly changing expression; Govina with his already hideous features diabolically distorted.

A cold smile dawned on Vin's once ruddy lips. He nodded at Mary's prone figure.

"Well, my son, she is there, helpless, at your feet . . . Burn her with your eyes . . . Tear her with your fangs . . . Or rip her with those nice long claws."

A low, rumbling growl answered him from the wolflike jaws; it was clear that the impulse to leap almost rent Govina's lean frame.

But he remained shivering where he stood, as if rooted.

Vin eyed him with a suggestion of idle, inimical amusement.

"So you see, my son, if you have Faith, my daughter, I have Mary, my wife."

A shocking transformation took place. Govina, dropping to all fours, howled in the blood-curdling and baleful fashion of his kind.

Vin examined his nails.

"If the faithful Anne hears that," he drawled, "her knees will be beating the devil's tattoo."

Govina, his jowl dripping, strained violently but uselessly towards Mary's unconscious form, then turning vanished through the bedroom door, which crashed. Vin, raising the prone woman with difficulty, staggered out on to the landing, where he came face to face with Anne, her cheeks chalk-white and the hand that held a candlestick shaking violently.

She tried to speak, in vain.

"Your mistress has fainted. Help me to get her upstairs."

But the maid still stood shivering, as if she had not heard.

"What was that howl?" she whispered.

"A dog in the garden next door."

"It sounded in the house."

"Noises travel curiously at night," Vin said. "Please pull yourself together and help me."

But at that instant Mary opened her eyes and started to scream, staring at Anne as if the flickering candle were the glaring eyes she feared and her plateless mouth the gaping jaws of Govina.

But Mary was no screamer, either by impulse or habit. Rather she was one well-equipped for crisis, her own or others.

The meaning of that grim scene into which, fortunately or unfortunately, she had blundered was all too clear. Disaster had overwhelmed her life just when it seemed the clouds were breaking. Terry, happiness, love—these, with their gentle forecasts, were as far behind her as the years of youth. What remained was the necessity to keep her will firm, her mind clear and her courage great.

"I can walk," she said harshly and with a force foreign to her usual considerate manner. "Anne, you go back to bed."

"But . . ."

"Do as you're told, please . . . I will come quite soon."

After some hesitation the elder woman, her candle dripping grease, which, ordinarily, would have filled her with horror, remounted the stairs.

"Will you come into my room?" Vin asked Mary in his quiet way, which contrasted so oddly with the impish manner and voice of those far off days.

It was significant of her new attitude to him that she consented without hesitation. In his room she had a surprise. It was bare to the degree of a cell. Everything that had stood for comfort had disappeared. She had her choice of a wooden chair or the floor. From a point of principle Mary had left the superintendence of Vin's two rooms to Anne, as silent as she was grim; and, though the latter had from time to time reported that Vin had asked for this, for that, to be removed, and had stripped his rooms, Mary had viewed this statement as exaggerated. But now she saw that, so far from being exaggerated, it fell short of the truth.

His door into the bedroom was open. Through it she could see a little black altar of which Anne had told her.

"There's always a dish with some rank-smelling stuff on it. Filthy stuff . . . But it's always there." So Anne had reported and now through the open door she could see the small black dish.

Vin closed the passage door. They were alone together for the first time in years and years. She sat on one wooden chair and Vin took another, facing her. Then he waited in silence for interrogation, as if he knew that now revelation was inevitable. Which it was.

A premonition of the truth was in her mind. Moreover, it was only too easy to interpret what she had seen and heard. Well, she was here; she had to begin; but it seemed to Mary that her soul was shaking. War, with its atrocities, its human degradation, had so far seemed to her the most sordid depth to which Man, with his boasted Immortal Soul, could sink; but now she knew she was wrong. There were things fouler; things that, maybe, accounted for the more obvious vileness to which men can and do sink.

She cleared her dry throat and for an instant closed her burning eyes.

"Who is this man, Govina?"

His face and eyes less eloquent than stone, Vin replied:

"Our son."

"Then ... that time when the thing came to the window ... and I cursed the son you expected ... It ... it ... photographed that image on ...?"

"Yes."

Unconsciously swaying in her horror, her gaze fixed upon Vin, Mary looked back.

"Then who is Don?"

"A baby I and the nurse substituted."

"Why did you do that?"

"I acted under some compulsion," Vin replied slowly.

He himself did not know, had never known, why he had so deliberately schemed to spare Mary the result of a curse to which he had driven her. It was not, he had always reminded himself, as if he had foreseen Faith, or that he wanted another man's son. But a shot and its grim complement had profoundly changed his outlook towards his human relationships. In that, or for infinitely more sinister reasons beyond even his occult knowledge, lay the explanation. On the face of it Mary was justified in assuming his action done to save her anguish.

"I am grateful for your compassion," she muttered.

But Vin made no reply.

"Is . . ." She stopped and nodded towards where Mr. Govina's rooms lay . . . "Is he abnormal in mind as well as body?"

"Absolutely."

"Mad?"

"You would call it so."

"What is its real appearance?"

"As you've just seen it."

"Those eyes—that mouth?"

"Yes."

"But why does it assume another appearance ... The bearded mouth and injured eyes?"

"It has hypnotic powers greatly developed. All the stupefying endowment of the preying world added to human will."

"Then it did kill that white-haired old man?"

"Don's true grandfather? Yes."

"And injure Terry?"

"Yes."

"And we did not truly see him sitting in his window?"

"No."

"The cat's eyes . . .?"

"Exactly."

"And Faith?"

"You heard. He has Faith."

"What does he want with Faith?"

"You must understand, Mary, he knows from the woman who brought him up as a freak on the Continent—and whom he has killed—that you are his mother, why he is a monster and that Faith is his twin. I know it will be quite useless to explain that he is abnormal to a non-human degree, but perhaps you can grasp this—that he believes he is immortal, in less exaggerated degree, as the fictional vampires are immortal. He has a natal adoration for his twin. He wants her to share his immortality. Perhaps that is only mania. If so, it is full of menace to Faith; for he believes that to attain life she must pass through death."

"You do not know where he has taken Faith?"

"No."

"Do you *believe* he has her? That letter from Mrs. Lessingham."

"She did not write it. She never invited Faith. If you got on the phone to her now, you would find she does not know anything about Faith's journey to stay with her."

"What about the police?"

"That would be fatal. You have seen him baffle the police. To call them in would be to condemn Faith to immediate death."

"Have you no . . . no influence with him?"

"Not influence *with* him. Some power *over* him. But I cannot say 'Bring Faith to me' with any hope of obedience. I can stop him, while at hand, from killing you."

"He means to kill me?"

"Apart from Faith, it is the foremost wish and the absolute intention of his mind."

"He said he would relinquish Faith for me."

"Yes."

There was silence. All this dark fantasy so little related to prosaic life required collating and assimilating. Never had Mary so longed for Terry's cool judgment and strong nature. Were he present, she could just turn over the whole complex problem to him. As it was, she had to deal with it alone.

"I must think, Vin," she said wearily. "I'll go to bed, though sleep seems improbable."

She moved to implement her purpose; but he stopped her.

"Mary." She turned towards him. "Make me up some sort of bed on your divan. I must sleep there until—this affair is settled."

"Why?"

"He cannot pass through to your bedroom while I am present."

She was about to utter trivial refusals; but suddenly refrained. She just nodded. For one thing—any excuse to get away, to consider this absurd yet awful problem, arrive at some decision.

Anne was awake and lifted her arrogant old head when Mary entered.

"Anne, I've asked my husband to sleep on the divan in the sitting-room."

"Good lor! Are you coming all over married?"

Mary ignored the familiar flippancy. Anne, old and well-loved, had many privileges.

"I told him I was nervous."

"Nervous!" The old woman looked round anxiously as if expecting evil faces to flower vilely among the floral extravagances of the wallpaper. "I never thought *this* house'd turn creepy; but it has. You get undressed; I'll make up his bed."

For Mary was rummaging in the huge bottom drawer where she usually kept some spare sheets and blankets.

"No, it's quite . . ."

"Do as you're told, M'm."

Mary, as often obedient to Anne as Anne to Mary, began to undress.

"What made you faint, M'm?"

"Oh, the strain of everything. Mr. Terry and . . ."

The old servant shot her mistress a shrewd glance.

"If I believed in the devil . . ." she began; but left her remark unended. "Didn't hear that howl, of course?"

"What howl?"

"Oh well, never mind!"

To prevent further questions Anne started to make Vin's bed. Suddenly she re-appeared.

"Listen, M'm, let him sleep there if you like—though it seems like asking the devil to keep his imps out of mischief—but I don't sleep with him in there unless our door's locked."

"We'll lock it, Anne," Mary agreed without humour.

Already her racked mind was wrestling with her problem. She was quickly in bed and was terse with Anne when she tried to express her growing alarm and feminine sense of outrage; she pretended great sleepiness, but actually had never felt so wide awake in her life before. Her head seemed full of white-hot wires and her mind so dense with confusion that it was a very long time before she could co-ordinate her thoughts to any degree at all.

It was amazing to think that the terrible nightmare which she had supposed past, but which, nevertheless, was too often present in her waking thoughts and in her dreams, was not present in concrete fact. In all the books she had read, in all the films she had witnessed, Mary had seen nothing so appalling as the raw truth obtaining in this house . . .

Now let me think, she kept saying , , ,

Don is *not* my boy. My own son I *did* curse . . . And curses come home to roost . . . This has . . . A mad monster in this house, teeming with the urge to rip me up, to debauch Faith's true nature . . . And how is he to be prevented? His hypnotic power's not marvelous, but easily understood; yet it's marvelous in its effective protection of him. More effective than a smoke screen in times of war. He must succeed. A voice in her mind soon began to assert itself: You can't just lie here and do nothing! Don't you understand that Faith is in this creature's power? You do not know to what vileness she may be subjected. She thought of Faith's dreamy beauty, of her lovable helplessness. An experience such as this was sufficient to wreck a stronger mind than Faith's. How could she continue to lie still without knowing where her daughter was?

Desperation surged over her. Inaction became abruptly impossible. She would speak to Vin, demand that something should be done . . . And, if Vin could not or would not do anything, then she'd tackle the thing that was her son. She must. If he would consent to return Faith to safe-keeping in exchange for her own life, the bargain should be made. Clearly, in regard to that, she had no choice. Faith was an utterly innocent party; she herself was aware of guilt. Plainly, calm reason declared, to curse a child in the early days of its conception is a grievous sin. Had she cursed Vin, she would have been justified, but the child . . .

She would do something, confront it; and if she could achieve nothing that way, she'd rouse the countryside.

Mary listened carefully to Anne's breathing. There were two stages of the old woman's sleep, when she had gone off but was rousable by even light noises, and when she had sunk into a deeper slumber and was hard indeed to rouse. From the depth and stertorous rhythm that proceeded from the other bed, Anne had reached her second stage and it would be safe for Mary to venture.

She and Anne slept with their curtains drawn. The moonlight streamed in. It was a hard night. All cloud had withdrawn from the sky, which was fully dominated, like the earth below, by aloof silver. A night without a sympathetic note.

With soft movements she donned her dressing-gown—more beautiful in this tempered radiance than the girl she called lovely—and stole to the door. Here she listened, but heard no sound from Vin's made-up bed; no breathing. No restless movements. She ventured the door, opening it slowly and with infinite caution.

Vin lay upon his back. She eyed him, making little tentative movements of entry . . . He was impressively still—still as a corpse; eyes as glassy. Mary had seen the dead and did not think that he was in truth a corpse . . . rather he gave her the impression of *suspension*. He looked not asleep but void, as if his spirit were not with his body. She moved more boldly. He did not stir.

Even when Mary had with a little unavoidable squeaking opened the passage door, a backward glance showed her Vin still as remote as an effigy at some waxworks.

The passage, too, was palely alight, as if her way were being lit by ghostly purpose. And each step downward was like dipping her feet into an immaterial stream.

At Govina's door courage failed her. For the first time terror welled up. But she welcomed the fear—as now she knew she welcomed the full frightfulness of this ordeal and its possible consequences. Thus she could purge her soul of a guilty feeling. What sin, she asked herself, can equal sin against the unborn, prejudicing lives not yet shaped? For this reason, though in turning the knob her hand trembled, it did not falter. She went in. The sitting-room was empty. With feet weighted and slow she crossed to the second door and tapped. But no answer came. She tapped again—many times . . .

She had an overmastering impulse to peep in; but a terror of doing so equally as strong. What might she not see? More death, more and more terrible death? Those deadly eyes? That ghastly mouth? Things blasphemous against the common beliefs of life?

In obedience to her less considered urge she did open the door to find an empty room . . .

How she was being baulked! Ten thousand times harder is the pursuing of a sacrifice when the impulse seeking its consummation has to endure by artificial means.

She *would*, however, see Govina.

She did.

He stood behind her muffled up as was his habit on his journeys to and from the house.

~ ~ ~ ~ ~

"Where has he come from? What has he come from doing?"

These were her first thoughts. Killing? Has he been killing? As he killed that old man. As he would have killed

Terry . . . As his dreadful prototype killed . . . to all seeming purposely . . . Unless there were some terrible explanation for these crimes that would show them far from objectless.

Well, soon he would kill her. She trembled in this muffled presence—kin of hers yet as alien as spirit to matter. The dread of immediate and violent death tied her tongue, dried her mouth. She stood merely trembling, ignorant of what might be happening behind those goggles and that black silk fall. She could not, somehow, identify this woman, trembling in strange circumstances to Miltonian aspects, with the Mary she had known from infancy.

She began to falter words, staring at the material of his wrappings.

"Your father has explained about you . . . I find it exceedingly hard to put into words what I feel . . . Contrition for the great wrong that I feel my curse has done you is what I most want to express . . . Any mother in such circumstances would wish to say . . ." Her voice faded. She was aware Govina shook. Was he laughing? Did he shake through rage? "Amends . . . if in any way I can make amends . . . There is *nothing*"—her voice deepened under the stress of her feelings—"*nothing* I would not do . . ."

She began to pour out words; the verbal flood fell from her lips like a fall fed by rain. Let him return Faith. Just say where she was. Assure Mary the girl was safe . . .

But her pleadings faltered . . . for he began to draw off his glove . . . The claws glistened in the moonlight. As Mary Queen of Scots must have gazed fascinated upon the instrument of her doom when they led her to the scaffold, so this Mary could not drag her gaze from those shining claws.

And then—he uncovered his fateful eyes. Staring into them, Mary surrendered her will, her identity, as Faith had done . . . and sank to her knees, pulling open her pyjama coat the better for his intention . . .

But, as abruptly as she had succumbed, she recovered, was aware of her supplicatory attitude, of her bared chest and rose, hurriedly buttoning up the undone jacket—as Vin, *coming from Govina's room*, stood beside his son, back to Mary . . .

From Govina's room . . . Then what was that lying in the made-up bed? The corpse-like shell. The . . . How could Vin have come through Govina's door . . . Unless from somewhere he had procured a ladder and burgled his son's window? And why should he do that when he'd only to descend a few ordinary, shallow stairs? Besides, when she had looked in Govina's room, it had been empty and the shutters fast.

It seemed as if her heart were forcing its way out of her breast . . .

And now Vin turned round, was his ordinary self—except that his smile seemed profoundly sweet.

"Did you not understand, Mary, that in trusting yourself to this son of ours you were trusting yourself to the instincts of a beast."

"I want Faith back," she said wildly.

"But you've gone the wrong way to obtain her. If you sacrifice yourself, you sacrifice her. Sacrifice yourself by all means—but see he does not betray you; and how are you going to make sure of that? Beasts have no sense of honour."

She looked from father to son . . . Astounding above all else was her discovery that, now Vin had come, the ungoggled, flaming eyes had no power to influence her, had indeed no more than a pale amber glow.

She faced Vin, looking very straight and young in her infinite eagerness.

"Faith must come back. If he harms her, it will punish me beyond my desserts . . . I don't want to die; I dread dying in his way; but I'd rather die a thousand awful deaths than that Faith should suffer for my idle words, spoken in a fit of fury for which you alone were responsible."

He stared at her gravely.

"Very well. We will arrange it like that. But nothing can be done to-night. Come."

Two things astounded Mary: the authoritative nature of Vin's tone and the instant obedience it commanded in her own mind; the utter lack of protest from Govina, who indeed turned deliberately and vanished into his bedroom.

She followed out the man to whom for years she, if in a very gentle way, had dictated.

"I can't go back to bed until I am reassured about Faith," she said urgently, plucking at his silk gown.

He stopped, looked almost unseeingly down at her and opened the door of his own room. She followed him in, but did not close the door. Once more she sat facing him on a wooden chair. Her quick glance round showed her a little stone jar added to the altar's contents. On it was painted a curious symbol.

"I thought *you* loved Faith!" she said stormily.

He was some time in answering; then he said:

"I love Faith, but I don't love you."

"I did not expect that you did. I don't ask help for myself; but I do for Faith. If you really love her, won't you help her?"

"I have not the power to compel our son to release his sister."

"Then you're going to let her die?" She sprang up. "I'm a fool to discuss the matter with either of you. Both are mad." She paused, looked again at Vin and said, "But of course you're mad. The two of you. I must be mad myself. I'm going to phone to the police station."

"Mary!"

Against her will she stopped to listen.

"You have been talking very nobly, according to your lights, about saving Faith—even at the cost of your own life."

"Well?"

"And now you're purposing to destroy her."

"What d'you mean?"

"I mean that you cannot more certainly condemn Faith to death than by phoning the police station. He has her in his power in a way that is beyond police jurisdiction. You yourself have experienced the power of his eyes. If you phoned the station and if they found Faith, they could not restore her mind, nor compel him to restore her mind. He alone, of his own free wish, can do that. And remember, we do not know where he has her hidden. Be quite certain of this, before your routine-loving police had found where she is, *she would be dead.*"

His quiet reasoning convinced her. She came back to her wooden chair.

"Then what can be done?"

"I thought you had solved that riddle?"

Her cheeks grew ashen. Human to the last beat of her heart, Mary did not wish to die more than any other of her kind; and now there was so much to live for. In one second she saw her whole life in retrospect, saw her possible future and present problem.

"Do you mean, seriously and sensibly, that is the only way?" she asked hoarsely.

"I'm afraid it is."

There was a tremendous long and tremendously significant silence.

"Can you guarantee that he'll release Faith, both mentally and physically?"

"Yes."

"Will you?"

"Yes."

" . . . Very well. Make that arrangement."

She nearly added "And break Faith's heart. How d'you think she's going to live without me, whom she adores? And will she love you when she finds that indirectly you are my murderer?" But she choked back the words. Definitely she could not now afford to antagonize Vin.

"I will see our son and tell you to-morrow what arrangements I've made. In the meantime, get what rest you can."

She laughed.

"Does rest matter any more?"

Vin shrugged.

"Even condemned prisoners sleep soundly, I understand."

He escorted Mary to her room and, with a smile, heard her relock the intervening door.

Then he returned, very slowly, to Govina's rooms.

CHAPTER VII

AS HE QUIETLY ENTERED by the passage door, Govina entered from the bedroom. He was without both goggles and fall and his face wore an exceedingly malicious expression.

"Your mother," Vin said politely, "consents."

A vivid contortion twisted Govina's face and his animal jaw smiled in a way that sat grotesquely on such a visage.

"She quite understands?" he asked in his grating voice.

"Oh, fully. She quite understands, too, that you alone can break the control which no doubt you've imposed upon your sister."

The long, lean jaws grunted.

"And she also understands, Mr. Govina, that neither you nor I can betray each other, since we have each too many uncommon resources."

"If my sister were in this house," Govina said slowly, "she'd be my prisoner as completely . . ."

"As if confined in a dungeon thousands of miles away."

"It is not a matter whether or not *she* consents, it's whether *you* consent. *We* understand that."

"Quite."

"And you do?"

"I want Faith."

"Well?"

"Where is my daughter?"

Govina—so far as his peculiar appearance permitted—indulged a grin.

"In the cellar next door."

"Oh—indeed! I like your sense of humour. That certainly simplifies matters. I will bring your mother to the house at midnight to-morrow—though, of course, it is to-morrow now. She will be under my protection until Faith is not only released from your thrall, but safely back in her own home. Then and then only will I deliver my wife into your keeping."

Govina rose with a curious gesture that said most effectively: "I accept your conditions and the interview is ended."

At the door Vin turned.

"At twelve precisely, midnight, I shall cross the threshold of next door with my wife. Not less than ten minutes later Faith must be back, normal and safe in this house. Treachery will mean extermination of your immortality."

Despite his gruesome face and menacing manner, Govina's terribleness faded to insignificance before that which quite suddenly flamed in Vin's—to fade at once.

He went out into the passage, leaving a curiously cowed Govina eyeing the door with flaming eyes.

Approaching Mary's sitting-room, he heard a quiet voice say "Father."

Looking back, he saw it was Don—and laughed.

How completely he and Mary had forgotten this young man!

"Hello, Don! Just come in?"

"Yes. Anything the matter?"

"No. Why should there be?"

"Oh . . . I don't know. Only . . . things seem queer lately—since this lodger's come."

"There's nothing of consequence the matter. Your mother and Anne had wind-up about the murder of that old man. You've heard of it?" Don nodded. "Well, I've been having a look round to reassure her. Good night."

Don had always been baffled by Vin's aloof jocularity, and, having experienced nothing but kindly consideration at his hands, found it hard to resent a distinct lack of the sympathy which, however, was, he noticed accorded generously to Faith. He set off disgruntled for his room.

So passed the night.

~ ~ ~ ~ ~

And, strangely enough, Mary did sleep. The fact astounded her. More, it rather disgusted her. To sleep in such circumstances was not worthy of the dignity of tragedy; nor worthy of her concern for Faith. Nor was it suitable to a woman condemned to die—die a foul and horrible death. Waking to a bright day, she shuddered as memory played its little tricks upon her . . . Sudden nausea troubled her stomach . . . She hid her face in the pillows and shed tears of pity for her suddenly young life . . . Tears for her lost Terry, who could not even say good-bye.

Yet it was with a calm face and air that she descended to preside over a breakfast terribly distasteful to her. Don, she noticed, was present and eyed her curiously. But she avoided his gaze and watched his departure with relief.

Vin, too, rose.

"I shall not be going to business in the circumstances," he said softly.

"When . . . what . . . have you arranged?"

"I shall take you to our son at midnight . . . your eyes will be bandaged . . ."

"And Faith?"

"Faith will be restored as you wish. You shall see her departure before I leave you with him."

A sob stuck in her throat.

"Thank you," she muttered. "I'm going to tell Anne she's to sleep alone to-night and that I'm returning to bed now . . . Will you see she does not disturb me, the whole day?"

"Yes, I'll do that."

"I want to write to Faith . . . Don and . . . Terry. My will—you'll find it in the little desk in my sitting-room."

"Very well."

Her mouth opened and shut several times as if she wanted to ask his help . . . But she said nothing and went quietly out.

~ ~ ~ ~ ~

"God knows what's coming to this house!" Anne told the kitchen dresser during the morning. "I'm not to sleep with her ladyship to-night, if you please," she confided to the kettle. "No food! Did you ever hear the like . . . *And* her door locked . . . Thinks I can't hear her crying," she added mopping her own streaming eyes. "Me who's been her friend . . . not just her servant . . . And that man wandering about the house all day like a lost dog. And *he* wants no dinner, neither, mind you!" She turned away, with an angry glance at her own untasted dinner on the kitchen table.

~ ~ ~ ~ ~

At fifteen minutes to twelve that night the house seemed composed in perfect order. Don slept unsuspiciously and heavily. Anne, in her strange bed, found complete and unexpected rest. Mr. Govina had gone out late and not returned. Mary, her door still locked, was quiet in her room. Only Vin was up and about, wandering, as Anne had said, like a lost dog, into this room, into that. His face might have been carved from flint. Thus it had been all day, except for a short while when he had gone out for not more than twenty minutes.

But as the silver-voiced clock in Mary's hall, by striking a quarter to twelve, midnight, told him the hour for his nocturnal expedition with Mary was near he became calm in gait as well as in manner; and did a strange thing; for he mounted softly to the door of Mary's sitting-room and locked it on the outside.

He stood an instant looking at the turned key and smiled. Then with a little gay gesture of farewell turned away . . . with the key in his pocket.

But his face was not gay when he entered his own sitting-room and moved swiftly from it into the bedroom beyond.

Here he crossed to the little black altar and laid his hand gently on the small stone jar that had attracted Mary's notice. For a while he stood silent; but presently, raising his head, looked at the wall, as if seeing through it into the past, maybe into the future.

Suddenly he turned away from the little altar, moved to his mirror and gazed at his reflection inscrutably; first full face, then profile. Satisfied, he returned to the altar and took the small stone jar in his hands, murmuring several curious words.

He opened the jar, but this was a complicated task that involved twisting the top this way and that. When it was open, he laughed and stared at the contents, which, presently, he drank. A voltaic shock all but lifted him from the floor and for a while he was in the grip of an extraordinary spasm.

It ceased . . . Border crossed again to his mirror, staring in.

He saw nothing—but the reflected room in which was no human being.

~ ~ ~ ~ ~

Without his goggles and fall, Govina, as if Vin's abandoned restlessness had fallen upon him, paced the hall of Terry's house. His eyes gleamed. His mouth hung open. The long, thin tongue lolled out. His loping gait seemed more than usually pronounced; for he moved ceaselessly and very fast—to the limits of his run, turning violently and away to the new far end.

On and on.

Suddenly he paused. The wind (west) had carried a sound to his ears. Twelve chimes from the Town Hall clock.

A raucous shrilling far behind him rent the stillness. Someone had rung the back door bell.

He paused. Then ran wolflike. But, the door reached, Govina paused, becoming both rigid and still.

He opened the door.

On the threshold he saw—Vin and Mary, whose eyes were bandaged.

All three stood quite still staring at one another. Then Govina moved from the door, Vin and Mary following.

In the hall, Vin spoke.

"Faith must not see her mother."

Trembling, Govina nodded. He seemed hungry with impatience.

"I will take your mother upstairs. Come with us."

All three ascended, Govina leading. Mary, blindfolded, following and Vin coming last.

~ ~ ~ ~ ~

Presently the two men came down.

"That was the strong room," Vin explained pleasantly as they descended. "In the old days, Lawyer Cliffe had his office here. You are satisfied that your mother cannot escape?"

"Yes."

"Very well. You may be sure I can play you no tricks. I'll come with you to the cellars, too; so you will have your eye on me continuously until the girl leaves. Keep your spell on Faith until we're back in the hall."

There was the same uncertain light in the foul cellar. Rats fled at their entry and peeped bright-eyed from various holes.

The girl lay prone, breathing heavily. At a word from Govina she rose, wearing a contented smile, but ignoring Vin as if they two had never met before.

Another procession of three.

In the hall, Vin said softly:

"Take her near the front door."

Govina obeyed.

"Now open the door. Thank you . . . Well, my son, release her."

Govina turned his flaming gaze upon the girl and stared into her vacant eyes.

As suddenly as light, come at the pressing of a switch, her expression changed from its pleased vacancy to alert intelligence. She stared in consternation at Vin; at the averted form of Govina. It was evident she remembered nothing of what had befallen her.

"Do you know where you are, Faith?" Vin asked.

She stared round.

"Next door?" she asked, astounded.

"Yes. Do you know how you came here."

"No . . . Have I walked in my sleep *again*?"

"I'm afraid so. You must go home at once. You understand?"

"Yes, Father."

Vin drew from his pocket a little silver whistle and handed it to Faith.

"Go straight in. Before you close the front door, blow this whistle. Is that clear?"

"Yes, Father."

"Very well, go."

"But aren't you coming?"

"All in good time. We think someone's got in here and we're going over the house. Be off with you."

She gave a puzzled glance at Govina's back and ran out.

The two men sustained their postures exactly until the sharp-shrill blast reached their ears. Then Vin turned abruptly to his son and said curtly:

"You wait here an instant. Then we'll go up."

The other swung round, met his father's steady gaze and mumbled an uncertain affirmative.

Vin moved swiftly down the small passage leading to the kitchen quarters; but had hardly been gone a minute before he came back.

"Now, my son," he said smoothly, "we'll go up." As they began to mount he said: "This, then, is the first time you've ever seen a combination lock? You can't work it unless you know the key-word. Our friend, Terry, confided it to me long ago, before you were thought of . . . Well, here we are."

He turned the knob of Terry's strong-room unhurriedly, smiling wider and wider until his smile changed to an audible giggle.

The heavy door swung smoothly open.

Propelled by Vin, Govina stumbled over the dark threshold. His luminous eyes created a little glow. Vin, too, crossed the threshold. The great door crashed to.

"We're in, Meredith," Vin cried with a loud laugh. "That's a saying humans have . . . Here we are then, fast in the strong-room . . . *And We Can't Get Out.*"

His laughter increased—becoming shrill; but Govina seemed not to comprehend his father's meaning, for he said:

"Light."

The terse word still further amused Vin.

"What on earth does an immortal being want with light? Where are your magical powers? However, as ever, I oblige."

He took a small torch from some pocket and switched on its powerful rays. Govina turned savagely to grip his prey, but, except for Border and himself, the stout chamber was empty.

He looked wildly round at his madly laughing father.

"Where is she?" he demanded harshly.

"Not *here*, my son. Just a little magic of my own, dear boy. Just a little joke. I always had a fantastic sense of humour and always did laugh at serious situations. I was laughing when I drove the stake through your grandfather's heart. How he screamed! But fire is just as effective for destroying eternally malign beings like you and me. And we'll scream, too, when the flames get us . . . I set the house on fire when I left you, son. It was all prepared. Straw and rubbish and petrol. We can't hear the flames through these strong walls, but they're roaring below . . . The thought of roast Borders excites me . . . I'd like to dance and dance . . ."

~ ~ ~ ~ ~

Item, which, some months later, appeared in the gossip page of *The Weekly Record*:

"Mr. Terry Cliffe, who has now quite recovered from the inexplicable attack that condemned him to several weeks in hospital, is, we understand, to be quietly married next week to his oldest friend, Mrs. Mary Border, whose late husband was so tragically burned to death in the mysterious fire which reduced Cliffe House to a smouldering mass of ruins. Readers will recall that the house in question was empty, which rendered the cause of the fire a complete enigma. However, it was understood at the time that the late Mr. Border, together with a guest staying in his house, went to investigate certain signs of intrusion they had detected in Cliffe House, and were trapped in the old strong-room where once Mr. Terry Cliffe's forebears stored legal documents. How the house came subsequently to catch fire none will ever be able to say, but it was assumed, at the time, that a tramp had been responsible.

"Our readers, we feel sure, will join us in wishing the prospective bride and bridegroom every happiness."

THE END

RAMBLE HOUSE's

HARRY STEPHEN KEELER WEBWORK MYSTERIES

(RH) indicates the title is available ONLY in the RAMBLE HOUSE edition

The Ace of Spades Murder
The Affair of the Bottled Deuce (RH)
The Amazing Web
The Barking Clock
Behind That Mask
The Book with the Orange Leaves
The Bottle with the Green Wax Seal
The Box from Japan
The Case of the Canny Killer
The Case of the Crazy Corpse (RH)
The Case of the Flying Hands (RH)
The Case of the Ivory Arrow
The Case of the Jeweled Ragpicker
The Case of the Lavender Gripsack
The Case of the Mysterious Moll
The Case of the 16 Beans
The Case of the Transparent Nude (RH)
The Case of the Transposed Legs
The Case of the Two-Headed Idiot (RH)
The Case of the Two Strange Ladies
The Circus Stealers (RH)
Cleopatra's Tears
A Copy of Beowulf (RH)
The Crimson Cube (RH)
The Face of the Man From Saturn
Find the Clock
The Five Silver Buddhas
The 4th King
The Gallows Waits, My Lord! (RH)
The Green Jade Hand
Finger! Finger!
Hangman's Nights (RH)
I, Chameleon (RH)
I Killed Lincoln at 10:13! (RH)
The Iron Ring
The Man Who Changed His Skin (RH)
The Man with the Crimson Box
The Man with the Magic Eardrums
The Man with the Wooden Spectacles
The Marceau Case
The Matilda Hunter Murder

The Monocled Monster
The Murder of London Lew
The Murdered Mathematician
The Mysterious Card (RH)
The Mysterious Ivory Ball of Wong Shing Li (RH)
The Mystery of the Fiddling Cracksman
The Peacock Fan
The Photo of Lady X (RH)
The Portrait of Jirjohn Cobb
Report on Vanessa Hewstone (RH)
Riddle of the Travelling Skull
Riddle of the Wooden Parrakeet (RH)
The Scarlet Mummy (RH)
The Search for X-Y-Z
The Sharkskin Book
Sing Sing Nights
The Six From Nowhere (RH)
The Skull of the Waltzing Clown
The Spectacles of Mr. Cagliostro
Stand By—London Calling!
The Steeltown Strangler
The Stolen Gravestone (RH)
Strange Journey (RH)
The Strange Will
The Straw Hat Murders (RH)
The Street of 1000 Eyes (RH)
Thieves' Nights
Three Novellos (RH)
The Tiger Snake
The Trap (RH)
Vagabond Nights (Defrauded Yeggman)
Vagabond Nights 2 (10 Hours)
The Vanishing Gold Truck
The Voice of the Seven Sparrows
The Washington Square Enigma
When Thief Meets Thief
The White Circle (RH)
The Wonderful Scheme of Mr. Christopher Thorne
X. Jones—of Scotland Yard
Y. Cheung, Business Detective

Keeler Related Works

A To Izzard: A Harry Stephen Keeler Companion by Fender Tucker — Articles and stories about Harry, by Harry, and in his style. Included is a compleat bibliography.

Wild About Harry: Reviews of Keeler Novels — Edited by Richard Polt & Fender Tucker — 22 reviews of works by Harry Stephen Keeler from *Keeler News*. A perfect introduction to the author.

The Keeler Keyhole Collection: Annotated newsletter rants from Harry Stephen Keeler, edited by Francis M. Nevins. Over 400 pages of incredibly personal Keeleriana.

Fakealoo — Pastiches of the style of Harry Stephen Keeler by selected demented members of the HSK Society. Updated every year with the new winner.

Strands of the Web: Short Stories of Harry Stephen Keeler — 29 stories, just about all that Keeler wrote, are edited and introduced by Fred Cleaver.

RAMBLE HOUSE's LOON SANCTUARY

A Clear Path to Cross — Sharon Knowles short mystery stories by Ed Lynskey.

A Corpse Walks in Brooklyn and Other Stories — Volume 5 in the Day Keene in the Detective Pulps series.

A Jimmy Starr Omnibus — Three 40s novels by Jimmy Starr.

A Niche in Time and Other Stories — Classic SF by William F. Temple

A Roland Daniel Double: The Signal and The Return of Wu Fang — Classic thrillers from the 30s.

A Shot Rang Out — Three decades of reviews and articles by today's Anthony Boucher, Jon Breen. An essential book for any mystery lover's library.

A Smell of Smoke — A 1951 English countryside thriller by Miles Burton.

A Snark Selection — Lewis Carroll's *The Hunting of the Snark* with two Snarkian chapters by Harry Stephen Keeler — Illustrated by Gavin L. O'Keefe.

A Young Man's Heart — A forgotten early classic by Cornell Woolrich.

Alexander Laing Novels — *The Motives of Nicholas Holtz* and *Dr. Scarlett*, stories of medical mayhem and intrigue from the 30s.

An Angel in the Street — Modern hardboiled noir by Peter Genovese.

Automaton — Brilliant treatise on robotics: 1928-style! By H. Stafford Hatfield.

Away From the Here and Now — Clare Winger Harris stories, collected by Richard A. Lupoff.

Beast or Man? — A 1930 novel of racism and horror by Sean M'Guire. Introduced by John Pelan.

Black Beadle — A 1939 thriller by E.C.R. Lorac.

Black Hogan Strikes Again — Australia's Peter Renwick pens a tale of the 30s outback.

Black River Falls — Suspense from the master, Ed Gorman.

Blondy's Boy Friend — A snappy 1930 story by Philip Wylie, writing as Leatrice Homesley.

Blood in a Snap — The *Finnegan's Wake* of the 21st century, by Jim Weiler.

Blood Moon — The first of the Robert Payne series by Ed Gorman.

Bogart '48 — Hollywood action with Bogie by John Stanley and Kenn Davis.

Calling Lou Largo! — Two Lou Largo novels by William Ard.

Cornucopia of Crime — Francis M. Nevins assembled this huge collection of his writings about crime literature and the people who write it. Essential for any serious mystery library.

Corpse Without Flesh — Strange novel of forensics by George Bruce.

Crimson Clown Novels — By Johnston McCulley, author of the Zorro novels, *The Crimson Clown* and *The Crimson Clown Again*.

Dago Red — 22 tales of dark suspense by Bill Pronzini.

Dark Sanctuary — Weird Menace story by H. B. Gregory.

David Hume Novels — *Corpses Never Argue, Cemetery First Stop, Make Way for the Mourners, Eternity Here I Come*. 1930s British hardboiled fiction with an attitude.

Dead Man Talks Too Much — Hollywood boozer by Weed Dickenson.

Death Leaves No Card — One of the most unusual murdered-in-the-tub mysteries you'll ever read. By Miles Burton.

Death March of the Dancing Dolls and Other Stories — Volume Three in the Day Keene in the Detective Pulps series. Introduced by Bill Crider.

Deep Space and other Stories — A collection of SF gems by Richard A. Lupoff.

Detective Duff Unravels It — Episodic mysteries by Harvey O'Higgins.

Diabolic Candelabra — Classic 30s mystery by E.R. Punshon

Dictator's Way — Another D.S. Bobby Owen mystery from E.R. Punshon

Dime Novels: Ramble House's 10-Cent Books — *Knife in the Dark* by Robert Leslie Bellem, *Hot Lead* and *Song of Death* by Ed Earl Repp, *A Hashish House in New York* by H.H. Kane, and five more.

Doctor Arnoldi — Tiffany Thayer's story of the death of death.

Don Diablo: Book of a Lost Film — Two-volume treatment of a western by Paul Landres, with diagrams. Intro by Francis M. Nevins.

Dope and Swastikas — Two strange novels from 1922 by Edmund Snell

Dope Tales #1 — Two dope-riddled classics; *Dope Runners* by Gerald Grantham and *Death Takes the Joystick* by Phillip Condé.

Dope Tales #2 — Two more narco-classics; *The Invisible Hand* by Rex Dark and *The Smokers of Hashish* by Norman Berrow.

Dope Tales #3 — Two enchanting novels of opium by the master, Sax Rohmer. *Dope* and *The Yellow Claw.*

Double Hot — Two 60s softcore sex novels by Morris Hershman.

Double Sex — Yet two more panting thrillers from Morris Hershman.

Dr. Odin — Douglas Newton's 1933 racial potboiler comes back to life.

Evangelical Cockroach — Jack Woodford writes about writing.

Evidence in Blue — 1938 mystery by E. Charles Vivian.

Fatal Accident — Murder by automobile, a 1936 mystery by Cecil M. Wills.

Fighting Mad — Todd Robbins' 1922 novel about boxing and life

Finger-prints Never Lie — A 1939 classic detective novel by John G. Brandon.

Freaks and Fantasies — Eerie tales by Tod Robbins, collaborator of Tod Browning on the film FREAKS.

Gadsby — A lipogram (a novel without the letter E). Ernest Vincent Wright's last work, published in 1939 right before his death.

Gelett Burgess Novels — *The Master of Mysteries, The White Cat, Two O'Clock Courage, Ladies in Boxes, Find the Woman, The Heart Line, The Picaroons* and *Lady Mechante.* Recently added is A Gelett Burgess Sampler, edited by Alfred Jan. All are introduced by Richard A. Lupoff.

Geronimo — S. M. Barrett's 1905 autobiography of a noble American.

Hake Talbot Novels — *Rim of the Pit, The Hangman's Handyman.* Classic locked room mysteries, with mapback covers by Gavin O'Keefe.

Hands Out of Hell and Other Stories — John H. Knox's eerie hallucinations

Hell is a City — William Ard's masterpiece.

Hollywood Dreams — A novel of Tinsel Town and the Depression by Richard O'Brien.

Hostesses in Hell and Other Stories — Russell Gray's most graphic stories

House of the Restless Dead — Strange and ominous tales by Hugh B. Cave.

I Stole $16,000,000 — A true story by cracksman Herbert E. Wilson.

Inclination to Murder — 1966 thriller by New Zealand's Harriet Hunter.

Invaders from the Dark — Classic werewolf tale from Greye La Spina.

J. Poindexter, Colored — Classic satirical black novel by Irvin S. Cobb.

Jack Mann Novels — Strange murder in the English countryside. *Gees' First Case, Nightmare Farm, Grey Shapes, The Ninth Life, The Glass Too Many, Her Ways Are Death, The Kleinert Case* and *Maker of Shadows.*

Jake Hardy — A lusty western tale from Wesley Tallant.

Jim Harmon Double Novels — *Vixen Hollow/Celluloid Scandal, The Man Who Made Maniacs/Silent Siren, Ape Rape/Wanton Witch, Sex Burns Like Fire/Twist Session, Sudden Lust/Passion Strip, Sin Unlimited/Harlot Master, Twilight Girls/Sex Institution.* Written in the early 60s and never reprinted until now.

Joel Townsley Rogers Novels and Short Stories — By the author of *The Red Right Hand: Once In a Red Moon, Lady With the Dice, The Stopped Clock, Never Leave My Bed.* Also two short story collections: *Night of Horror* and *Killing Time.*

John Carstairs, Space Detective — Arboreal Sci-fi by Frank Belknap Long

Joseph Shallit Novels — *The Case of the Billion Dollar Body, Lady Don't Die on My Door-step, Kiss the Killer, Yell Bloody Murder, Take Your Last Look.* One of America's best 50's authors and a favorite of author Bill Pronzini.

Keller Memento — 45 short stories of the amazing and weird by Dr. David Keller.

Killer's Caress — Cary Moran's 1936 hardboiled thriller.

Lady of the Yellow Death and Other Stories — More stories by Wyatt Blassingame.

League of the Grateful Dead and Other Stories — Volume One in the Day Keene in the Detective Pulps series.

Library of Death — Ghastly tale by Ronald S. L. Harding, introduced by John Pelan

Malcolm Jameson Novels and Short Stories — *Astonishing! Astounding!, Tarnished Bomb, The Alien Envoy and Other Stories* and *The Chariots of San Fernando and Other Stories.* All introduced and edited by John Pelan or Richard A. Lupoff.

Man Out of Hell and Other Stories — Volume II of the John H. Knox weird pulps collection.

Marblehead: A Novel of H.P. Lovecraft — A long-lost masterpiece from Richard A. Lu-poff. This is the "director's cut", the long version that has never been published before.

Mark of the Laughing Death and Other Stories — Shockers from the pulps by Francis James, introduced by John Pelan.

Master of Souls — Mark Hansom's 1937 shocker is introduced by weirdologist John Pelan.

Max Afford Novels — *Owl of Darkness, Death's Mannikins, Blood on His Hands, The Dead Are Blind, The Sheep and the Wolves, Sinners in Paradise* and *Two Locked Room Mysteries and a Ripping Yarn* by one of Australia's finest mystery novelists.

Money Brawl — Two books about the writing business by Jack Woodford and H. Bedford-Jones. Introduced by Richard A. Lupoff.

More Secret Adventures of Sherlock Holmes — Gary Lovisi's second collection of tales about the unknown sides of the great detective.

Muddled Mind: Complete Works of Ed Wood, Jr. — David Hayes and Hayden Davis deconstruct the life and works of the mad, but canny, genius.

Murder among the Nudists — A mystery from 1934 by Peter Hunt, featuring a naked Detective-Inspector going undercover in a nudist colony.

Murder in Black and White — 1931 classic tennis whodunit by Evelyn Elder.

Murder in Shawnee — Two novels of the Alleghenies by John Douglas: *Shawnee Alley Fire* and *Haunts*.

Murder in Silk — A 1937 Yellow Peril novel of the silk trade by Ralph Trevor.

My Deadly Angel — 1955 Cold War drama by John Chelton.

My First Time: The One Experience You Never Forget — Michael Birchwood — 64 true first-person narratives of how they lost it.

Mysterious Martin, the Master of Murder — Two versions of a strange 1912 novel by Tod Robbins about a man who writes books that can kill.

Norman Berrow Novels — *The Bishop's Sword, Ghost House, Don't Go Out After Dark, Claws of the Cougar, The Smokers of Hashish, The Secret Dancer, Don't Jump Mr. Boland!, The Footprints of Satan, Fingers for Ransom, The Three Tiers of Fantasy, The Spaniard's Thumb, The Eleventh Plague, Words Have Wings, One Thrilling Night, The Lady's in Danger, It Howls at Night, The Terror in the Fog, Oil Under the Window, Murder in the Melody, The Singing Room.* This is the complete Norman Berrow library of locked-room mysteries, several of which are masterpieces.

Old Faithful and Other Stories — SF classic tales by Raymond Z. Gallun

Old Times' Sake — Short stories by James Reasoner from Mike Shayne Magazine.

One Dreadful Night — A classic mystery by Ronald S. L. Harding

Pair O' Jacks — A mystery novel and a diatribe about publishing by Jack Woodford

Perfect .38 — Two early Timothy Dane novels by William Ard. More to come.

Prince Pax — Devilish intrigue by George Sylvester Viereck and Philip Eldridge

Prose Bowl — Futuristic satire of a world where hack writing has replaced football as our national obsession, by Bill Pronzini and Barry N. Malzberg.

Red Light — The history of legal prostitution in Shreveport Louisiana by Eric Brock. Includes wonderful photos of the houses and the ladies.

Researching American-Made Toy Soldiers — A 276-page collection of a lifetime of articles by toy soldier expert Richard O'Brien.

Reunion in Hell — Volume One of the John H. Knox series of weird stories from the pulps. Introduced by horror expert John Pelan.

Ripped from the Headlines! — The Jack the Ripper story as told in the newspaper articles in the *New York* and *London Times*.

Rough Cut & New, Improved Murder — Ed Gorman's first two novels.

R.R. Ryan Novels — Freak Museum and The Subjugated Beast, two horror classics.

Ruby of a Thousand Dreams — The villain Wu Fang returns in this Roland Daniel novel.

Ruled By Radio — 1925 futuristic novel by Robert L. Hadfield & Frank E. Farncombe.

Rupert Penny Novels — *Policeman's Holiday, Policeman's Evidence, Lucky Policeman, Policeman in Armour, Sealed Room Murder, Sweet Poison, The Talkative Policeman, She had to Have Gas* and *Cut and Run* (by Martin Tanner.) Rupert Penny is the pseudonym of Australian Charles Thornett, a master of the locked room, impossible crime plot.

Sacred Locomotive Flies — Richard A. Lupoff's psychedelic SF story.

Sam — Early gay novel by Lonnie Coleman.

Sand's Game — Spectacular hard-boiled noir from Ennis Willie, edited by Lynn Myers and Stephen Mertz, with contributions from Max Allan Collins, Bill Crider, Wayne Dundee, Bill Pronzini, Gary Lovisi and James Reasoner.

Sand's War — More violent fiction from the typewriter of Ennis Willie

Satan's Den Exposed — True crime in Truth or Consequences New Mexico — Award-winning journalism by the *Desert Journal*.

Satans of Saturn — Novellas from the pulps by Otis Adelbert Kline and E. H. Price

Satan's Sin House and Other Stories — Horrific gore by Wayne Rogers

Secrets of a Teenage Superhero — Graphic lit by Jonathan Sweet

Sex Slave — Potboiler of lust in the days of Cleopatra by Dion Leclerq, 1966.

Sideslip — 1968 SF masterpiece by Ted White and Dave Van Arnam.

Slammer Days — Two full-length prison memoirs: *Men into Beasts* (1952) by George Sylvester Viereck and *Home Away From Home* (1962) by Jack Woodford.

Slippery Staircase — 1930s whodunit from E.C.R. Lorac

Sorcerer's Chessmen — John Pelan introduces this 1939 classic by Mark Hansom.

Star Griffin — Michael Kurland's 1987 masterpiece of SF drollery is back.

Stakeout on Millennium Drive — Award-winning Indianapolis Noir by Ian Woollen.

Strands of the Web: Short Stories of Harry Stephen Keeler — Edited and Introduced by Fred Cleaver.

Summer Camp for Corpses and Other Stories — Weird Menace tales from Arthur Leo Zagat; introduced by John Pelan.

Suzy — A collection of comic strips by Richard O'Brien and Bob Vojtko from 1970.

Tales of the Macabre and Ordinary — Modern twisted horror by Chris Mikul, author of the *Bizarrism* series.

Tales of Terror and Torment #1 — John Pelan selects and introduces this sampler of weird menace tales from the pulps.

Tenebrae — Ernest G. Henham's 1898 horror tale brought back.

The Amorous Intrigues & Adventures of Aaron Burr — by Anonymous. Hot historical action about the man who almost became Emperor of Mexico.

The Anthony Boucher Chronicles — edited by Francis M. Nevins. Book reviews by Anthony Boucher written for the *San Francisco Chronicle,* 1942 – 1947. Essential and fascinating reading by the best book reviewer there ever was.

The Barclay Catalogs — Two essential books about toy soldier collecting by Richard O'Brien

The Basil Wells Omnibus — A collection of Wells' stories by Richard A. Lupoff

The Beautiful Dead and Other Stories — Dreadful tales from Donald Dale

The Best of 10-Story Book — edited by Chris Mikul, over 35 stories from the literary magazine Harry Stephen Keeler edited.

The Black Dark Murders — Vintage 50s college murder yarn by Milt Ozaki, writing as Robert O. Saber.

The Book of Time — The classic novel by H.G. Wells is joined by sequels by Wells himself and three stories by Richard A. Lupoff. Illustrated by Gavin L. O'Keefe.

The Case in the Clinic — One of E.C.R. Lorac's finest.

The Strange Case of the Antlered Man — A mystery of superstition by Edwy Searles Brooks.

The Case of the Bearded Bride — #4 in the Day Keene in the Detective Pulps series

The Case of the Little Green Men — Mack Reynolds wrote this love song to sci-fi fans back in 1951 and it's now back in print.

The Case of the Withered Hand — 1936 potboiler by John G. Brandon.

The Charlie Chaplin Murder Mystery — A 2004 tribute by noted film scholar, Wes D. Gehring.

The Chinese Jar Mystery — Murder in the manor by John Stephen Strange, 1934.

The Cloudbuilders and Other Stories — SF tales from Colin Kapp.

The Compleat Calhoon — All of Fender Tucker's works: Includes *Totah Six-Pack, Weed, Women and Song* and *Tales from the Tower,* plus a CD of all of his songs.

The Compleat Ova Hamlet — Parodies of SF authors by Richard A. Lupoff. This is a brand new edition with more stories and more illustrations by Trina Robbins.

The Contested Earth and Other SF Stories — A never-before published space opera and seven short stories by Jim Harmon.

The Crimson Query — A 1929 thriller from Arlton Eadie. A perfect way to get introduced.

The Curse of Cantire — Classic 1939 novel of a family curse by Walter S. Masterman.

The Devil and the C.I.D. — Odd diabolic mystery by E.C.R. Lorac

The Devil Drives — An odd prison and lost treasure novel from 1932 by Virgil Markham.

The Devil of Pei-Ling — Herbert Asbury's 1929 tale of the occult.

The Devil's Mistress — A 1915 Scottish gothic tale by J. W. Brodie-Innes, a member of Aleister Crowley's Golden Dawn.

The Devil's Nightclub and Other Stories — John Pelan introduces some gruesome tales by Nat Schachner.

The Disentanglers — Episodic intrigue at the turn of last century by Andrew Lang

The Dog Poker Code — A spoof of *The Da Vinci Code* by D.B. Smithee.

The Dumpling — Political murder from 1907 by Coulson Kernahan.

The End of It All and Other Stories — Ed Gorman selected his favorite short stories for this huge collection.

The Fangs of Suet Pudding — A 1944 novel of the German invasion by Adams Farr

The Finger of Destiny and Other Stories — Edmund Snell's superb collection of weird stories of Borneo.

The Ghost of Gaston Revere — From 1935, a novel of life and beyond by Mark Hansom, introduced by John Pelan.

The Girl in the Dark — A thriller from Roland Daniel

The Gold Star Line — Seaboard adventure from L.T. Reade and Robert Eustace.

The Golden Dagger — 1951 Scotland Yard yarn by E. R. Punshon.

The Great Orme Terror — Horror stories by Garnett Radcliffe from the pulps

The Hairbreadth Escapes of Major Mendax — Francis Blake Crofton's 1889 boys' book.

The House That Time Forgot and Other Stories — Insane pulpitude by Robert F. Young

The House of the Vampire — 1907 poetic thriller by George S. Viereck.

The Illustrious Corpse — Murder hijinx from Tiffany Thayer

The Incredible Adventures of Rowland Hern — Intriguing 1928 impossible crimes by Nicholas Olde.

The Julius Caesar Murder Case — A classic 1935 re-telling of the assassination by Wallace Irwin that's much more fun than the Shakespeare version.

The Koky Comics — A collection of all of the 1978-1981 Sunday and daily comic strips by Richard O'Brien and Mort Gerberg, in two volumes.

The Lady of the Terraces — 1925 missing race adventure by E. Charles Vivian.

The Lord of Terror — 1925 mystery with master-criminal, Fantômas.

The Melamare Mystery — A classic 1929 Arsene Lupin mystery by Maurice Leblanc

The Man Who Was Secrett — Epic SF stories from John Brunner

The Man Without a Planet — Science fiction tales by Richard Wilson

The N. R. De Mexico Novels — Robert Bragg, the real N.R. de Mexico, presents *Marijuana Girl, Madman on a Drum, Private Chauffeur* in one volume.

The Night Remembers — A 1991 Jack Walsh mystery from Ed Gorman.

The One After Snelling — Kickass modern noir from Richard O'Brien.

The Organ Reader — A huge compilation of just about everything published in the 1971-1972 radical bay-area newspaper, *THE ORGAN*. A coffee table book that points out the shallowness of the coffee table mindset.

The Poker Club — Three in one! Ed Gorman's ground-breaking novel, the short story it was based upon, and the screenplay of the film made from it.

The Private Journal & Diary of John H. Surratt — The memoirs of the man who conspired to assassinate President Lincoln.

The Ramble House Mapbacks — Recently revised book by Gavin L. O'Keefe with color pictures of all the Ramble House books with mapbacks.

The Secret Adventures of Sherlock Holmes — Three Sherlockian pastiches by the Brooklyn author/publisher, Gary Lovisi.

The Shadow on the House — Mark Hansom's 1934 masterpiece of horror is introduced by John Pelan.

The Sign of the Scorpion — A 1935 Edmund Snell tale of oriental evil.

The Singular Problem of the Stygian House-Boat — Two classic tales by John Kendrick Bangs about the denizens of Hades.

The Smiling Corpse — Philip Wylie and Bernard Bergman's odd 1935 novel.

The Spider: Satan's Murder Machines — A thesis about Iron Man

The Stench of Death: An Odoriferous Omnibus by Jack Moskovitz — Two complete novels and two novellas from 60's sleaze author, Jack Moskovitz.

The Story Writer and Other Stories — Classic SF from Richard Wilson

The Strange Case of the Antlered Man — 1935 dementia from Edwy Searles Brooks

The Strange Thirteen — Richard B. Gamon's odd stories about Raj India.

The Technique of the Mystery Story — Carolyn Wells' tips about writing.

RAMBLE HOUSE

Fender Tucker, Prop.   Gavin L. O'Keefe, Graphics
www.ramblehouse.com   fender@ramblehouse.com
228-826-1783   10329 Sheephead Drive, Vancleave MS 39565

www.ingramcontent.com/pod-product-compliance
Lightning Source LLC
Chambersburg PA
CBHW030402020726
47493CB00003B/915

* 9 7 8 1 6 0 5 4 3 7 1 4 9 *